I0702784

I Suck at Titles

Ellen Taylor

Copyright © 2023 by Ellen Taylor

ISBN: 979-8-9892076-1-9

All rights reserved.

No part of this publication may be reproduced, distributed, or transmitted in any form or by any means, including photocopying, recording, or other electronic or mechanical methods, without the prior written permission of the publisher, except as permitted by U.S. copyright law. For permission requests, contact ellentaylorbooks@gmail.com

The story, all names, characters, and incidents portrayed in this production are fictitious. No identification with actual persons (living or deceased), places, buildings, and products is intended or should be inferred.

Cover design by Getpremades.com

Map by emach55

First edition 2023

CONTENTS

South
Island
Wastelands
Drakehaven

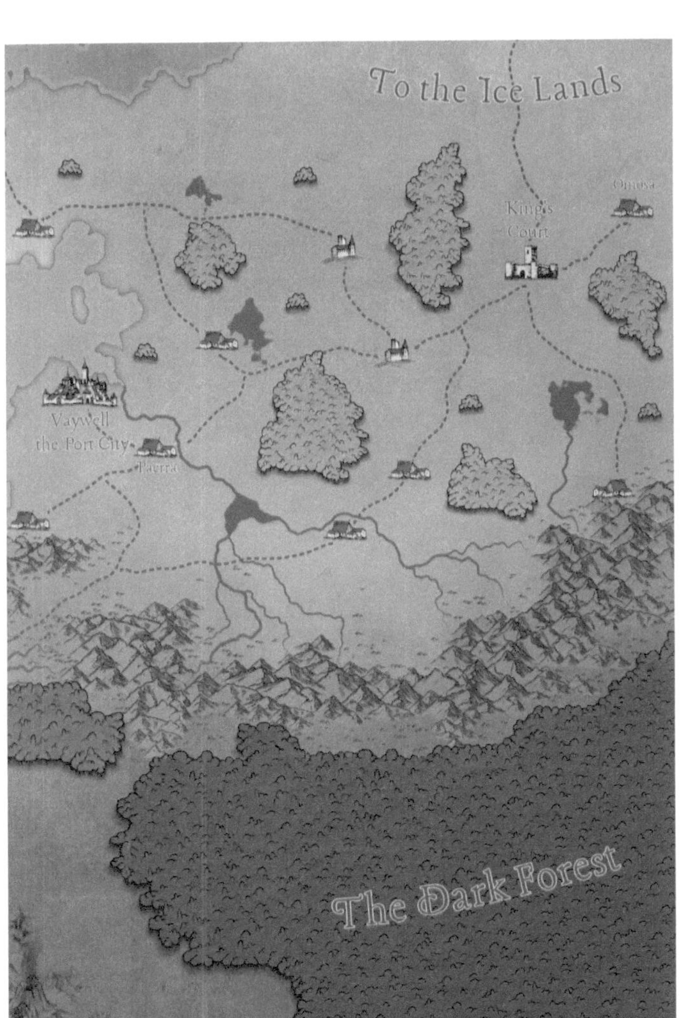

To the Ice Lands
Omdsa
King's Court
Vaywell
the Port City
Tavria
The Dark Forest

Chapter One

THE DRAGON STRIKES

Dread filled the town when the dragon's wing darted into view. Fear at the glint of colossal teeth in the moonlight. When the fire burst from her mouth, chaos joined. Three simple sentences I spent months perfecting. Then I ruined it by mentioning how I sat up, confused, in the middle of the chaos.

I straightened my glasses as people screamed around me. The town was ablaze, warming the autumn night. It was a chaos of broken buildings and crunching bodies. My jaw slackened as villagers ran every which way, saving women and children. Which made complete sense. I just didn't understand why *I* was here. Perhaps I should, as a man in medieval times, start saving them too, but I was still in shock.

My hands patted my chest and stomach, feeling my university t-shirt and shorts. I should be in my office narrating this story. But since I'm here, the narration device would focus on me. It would pick up my internal dialogue to use as narration since no one was up there dictating what it should do. Which meant all I had to do was think about it and my thoughts would play out for anyone in the real world to read. I'd have to be careful, or else everyone would find out about gym class in seventh grade when I—

You know what? Let's *not* think about it.

Pavaldri the dragon swooped low, fire erupting far too close to me. I scooted away before scrambling to my feet and sprinting to the nearby forest. Fire crackled overhead, and people shrieked in pain. My brain sputtered with adrenaline as I tried to remember if I accidentally said the code. But they designed the code so narrators *never* accidentally said it. It didn't matter. I'd say it now.

"Narration code 0000! I leave my story," I hollered to the sky.

Screams reverberated around me. Fire inching toward my flesh reminded me how I was here, in a town I set up, with a dragon I created, in the opening scenes of which I knew the ending.

"And then I did *not* enter my story!" I willed my office to appear. My nice, cushy, not burning office. With my breakfast on the...

Was my stove still on?

Pavaldri slammed to the earth, roaring. I covered my ears, falling to my knees. The townsfolk shrieked, clambering over each other to escape her terrible claws. If I was in my office, I'd describe the townsfolk's cries, but I ran in the opposite direction instead. I couldn't stay here; this would mess everything up. Not only did stumbling into my story ruin it, but it also broke every law of narration and would ban me from creating future stories. If I ever got out.

The dragon rammed her claws into buildings, toppling them as she roared. Jets of flame covered the town, cutting off hundreds of screams.

Sweat poured down my face as I closed my eyes, trying to will myself back to my office. This was one hundred percent going to ruin my story. Case in point, my medieval fantasy didn't know what one hundred percent meant. There was no reset button on the narration device. I needed to get out now before my story drastically changed.

My sprinting carried me behind a tree, which was stupid because trees burned, but I needed somewhere to think. When I was in my office, I remembered starting my story. I turned toward the device because I thought sparks were coming out of it. Then I woke up here.

An inferno blasted through the village, my brown hair moving with the heat wave. I instinctively ducked.

"Come, my good man! We must fight back!" a villager called to me, holding a pitchfork.

Panic seized me as I remembered how this scene would play out. "No, wait!"

The stubborn fighters shouted, heading for the dragon. She turned her long, snake-like neck toward them, and I sprinted out of the way of the inevitable blast. The fire came because my outline required it. The outline which was printed out and sitting on my desk by my coffee. Where my body was most likely slumped over in a coma.

Pavaldri blasted them with a flame so hot it incinerated them on the spot. I gagged, smelling other people's burning flesh before the blast moved toward me. I prepared for complete destruction of my body, yet felt nothing. Despite feeling the heat, a direct stream of death made me feel nothing. I worked some air into my lungs and gathered my courage. Despite being hit by lava hot flames, I couldn't die in my story. Not unless I let it. It didn't stop me from producing adrenaline as flames devoured me, the heat somehow not melting my bones.

The dragon would find me unharmed and try to kill me, as it was in her character, so I ran with the blast toward some trees catching on fire. The flame disappeared, and I once again patted my chest. People were moving, but not fast enough.

Pavaldri used her scarlet tail to wipe out the statue of the founder, her scales gleaming in the moonlight. If Pavaldri was sleeping, I would have spent paragraphs describing her. Since she was not, I didn't want to ponder the best way to capture her terrifying essence in words. If this were my actual life and a scarlet dragon started wreaking havoc on my city, I'd have run in the opposite direction screaming at a pitch more suitable for a preteen girl. Since I couldn't die, it helped me sound more like the twenty-nine-year-old male that I am. Mostly.

"Watch out!" I shouted at a little girl who was trying to run from falling debris. As the dragon rammed her tail against the house, I grabbed the little girl's waist and covered her with my body. Bricks hit me instead. It felt like a pathetic pillow fight. The bricks settled on the ground as the little girl sobbed.

"Run for the forest. Get out of here," I ordered, cleaning my glasses on my dirty shirt before placing them back on again, which worsened my vision.

She nodded, then leapt out of my arms, racing into the forest. I didn't know how much of her speed came from fear or the subconscious need to obey the narrator. I watched her disappear behind a tree before I faced the destruction. Pavaldri had either smashed the houses or set them ablaze. The comfortable warmth of the white-hot flames licked my face, arms, and legs. This destruction needed to happen because it was in my outline, but being in the middle of it gave me a different perspective. And burning flesh reeked.

The four-story building to my right moved. No, wait, that was Pavaldri. She swung her head and stared right at me. My blue eyes widened as I met her yellow ones. The horns shaped her face, making it twice the size of my body. Her red scales shimmered in the flames. She opened her mouth and growled to reveal teeth the size of my legs. Staring into her eyes, her thoughts tumbled into my mind. It surprised me at first, but then again, as her creator I would understand everything about her, even if her thoughts were to...

I turned and ran. "Nope, nope, nope, nope, nope."

No, I couldn't die, and no, I wouldn't feel pain when she tried to eat me, but I didn't want to experience it either.

The ground trembled under her steps. I sprinted past burning buildings, burning bodies, burning *everything* before teeth surrounded me on every side. I looked up to see Pavaldri's mouth instead of the sky. "Nope, nope, nope, nope, NOPE!"

She clamped down, chewing as she lifted into the air. I screamed in a pitch I refused to elaborate on. The razor-sharp teeth tried to pierce my skin, but never succeeded. My overactive imagination wondered what it would feel like to be eaten by a dragon, and somehow my entire body went numb.

Pavaldri kept trying to eat me, and I did little else but hold my glasses to my face as I wriggled out of the spaces between her teeth. I landed on her tongue, gasping. Her mouth was hot. She burned down an entire village, so of course it was, but it still surprised me.

She was unsure about the man trying to keep his balance on her tongue. She tried to get me to fall on her teeth again. Instead, I wrapped my arms around her thin, forked tongue, keeping my eyes closed. As my glasses hung askew on my nose, I realized this was never a paragraph I wanted to say. Ever.

Through the gaps of her teeth, I watched the destroyed village become a small smoking matchbox as she flew higher in the air. I weighed my options of either leaping out of a dragon's mouth or end up in her stomach. Pavaldri decided for me by snapping her tongue, propelling me to the back of her throat.

Chapter Two

THE AFTERMATH

A few situations in life compel a person to ponder how you reached this low. Being devoured by a dragon is one of them. Divorced before thirty is another. Now that I've experienced both, I wondered which was worse, though either would be a horrible way to start a conversation once I get back into the dating game.

On the plus side (if there is a plus side to sitting in the stomach of a dragon), I could now consider my ex-mother-in-law's advice. Once Esme and I officially signed the papers, her mother smiled at me and said, "Now that you are surrounded by the ashes of your old life, take the time to reach into your soul and root out the imperfections in your personality that caused a perfect girl like Esme to leave." My ex-mother-in-law never understood how her blatant disregard for Esme's flaws was one reason our divorce happened.

Oh, wait, was she going to read this?

There was no light in Pavaldri's stomach, but I was the all-powerful narrator who lost his glasses, so light magically appeared. It was hot; it was slimy. There were things in various stages of digestion. And it stank.

I pulled my glasses out and almost placed them on my nose before dry heaving. I about covered my mouth with my shirt, but found it soaked in the same stuff. So was my hand.

"This day is the worst," I said to no one. Well, not to no one, since there were bodies currently being digested. Kind of insensitive, I realized after the fact. After taking a poll from people in the immediate vicinity, they clearly had a worse time. "Sorry," I mumbled to the unattached arm floating in the stomach juices. Which didn't help. Seeing it made me dry heave all over again.

Alright. Focus. A part of my shoulder housed a clean enough section of shirt to wipe my glasses off. Once they were clean-ish, I put them back on my nose. Now that the destruction was done, I needed to sit, ponder, and figure out what happened. Not about my divorce, but the current issue about being stuck in my story.

Wait a second, Aimee wouldn't read this. It had dragons in it. She and Esme both opposed my career choice.

Hey, Aimee, you spell your name funny, and you should worry about the direction of your own life.

I settled against the stomach wall, pretending this was a hot tub. Of slime. With random chunks. From my understanding of the narration device, entering a story would alert the four Guardians and make them aware of my position in the real world, and they'd figure something out.

When the Guardians sent me a narration device two months ago, it didn't work. I tried everything, even opening the lid of the small black box to check the wiring inside, pretending like I knew how to fix it. Nothing turned it on. When I called the Guardians, the secretary ran through the list of questions reserved for emergencies. Were there characters I didn't create in my story? Did my characters deviate from my original outline? Did I suspect the Rogue Narrator might target my book to cause further chaos and destruction? Do background extras somehow have the hero's face? Did I double check the coding to see if there were any mistakes? I assured them none of that happened, because I couldn't turn the thing on in the first place. The Guardians were overly cautious, but I didn't blame them. The device was terrifyingly powerful with its dangerous yet alluring combination of artificial intelligence and virtual reality.

The Guardians could have simply sent another device, but instead, they asked me to fly to their headquarters in the city. They set me up in one of their apartment complexes, usually reserved for narrators working on their first story, or narrators having issues with their devices. Ninety-nine percent of the issues were always small, like random sparking, or the screens unable to focus. Or, in my case, one incapable of turning on. They gave me a new one, asking me to live in the apartment while I narrated my story. I didn't mind. After all, my dignity demanded I get out of my parents' basement before I turned thirty.

Since Esme and I finalized our divorce, it wasn't hard to pack up and move. Which was super awkward to mention to the Guardian, Jim, who gave me a tour of the apartment and helped set up the device. He was a year or two younger than me with his life in order. Girlfriend. Member of the Guardians. A life ahead of him. Not divorced. Not living in his parent's basement. Not sitting among partially digested filler characters.

Oh, wait, Jim would definitely read this. Awkward.

Anyway, once they set up the device, I spent weeks using the proper codes to build my characters. I met them in the device's interview room, the closest I legally could be to meeting my characters. After each interview, the device broke it down into proper characterization code for the beginning of the story before suppressing the information of me, their narrator. If they knew they were characters in an epic fantasy novel, they would have an existential crisis.

Soon, everything was ready. Well, no, not everything. Not the title. I had a thousand-page outline and no idea how to find the perfect string of words to help readers understand the essence of it. The Guardians assured me a title was easy to change on a finished product. So, I slapped my go-to title for any work in progress, because I really do suck at titles.

Besides the issue with the title, everything went as planned until I put on the headset for the first time. I didn't even speak a word of the story, and something in the device sparked. Next thing I knew, I woke up here.

Pavaldri landed, and the shock of it threw my balance. I dipped into the digestive soup of nastiness before scrambling to my feet and sputtered, making sure my glasses remained securely on my face. I did not want to fish them out again.

My feet were unstable in Pavaldri's stomach as water descended from above. I closed my eyes and got drenched, but this was cleaner than anything in here. Once the waterfall stopped, I pushed my glasses up my nose and thought about the choice before me. If I knew Pavaldri (and I did since I created her), she would fly to her mountain cave protected by the dark forest where she would sleep until the heroes accidentally woke her, beginning the epic fight. Which meant I would sit here, cramped in this stomach, since I was impossible to digest, until the Guardians sorted out my situation. Then I'd return to my office to keep narrating the story. Time for a pros and cons list.

Pros: This would keep my story outline mostly intact because I wouldn't be there to mess it up. If (or when) I returned to my office and the Guardians fixed the device, I could locate my characters and keep narrating from there. Though if I concentrated hard, maybe I could keep narrating from inside the dragon.

I closed my eyes, already sensing my main character. Actually, he was kinda close. This might work. It shouldn't be too confusing. We'll just jump into the actual story now, to not confuse the readers.

What readers, though? After this horrible fiasco, there was no way my story would get published. My story, my characters, never to be read.

A gurgling noise demanded my attention, and I frowned, seeing a hole open. It pulled a bit of the juice from the stomach into...

Oh *poop*.

Cons: No need to make a list. I am not staying here. And I won't travel through the intestines, either.

As the creator, there were ways to get out, but I needed to be careful. Narrators writing themselves into their own novels was the reason the government created the Guardians. And why no one received a device until they got a Narration degree. Becoming an all-powerful being in one's own creation could eventually cause people to go mad with God-like power. If I couldn't get out, then I needed to pretend I wasn't anyone special. Blend in with the background.

Shouldn't be too hard, a part of me said to myself. The part who listened too much to Esme. *Curse you, Esme,* I added for good measure.

I'll use my power and risk my sanity just this once; then be done. I grabbed Pavaldri's stomach wall and pried it open, trying not to think too hard about how my fingers possessed the ability to rip open a dragon. Pavaldri's bellows rocked the forest. Breaking through scales, I shimmied out of the hole, gasping. The fresh autumn air froze my face after being in the humid stomach. Bursts of flame escaped Pavaldri's mouth as she writhed. Fine, I also needed to use my power to heal the wound, then I wouldn't use them anymore.

The ground appeared faster than expected and I sensed an audience. Two people were watching me, and they were all too familiar.

Paldric got off his horse, staring at me slack jawed. Unlike me, he could get hurt. My other character was in the trees just above the thrashing dragon.

"No! Wait!"

Alwin dropped from the trees and landed with a light foot on Pavaldri's head. The dragon jerked around, hardly aware of Alwin, but it took more than that to threaten his balance. The razor-sharp scales cut his feet as he rammed his sword into her eye with such force it hit her brain. I gasped and backed away. The dragon roared, and Alwin jumped back into the trees. Paldric ran forward with his own sword, bringing it down hard against the dragon's neck before it bounced off harmlessly. He frowned before trying again. And again. If my dragon wasn't worried about a sword sticking out of her brain, she would have flicked him away. A fraction of steel chipped off Paldric's sword before he decided it wasn't worth it.

Air escaped my lungs and reentered, the noises higher in pitch as my dragon gave a dying cry, collapsing on the ground, the sword still sticking out of her eye.

"I... that was... you were supposed to..." I clutched my hair, eyes wide. "That was the epic finale. You killed her. A thousand pages before you were supposed to!"

This was the shortest epic fantasy ever.

Chapter Three

Now I Have to Rename These Stupid Chapter Titles Too

"A thousand pages." It sounded more like breath escaping from my lungs instead of intelligible words. "You were... that was supposed to..." The scarlet scaled body let gravity take over and her one remaining eye turned glassy. "You were part of a theme," I said, pointing to Paldric, who didn't hear me. "A nobody from a nothing town, defeating a dragon and saving the world." My voice fluctuated in strange pitches. Paldric nudged the dragon's head with his boot, wincing as the scales cut into the leather. Alwin dropped from the trees and grabbed the hilt of his sword, giving it a firm tug. It squelched as it came out. "Alwin was going to do a half somersault through the cavern and launch a dozen arrows into the air, barely dodging fire blasts." I fell to my knees. "Nine years of work. Writing, outlining, researching, world building. Down the drain. Gone. This story... my one constant while going through my divorce. The flickering light at the end of the tunnel while everything else in my life hit rock bottom." I covered my face with one hand. "The only thing actually going for me." I patted the dragon in a complete state of shock. "You're dead." I let out a groan that sounded more like a cow being strangled. "The story has no point."

Paldric wanted to talk to me about how I escaped a dragon's innards, but didn't feel comfortable approaching me yet. Instead, he held his hand out to Alwin. "Hello. I'm Paldric."

After the brief handshake, Alwin took out a handkerchief to clean his blade. "I'm Alwin."

Paldric watched him work. "You must be the man my father sent me to find. Do you know Don?"

"Yes, of course. I consider him a brother to me."

Confusion flickered so quickly past Paldric's face, I almost missed it. Alwin was genuine about his friendship, yet Paldric assumed the supposed man in front of him was the same age as him, about twenty-four years.

Alwin finished cleaning his sword and sheathed it before walking forward tenderly enough for Paldric to notice. "Are your feet alright?"

"I wrapped them while I was in the trees. Dragon scales truly are sharp."

"You wrapped them?" Paldric glanced toward the treetops. "While up there?"

Alwin gave no answer. It was then that Paldric noticed his big toe sticking out of his fine leather boots, and all he did was gently nudge the dragon. The two of them looked at me. I was still in a state of shock with my hand on my dead dragon's belly. Always the cautious one, Alwin kept a hand on the hilt of his sword, but didn't feel too threatened.

"No point." I stared at nothing and remained on my knees beside my dead dragon. "Nine years, and it's gone. If my stove is still on, it'll burn my outline. Might as well. My story is first person now. First person is the worst. I've unraveled everything." I covered my face and moaned. My sprawling epic was reduced to less than twenty pages. It didn't matter if I got back. The device allowed my characters to be coded in once, and this story was it. They had to be different enough, because the database couldn't handle characters that were too similar. Not even the same character with black hair instead of brown. This was what made them original and new, and now I ruined it like everything else in my life. "Nine years," I breathed again. "Ruined."

This hurt worse than a divorce. Maybe this clear priority was why Esme left me.

"Are you alright?" Paldric asked, placing his hand on my shoulder.

"Don't!" Alwin shouted.

It was my main character's scream of pain that made me finally lift my head from my hands. Paldric backed away with his gauntlet burned straight through as the scent of burning flesh hit the air again. Pulling out his waterskin, Alwin dumped it on the smoking palm before cutting the gauntlet off. Paldric hissed as he closed his eyes and gritted his teeth. "What was that?"

"He's surrounded by, and covered in, dragon fluid." Alwin rummaged through his pack for some cloth.

"Then how is he still alive?"

My characters looked at me, waiting for an answer, but I gave none. If I told the truth, they might have an existential crisis that drastically altered their characters. I didn't want them to change any more than what had already happened.

"I'm, uh…" My characters took in my appearance. Plastered brown hair stuck to my head, the hopelessness in my blue eyes, glasses I could barely see through, and modern clothes that didn't change when I stumbled into my story. My university t-shirt and shorts would stick out in a medieval fantasy.

My gaze returned to Paldric and Alwin, who still stared at me, waiting for me to answer. "I… don't… remember…" I said before wincing. Derailing a nine-year outline wasn't enough for me. My beautiful epic fantasy was now a soap opera with an amnesia trope. I kept one eye open to watch Paldric and Alwin's reactions.

Is the narration device working now? Can I wake up in my office? Please?

I was still next to a dead dragon, telling my beloved characters I didn't know who I was. Perfect.

Alwin found a cloth bandage and poured healing ointment on it. "Maybe the stomach poison hurt his memories instead of his skin." He motioned Paldric closer before wrapping the bandage around his hand. Paldric nodded, taking the suggestion from a stranger too well. Alwin finished tying the bandage as I struggled to my feet. My main character walked forward, ready to help me up, but Alwin grabbed his shoulder and pulled him back, pointing at the digestive juices killing the grass.

"Well…" I watched the dawn light glisten off her scales. Saw the razor-sharp teeth that should have killed me in an instant. She was a terrifying beast, not even at her full potential. Tears filled my eyes. "It is… so good of you brave men to… to save me from Pavaldri." A sob traveled through me. "So glad you took her out… when I weakened her." I rubbed tears from my eyes, the scent of her stomach lingering. "Instead of when she was better. Even though you should have waited."

"Good sir, are you alright?" Paldric asked.

My hand trembled as I pointed at Paldric. "You share a similar name spelling with her. It was so hard to convince my writing group to let me keep the two names. Pavaldri is such an awesome name." I patted her corpse. "So awesome."

"Do you remember... was she your pet?" Alwin's question was innocent enough, but he had a barrel of negative judgment ready to pour on me if I said yes.

"I don't think so." It was a safe enough answer. I dried my tears with my slimy hands. "She was terrifying and ate me."

We were silent as my characters exchanged worried glances. "Well, let's um... there's a river over there. Let's get you washed so you're not... covered in fluid," Alwin said.

I patted Pavaldri one last time as Alwin stared at my hands. Her crimson scales did not cut them to ribbons. I didn't have to see my characters to know they were trying to communicate their worries without talking. The two of them just met, but they bonded over this strange experience of killing a dragon and meeting an odd man who couldn't remember himself.

According to my original outline, Pavaldri wasn't supposed to be here. I caused the butterfly effect that I never wanted. My constant movement in her stomach made her nauseous, and she landed near my characters to take a drink. And now the story was done.

We walked to the river beyond the trees. My shoes, soaked in dragon acid, brought instant death to the grass. Paldric and Alwin stayed a safe distance away. I didn't know what to do anymore. The entire plot of the story was gone. Was I supposed to wait until the device let me return? My predicament should have alerted the Guardians by now. Narrators who entered their stories always did so willingly, not accidentally. The Guardians took preventive measures to fix even accidental entrances, so why didn't it work with me?

The river was icy as I stepped into it, but I didn't shiver. It was autumn time, and leaves fell into the water before being swept away. Death, letting go, a village destroyed, it was supposed to be symbolic. Now it was a symbol of my failure. For someone who failed a lot, I should get used to it, but it still stung.

I sank into the river fully clothed with my glasses on as Alwin and Paldric waited on the bank, whispering to themselves. Alwin sat on a fallen log and eased his shoes off, inspecting the bandages on his feet before grabbing more ointment.

"What do you think of him?" I could still hear Paldric's whispers despite dunking myself in the river. As his narrator, I already guessed how this conversation would go, but I let it play out.

Alwin glanced at me as I scrubbed my hair. "He climbed out of a dragon. Do you think he's somehow part dragon?"

Paldric caught a bundle of cloth that slipped out of Alwin's pack before kneeling to help wrap his foot. "How could he? Especially since the creatures have been gone for centuries."

"Well, not as absent as everyone thought." Alwin jerked his head toward the dead dragon, still visible from the trees.

My shoes were full of water as I picked out a mystery chunk from my hair and contemplated why anything mattered. I could lie down at the bottom of the river for hours, and nothing would happen. Maybe I *should* sink into the river. Get out of my characters' way. Let them live their lives. Boring and peaceful, now that the primary threat of the story was gone.

They finished wrapping Alwin's feet. "Do you think this is a sign? Are magical creatures returning?" Paldric asked.

"I don't know." Alwin tried to hide his excitement. Paldric didn't notice, but I did, because I knew Alwin was an elf, and he wanted magical creatures to return. The big reveal was cooler in my original draft, but everything's ruined now. I sighed and saw the scars around my elf's ears. He did it himself, using a collection of plants with burning properties in order to hide among the humans. Paldric's great-grandfather found him as a baby, and he lived with the family, since he had nowhere else to go. They never found whatever elf group left him. Alwin stayed with the family for a couple of generations and was almost one hundred and fifty years old. But no one in the village knew his secret. Lots of hijinks kept the townsfolk from suspicion until Alwin fled into the forest a couple of years after Paldric's birth to keep the family safe from the people and their growing hatred for the elves who abandoned them centuries ago.

My shoes squelched as I walked on the riverbank, picking something out of my ear.

"Do you have a name, sir?" Paldric asked.

"Um..." I couldn't give my actual name. If anyone said my real-world name, the device would shred the story down to its virtual atoms and transport it to the limbo world. It was a place that existed only to hold discarded worlds in a collective soup of shredded atoms, floating in nothingness.

With that beautiful image of oblivion, I did the responsible thing and forced myself to forget my name. Yes, I used my all-powerful God-like powers for it, because knowing my current streak of bad luck, I would accidentally mumble my name and throw us all into oblivion. It was better to have no recollection until I figured out how to leave.

"I don't remember," I said with all the confidence of someone with actual amnesia.

Alwin frowned, studying me. "Do I know you?"

"I don't know." I'd have to get used to that phrase. As I wrung out the bottom of my university tee, the surrounding grass took it in without dying.

"Something about you seems oddly familiar," Alwin said.

It was Paldric's turn to study my face. "I feel it too."

Despite the life draining experience of the last few hours, I glanced at my two characters and understood the feeling. I met these men doing interviews, but it was only my subconscious meeting them, unable to do much else but talk. Yet here I was, standing next to them. My characters. The people I created in my head, interacting with me. It was cool, now that the life-or-death situation ebbed away. Since I was their creator, they felt a sense of familiarity around me.

"I don't know," I whispered my go-to phrase.

"Looks like the wash did little good getting his memories back," Alwin said.

"Perhaps a change of clothes." Paldric didn't actually believe a change of clothes would return my memories, but he was happy to provide a distraction for me to help me feel better. He used his bandaged hand to brush my shoulder, and when it didn't burn, he gave me a firm pat. "Let's return to Omosa. My parents will welcome you and you'll be dry in no time."

I froze at the mention of his parents. Meaningful characters, but so small I only named the dad. How was I supposed to start this conversation? I stared at Paldric, trying to find the words, but keeping my mouth shut because there was no comfort to give. I knew the fate of his parents. That, unfortunately, still remained from my original outline.

The hesitancy on my face filled Paldric with confusion, then dread. He spun to see the dragon corpse in a new, dire light. "No!"

Chapter Four

I Question My Morals and Chat with the Sky

Paldric sprinted toward his horse, who wandered down to the water for a drink. My main character leapt onto it and left in a cloud of leaves and dust. Alwin whistled, and we heard hoofs from a different direction. My face dropped as a horse galloped into view. I'd never been near horses before. I'd researched them for this book, but that was it. Also, Alwin the elf always rode bareback. He climbed on before extending a hand to me. "Come, sir, you mustn't get lost. I'll make sure you're safe."

I took his hand, and he pulled me onto the horse before starting off. Alwin was strong and impossibly light. Any other person in this story would question why, but I was just relieved he would sense if I was falling off the horse. Even though I'd never die if I did. For the safety of my characters, I shouldn't get too comfortable with the idea of immortality. And invulnerability. And invincibility.

Okay, I need to stop.

My arms clutched Alwin's torso like a child on a scary amusement ride. Mortality was a tough concept to shake. We kept going, my elf patting the horse as the creature tired. If I wasn't here, he would have whispered to it.

We approached the massacre, and Alwin stopped the horse. He leapt off before helping me down, which I did as gracefully as possible. Since I wasn't someone used to horses, it ended in Alwin almost toppling over as he caught me.

"Go on." I pulled at my still wet clothes. "I'll be fine." He nodded before approaching Paldric, who knelt on the only patch of unburnt grass near Omosa.

The wind hardly moved, as though it too was terrified of what happened here. The entire town, the townsfolk, gone. Destroyed. The town square, the bakery, the bell tower. The buildings which held centuries of memories were now bits of broken brick and dust. All in one night.

Nice. Some of my original outline returned.

Alwin stood beside Paldric, surveying the destruction with tears in his eyes. Now was not the time to mention the dragon got spooked after detecting Alwin. That was for a later chapter where they'd have a fight in a tavern, testing their budding friendship. In my original outline, at least, when the dragon was still a threat.

"I am sorry," Alwin said as Paldric continued to stare in shock.

I truly felt sorry for Paldric. Parents' deaths always tugged at my heartstrings. Then again, I orchestrated the world for it to occur. That, too, I couldn't reveal to Paldric. The narration device brought its own debates and questions of morals since its invention almost thirty years ago. The characters beside me were hyper real simulations, so technically not alive in the same way I was. Pouring all my work and creativity into them made them real enough to me. Considering I was here now, did it mean I was a murderer for letting this happen? Plenty of activists believed I was, whether or not I was in my story.

This book was boring enough now that Pavaldri was dead. I wouldn't sit with a mirror and discuss morality in a virtual reality world too. I just needed to navigate this new situation and keep my sanity in check until I returned to the real world.

Alwin and I partially created this destruction while we stood searching for the words to ease an unquenchable pain. At least Alwin didn't know his contribution to it, yet. I folded my arms, still hearing the ghosts of the screams, and tried not to remember how I, too, should be dead. The sun rose as Alwin extended his hand and helped Paldric up. "We know what killed them."

"Well, you do now," I thought. The first chapter clued the reader in, but for my characters, the unseen being that pulverized a town and left no survivors was the driving mystery for a good chunk of chapters.

"And we took care of it. We need to make the next town aware of what happened. I doubt there's another dragon flying around, but we need to be prepared all the same," Alwin said.

Paldric nodded, drying the tears from his brown eyes. He also had brown hair. Did I mention that? Maybe I was too busy sobbing over the carcass of my epic finale to describe the physical appearances of my characters. There's some truth to those debates about protecting one's morals in a hyper realistic virtual reality world. Still not sitting with a mirror, though.

Alwin also had brown hair, and he figured out how to change his forest green eyes to be browner about a hundred years ago, which gave him a striking hazel color. Having green eyes that literally shifted to blend in with the deep green of the forest would have caused questions he didn't want to answer.

I reached for my phone to check the time, but my phone wasn't in my pocket. Inspection of my other pocket brought the same result. It must be with my real-life body, which was better. My phone wouldn't have worked in an epic fantasy setting, anyway.

My face reflected my grim feelings as I approached my characters. "I'm really sorry."

"Seriously?" I remember Esme saying after she finished the first few chapters of my book. *"Another orphaned fantasy hero? Is there a required checklist for fantasy authors? Why are they all orphans?"*

My head shook to physically remove those memories, but they remained, so I kept shaking my head.

"Are you alright?" Alwin asked.

"Fine. It was…" I trailed off, not wanting to blame the flies. Yes, flies buzzed everywhere here, but I didn't want to remind anyone why. Paldric's legs trembled as he took a few unsteady steps away from the town and leaned against a tree.

Standing beside Paldric instead of watching it from a screen, being an orphan meant something different. A twenty-four-year-old was mourning his parents. Even at my age of twenty-nine, I would have done the same. My parents were both still alive, and my thoughts drifted toward them. Did they hear the news yet? Was Mom already out the door to save me? Did Dad pack enough for the extended stay they would demand from the Guardians? How quickly did the message spread? This world moved in real time, and already a few hours passed. The Guardians would have alerted them already.

Hi Mom and Dad. A dragon ate me, but I got out alright. No one can kill me here, so I'll be safe. In fact, my characters are in the most danger. Because if I realize how much power I possess, I'll destroy this world and create another to do whatever I want, whenever I want.

I closed my eyes and ignored the possibilities flitting into my mind. Good thing my parents didn't raise a psychopath.

Alwin turned, his face full of compassion. "The next town is half a day's travel from here. Some people might help with the dragon body. Maybe something on the journey will help you remember who you are. If it's alright, perhaps we can think of a name for you."

As I studied Alwin's hazel eyes, my mind synchronized with his personality code, and I understood what he thought. To his understanding, I suffered the trauma of losing my entire identity, and Paldric suffered the loss of his parents. His suggestion of finding a name for me was a light topic to discuss as we walked to the next town. It was kind of him.

"I'd like that," I said.

"Come, we'll think of a name."

They led their horses around the destruction while Alwin suggested names. Paldric tried to get involved, saying names that did not belong to anyone in his village.

"HELLO, CAN YOU HEAR ME?"

I leapt out of my skin. Yes, figure of speech, but the masculine voice reverberated through the sky. My characters glanced at me.

"Are you alright, sir?" Paldric asked.

"Fine." I tried to smile, rubbing my ears. They clearly didn't hear the voice, and since the horses weren't sprinting for the next town, none of the animals must have heard it either. Once the shock subsided, the voice sounded familiar.

"Is this better?" His voice wasn't nearly as loud, though it still came from the sky. His question caused another sinking realization.

Can you hear my thoughts, man in the sky?

"I can. I'm reading them as they are coming in on the screen here."

Wait, you're that Guardian, right? The one I've been in contact with since I got the new device?

"Yes. I'm Devin."

Can you fix this?

"Your situation is our top priority. We'll get you out as soon as possible."

Which means you haven't figured it out yet.

"We don't know how this happened, and all our usual codes to pull you out aren't working. This level of faultiness never should've gotten past us, and we will not rest until we figure it out."

Did you turn off my stove, by any chance?

"What?" The sky paused as Alwin and Paldric tried some other names. **"Yes, someone did. You're here at the hospital, hooked up to some machines to keep you alive while you're in there."**

Oh, thanks. That's very kind of you.

"Believe me, none of us wanted you in this situation, and we are working tirelessly to get you out of it. I am now in charge of your case and will do my best to keep you informed. I'll monitor your story, too."

Right. Do you have suggestions to keep me from becoming a power-hungry God?

"I commend you for forgetting your name. My next suggestion is to lie low. Try not to mess around with your original outline too much."

Yeah, too late. My dragon died, so there's nothing left for my characters.

The sky sighed. **"I'm sorry. That does drastically change your outline, but it's wiser to not have a dangerous creature on the** loose, so you're not tempted to use your powers. The more you act like a regular human, the longer you will last."

Alright. I'll do my best to keep my sanity in check.

"Many people who entered their stories use their powers to create some sort of gauge or a percentage bar to help them know how close they are to going insane. I suggest you create something like that to keep yourself in check."

Alwin turned around and walked backwards to face me as we moved. "Do you like the name Gunther?"

"Uh, sure," I said, before realizing how strange a name it sounded. Do I look like a Gunther?

"Might as well take it. The likelihood of them guessing your real name may not seem high, but it's still possible."

I smiled to distract myself from thinking about the horrors of limbo. "Gunther is a great name."

"If you need to talk again, I've synchronized my phone to the narration device, so it will alert me if you say my name. I'll try to answer as fast as I can. Stay safe. We'll get you out. I promise."

Right. Thanks, Devin.

Alwin was still there, watching me as he walked backwards. "Until you remember your real name, of course."

I blinked, remembering Alwin couldn't hear Devin. Juggling two different conversations at the same time was hard. "Of course." Hopefully, I would be gone before they got suspicious about my fake amnesia.

"Perfect." He patted me on the shoulder, still walking backwards effortlessly. "Let's head to the next town." His smile dropped as he turned his head to one side, his walk slowing. At first, I was confused, but I understood his thoughts, and my heart rate quickened.

Paldric, who didn't understand Alwin's thoughts, was a few steps ahead when he noticed no one followed him. Half a mile away, Alwin heard a little girl crying.

Chapter Five

CHARACTER BONDING!

Alwin took out his sword and raced into the trees. I moved to follow Alwin as Paldric watched, confused. "He hears a little girl crying," I replied to the question he didn't ask out loud.

My main character didn't hesitate to race after Alwin, pulling out his own sword. My conversation with Devin resurfaced. Don't get in situations where I felt tempted to use my powers. However, it was a little girl in trouble. How could I not?

We jogged through the forest, dodging trees, Alwin far ahead of us. I heard the girl crying. My original outline didn't have this. What was going on?

Even though I couldn't see her, I almost sensed her. More importantly, I sensed no animal or creature around her, nor a life-threatening injury. Did sensing the world like this hurt my sanity?

We reached Alwin, who already sheathed his sword, his two hands out in an innocent gesture. "It's alright. We will not hurt you," Alwin said. The little girl's brown eyes peeked from behind the trunk of a tree. She saw Paldric and me before darting back again. The little girl, eight, trembled as she noticed the chip in Paldric's steel sword. She imagined many evil bandits owned jagged swords. Paldric went closer, oblivious to the fear she felt, and I motioned for him to sheath his sword. Paldric surveyed the small section of forest before putting it away, much to the little girl's relief.

It was like I was… omniscient. First person omniscient, to be exact. That had to be a rare point of view. This narrator ability weirded me out.

"Who are you?" the little girl asked from behind the tree.

"I'm Alwin. This is Paldric and Gunther." I waved, hoping it would calm her nerves, but it would have been more effective to wave to the tree. "We're here to help you."

The little girl peeked over to study Paldric's kind face now that he sheathed his chipped sword. Her eyes rested on me, and her nose crinkled. "I know you."

My other characters said the same thing, and I gave them no answer, either. However, their interviews took longer and were therefore more prone to familiarity in my presence. I didn't know this girl's name, which meant she was a filler character. It confused me how she felt the same as Paldric and Alwin. I gleaned information by looking at her face as I sensed her character code. Eight years old. Wide brown eyes. The wideness was important. Why was it important?

"You're the one who saved me from the dragon," she said.

Ohhh. Paldric was supposed to see the little girl's broken body on their way out of Omosa. Because of the dragon. The one I saved her from.

"Um, yes." Unease settled into my bones as I remembered why her wide brown eyes were so important. It helped fuel Paldric's horror at the annihilation of Omosa and give the reader an emotional gut punch at the sight of her dead, youthful face. I smiled at my characters, trying not to feel like a monster before focusing on the little girl. "Yes, I'm… I'm glad you're alive."

She rushed out from behind the tree and squeezed the air out of me with her frail arms. I hugged her back, patting her head. Honestly, it pleased me to know she survived. Knowing a child escaped last night's trauma helped ease the pain. Yes, the entire town died in my original outline, but that was before I entered my story.

Also, I'm not heartless. Just needed to add that.

"Do you know her?" Alwin asked Paldric.

"There are many children in Omosa." Paldric studied the little girl, grimacing. *Or there were.* It was the phrase he refrained from saying.

The girl let me go after I wiggled enough. She had little character development besides a gut-wrenching death, but I could access her code and deepen her so we wouldn't be responding to a flat character.

I knelt to be eye to eye with her and straightened my glasses. "What's your name?"

Her two sandy blonde braids were coming undone after running for her life and hiding behind a tree. Tears left salty paths down her dirty cheeks as she tried not to shed more.

This conversation needed to happen in the device's interview room, but I couldn't get there. Not without stopping the story, which couldn't happen unless I was out of it. "What is your name?" I asked again.

"I... I don't..." The terror of the dragon pressed on her mind, making it difficult to focus. She couldn't be a filler character for the rest of the story. She had to get more personality, or she wouldn't react to things properly, and my other characters would have questions.

I rested my hand on her shoulder. "You are safe. The dragon is dead. She won't hurt you anymore."

She nodded, trusting my words. "My name is...." The code opened, ready for me to suggest something. In the lexicon of names only I could sense, I searched through and picked one, pressing it on her mind. "Milla," she said, testing it out. I waited as the name settled, entering her code before she nodded again. "Milla."

"It suits you." She finally smiled, drying her tears. I was just happy it worked. "Tell me about yourself."

"I'm eight." She used the sleeve of her torn, light blue dress to dry her tears. "I only use manners when I'm in a good mood. When I'm nervous or scared, I forget to be ladylike." She frowned, almost embarrassed. "I... I don't know why I told you that."

My gaze remained on her so I wouldn't have to see how Paldric or Alwin reacted to her stilted speech. "It's alright. I want to know everything. We're going to the next town for help. Come along with us."

She nodded, choking up again. "Yes. Because my... my parents are..."

I wasn't entirely sure if they invented the piggyback during the medieval time period, but I didn't have any other means to help her. Paldric helped her settle on my back.

"It's going to be alright, now. Say whatever you want. I'm here to listen," I said.

We developed her character while we walked. She spoke about her life in Omosa, and I prompted her with ideas when she felt stuck. We made her the youngest, with four older brothers who picked on her but loved her deeply. It wasn't long before her emotions overtook her ability to speak. Paldric suggested a different topic.

These stories she told translated to code, deepening her character, making it easier for her to react without me prompting her. I didn't consider myself great at writing kids, though I corrected anything that might turn her into a brat. I refused to be stuck with a brat.

"Tell me your most embarrassing moment," I said.

"Most embarrassing moment?" Milla asked.

Paldric frowned, glancing behind him as we walked on the road. "What an odd question."

"You learn a lot about a person when you ask them about their most embarrassing moment. Like yours about—" I froze, realizing someone with amnesia wasn't supposed to know someone else's memories.

His eyes narrowed. "Yes?"

"I'm assuming I could learn a lot about you. If you ever wished to tell us a story you consider embarrassing."

Alwin patted his horse, curious. "Do you have this embarrassing life story Gunther speaks of?"

"It's, um…" Paldric's eyes bounced between me and Alwin. "I tripped while entering the house once, carrying a lot of furs my father wanted to sell. In front of a girl."

So much about Paldric's story confused Alwin. "I don't understand. Losing your balance is embarrassing?"

"Um, yes. Yes, it was."

"And why does a girl's involvement add to the embarrassment?" Alwin asked.

"It… you know…" Paldric said.

But Alwin didn't know. He never understood physical attraction, even when he spent time with humans.

It wasn't Paldric's actual embarrassing moment, but that, too, revealed a lot about his character. Overhearing his parents' fight about his choices, though more shame based, was something he considered embarrassing. Also, not something to share with a group of strangers.

"And you? Do you have one? An embarrassing moment?" Paldric asked my elf.

"I don't fully understand what this is," Alwin said, before panicking and trying to think of something so this group of strangers would consider him human. "I guess there was that time I, too, tripped."

Which was also true to Alwin's character, pretending he had an embarrassing moment when he didn't. He wasn't a snobbish elf; he simply didn't understand why he was more graceful and stronger than humans. Which, yes, made him a bit snobbish, but his intentions were pure.

Milla straightened, her chest puffing up in pride. "My brothers dared me to eat a snake's head, and I did. My older brother made me swear not to tell my parents, but then I vomited during the middle of family dinner, making my older brother vomit too. Because of the smell."

My two male characters stopped in their tracks to look at her. The story's candidness horrified and surprised Paldric, while Alwin listened curiously to all things human.

"You discovered much about her by this moment of her life?" my elf asked me.

She's not afraid to prove a point or get scared by a dare. Willing to do anything to prove her worth with people she looks up to and hiding from an authority figure until it becomes her undoing. Okay, maybe not that melodramatic. I shrugged. "A bit."

Alwin gazed at me, and I understood his thoughts. He yearned for me to be a mythical creature like him, forced into hiding. Maybe my amnesia was a coverup to keep me from revealing the truth. Except I wasn't an elf because Alwin kept thinking about how plain my features were, which... okay, fair. Nor was I a fairy or nymph. I had a peculiarity about me that wasn't just because of my modern clothes. For now, Alwin would wait and watch.

"Do you ride horses, Milla?" Paldric asked.

She thought this over, and I didn't prompt a reaction just to measure how much she'd developed. "I've ridden a few."

"Would you like a ride now?" Paldric asked.

"Sure!"

Being in an epic fantasy required a lot of walking, and I didn't notice if she was becoming heavy. I eased Milla off my back and Paldric helped her onto his horse.

"So, you were there when a dragon attacked Omosa?" Paldric asked. Milla nodded, not saying anything. "I'm sorry. The dragon is dead now. I'll make sure you stay safe." She nodded again, and it wasn't from lack of development. If she opened her mouth to talk, she would cry, and it would make her feel embarrassed.

Paldric and Milla tried to pretend they were simply going on a trip, and when they returned, Omosa would be back to how they remembered it, with their families waiting for them. I left them to their silent reverie.

Alwin fell in step with me, keeping his eyes on the road as his horse followed behind us. "You heard her crying too?" It was an innocent enough question, but I understood the implication. Milla had been sobbing softly at a range no human could hear.

"No, I didn't."

"You turned your head soon after I did."

"Alwin—" I wouldn't pretend to be an elf, because even he noticed I wasn't, but telling someone they were a character in a story, let alone that I was the guy in charge, might be detrimental to their mental wellbeing.

"So, you heard her," Alwin said.

Curious at our whispers, Milla turned to listen. She and Paldric were still in their quiet reveries, but well within range to overhear.

"You did too." My look helped him realize I knew his secret.

"Are you like me, then?" Hope trickled through his eyes.

"You know I'm not."

He took in my plain, human features, which had none of his grace. Despite already knowing it, my self-esteem still took a jab when I sensed the moment he acknowledged how plain I looked. "How do you know me, but not yourself?"

"It's, um…" He got me there. "I'm not sure." He didn't believe me, but for now, it would have to do.

Chapter Six

IT'S A TOWN!

We reached the next town, Isinter. I wanted to help Milla down from the horse, but decided Paldric should help instead.

"Where do we start?" Paldric asked.

"The tavern, of course. Where else do travelers go?" They gave me weird looks at my outburst, which prompted me to clear my throat. "Head for the tavern. I'll find a change of clothes."

The townsfolk gave my clothes strange looks, and there would only be more. I waited until my characters arrived at the tavern before returning to the forest. Devin's advice about making a gauge was solid, but right now I needed to not wear my university t-shirt and shorts. I wiggled my fingers and my clothes transformed into dark pants and a cream-colored long sleeve shirt. My shoes turned into simple boots. It tempted me to heal my eyesight and lose my glasses since they were an oddity in a medieval fantasy, but something told me that differed from magically changing clothes. Changing my eyesight was physically altering me, and what would stop me from giving myself a six-pack? A chiseled jaw? Perfectly windswept hair all the time? Or—

I needed to stop.

Pushing my glasses up, I walked into the tavern to see my characters in a ring of townsfolk telling their story. In my original outline, they didn't know what caused the destruction and most of the townsfolk brushed them aside, but this was different. Now Alwin and Paldric had a dragon body. Paldric unsheathed his sword to reveal the chip in the steel. The leaders of the town gathered a group to study the corpse tomorrow morning. No one saw a dragon for five hundred years, and now a dead one was in the next town with enough dragon scales to make them rich. If they could get them off.

Not wanting to bring attention to myself, I stayed in the back. When my characters noticed me, I gave them a thumbs up, until I realized they didn't know what the gesture meant, so I changed to encouraging nods.

The tavern keeper came with plates of bread and cheese. Milla began stuffing her mouth, as she had nothing for breakfast. The leaders ushered people out of the tavern while talking with swordsmen and scholars.

I sat next to Milla, smiling. She ignored me, focused on eating.

Paldric gestured toward my clothes. "Those look nice."

"Thanks." I straightened my shirt before studying the few patrons in the tavern. "Looks like you emptied the place." My original outline had it fuller, but it was also still early afternoon. In the original outline, the two of them arrived in the evening, which meant we got here fast. How was that possible? Paldric and Alwin killed the dragon and raced to Omosa instead of moseying back while getting to know each other, but Milla's detour should have evened it out.

Oh, right. We didn't save *her*. Just missed her kidnapping. That might be better. According to Esme, I'm a misogynistic pig who can't write a female character. Milla can be the female in our group.

The kind peddler woman who would send them on their journey to defeat the dragon was there in the corner, enjoying her ale. There would be no journey now. All that knowledge, and it was pointless.

Milla pointed at my face. "What is that?"

A glimmer of hope overcame me that maybe I was disappearing back to the real world, and something was happening to my face before I realized she meant my glasses. My fingers brushed against the frames. "They help me see better."

"I don't get it," Milla said.

I took off my glasses and handed them to her. Even in a medieval fantasy, this principle was universal. When people got comfortable enough in a group, they share glasses to showcase their eyesight. Milla placed them on her face, her eyes growing wide. "Whoa!" She looked around, almost cross-eyed. "Can you even see with this on?"

"They help correct my eyesight to see the same as you," I said.

"That's not how it works. I don't believe you." She took them off and blinked repeatedly.

Explaining the scientific reason why my eyesight was worse than hers was pointless, and not because I didn't know the exact science. Even if I did, she'd just stare at me.

Milla handed my glasses to Paldric, who barely placed them on before snatching them off, closing his eyes like he was in pain. "What eyes do you have, Gunther? Can't a healer help you?"

"I doubt it."

Alwin took a turn, frowning as he looked around in my glasses. I hated how hot they looked on him. Stupid, hot elves. "What a strange tool," he said before handing them back.

"Just trust me. They help me see better." I placed them back on my nose.

There was a beat of silence as we settled into the tavern. The smells of vegetable soup being made for dinner, the fresh bread coming out of the oven, the quiet patrons enjoying their late lunch.

"What will you do now?" Alwin asked.

Paldric finished his cheese. "Not sure. We'll figure out something, though. Make a new life here in Isinter."

"The forest is always welcome if anyone would like to visit me."

I sighed, staring at the table as my story ended. This small group we formed was already splitting up. With no epic adventure, what was the point? Living a mundane life in Isinter was the logical next step. A part of me ached for the strong friendship Alwin and Paldric would never form.

Alwin passed his portion of cheese to me. "I never liked cheese."

Paldric broke his bread in half and handed part of it to me. I wasn't here when they passed out the plates of food, and I didn't feel hungry, but their thoughtfulness touched me. "Thank you."

The old peddler woman walked over, giving us a strange look. I didn't know what to do, other than stare back, her one eye blue and the other white with cataracts. "You young men are certain you killed the only dragon?"

I frowned. There was only one dragon. Anything more was speculation (and to keep things open for a sequel if it did well). That was before the device threw me into the story. There couldn't be another dragon, and I couldn't chase one down, anyway. It'd be too tempting to use my powers.

"One dragon doesn't mean all the dragons have returned," Alwin said.

"You sound so sure," the woman said.

The woman's eye fascinated and scared Milla. Did the woman need glasses too? Milla didn't dare ask it out loud.

"It was the last of its kind," Paldric said.

"Are you prepared to gamble everyone's life on that belief?" the woman asked.

Paldric and Alwin exchanged glances. Milla turned toward her empty plate as the recent memories of the dragon attack flitted through her mind. I simply stared at this woman. She used that phrase in the original outline, but the dragon was dead now. *Why are we having this conversation?*

Studying my characters helped me realize I needed to ease the plot along. There would *not* be another dragon. My sanity couldn't take it. "Dragons are large. Yes, this one escaped our sight for five hundred years, but there is little chance a second one exists."

"Though a dragon is the least of your worries."

I faced the peddler woman, frowning. "Sorry?"

"Rumors are growing of an evil in the south."

My frown deepened. *What on earth was she talking about?*

"An... evil?" Paldric asked.

"The cursed creatures of old," the woman said.

Alwin lowered his mug. "But they were all banished by the elves, nymphs, and fairies almost a thousand years ago."

I swiveled to stare at Alwin. *What was* he *talking about?*

The woman pulled out a map. "Banished, but growing in power." She spread the map on the table. There was the main road, mountain ranges, the dark forest, and ocean. I spent hours creating this map, so when the peddler woman used her arthritic finger to point at the island I did *not* create, my mouth dropped open.

"How do you know this?" Paldric asked.

"I collect legends and folklore because there are grains of truth to every tale." She tapped the island I still stared at. "With the elves no longer protecting us, all they need is a leader to feed them thoughts of revenge."

"Where did you purchase this?" I asked, taking the map.

The peddler woman looked confused. "It's a standard map of Veniloria."

"But... but this island. How did you get a map with this island on it?"

"They added South Island to the map decades ago to make sure we remember it still exists," Paldric said.

My gaze shot to my main character with barely enough time to react. "You know about this island, too?"

"Perhaps it's your amnesia," Alwin said. My eyes bounced from Alwin to Paldric, sensing the truth. They knew about this the entire time. This island that somehow slipped from my recollection.

Or someone added it without my knowledge.

Color drained from my face. Milla examined the map and nodded. "My mother warned me if I misbehaved, goblins would steal me and force me to live in South Island forever."

I stared at Milla, ice racing through my blood. The little girl who barely got a deeper character already knew about this island. This couldn't happen. This story was mine. A person couldn't just add to my story. Unless...

I stumbled to my feet, heading toward the door of the tavern. "Please excuse me. I need to go write a letter. Or something."

Devin. I need to talk to you. Right now.

Chapter Seven

I'M TOO RATTLED TO THINK OF A CHAPTER TITLE

I scrambled outside before leaning against the tavern building, my mind jumbled.

Devin! You said your phone would alert you if I said your name. I really need to talk to you, so I'm sorry to do this. Devin, Devin, Devin, Devin.

No answer for now, at least. I closed my eyes, sick to my stomach. It was bad enough my outline became useless, and I had God-like powers tempting me to live out my wildest fantasies. But now? Now there was a possibility someone was messing with my story. They needed to get out. And I had a *terrible* feeling I already knew who it was.

"Hello?" a new voice asked.

Who are you?

"Jim Solomon from the Guardians."

I groaned. Jim. The guy a year or two younger than me with the life my ex-mother-in-law dreamed of for her daughter.

"Uh..."

And, as I forgot, able to read every thought being written out. Jim, be a good man and disregard what I said. Or... thought.

"Fair enough."

Ugh, he was a good man, too.

"Forgive me for stepping in. Devin went to bed early with instructions to only wake him in an emergency."

Early? It was only mid-afternoon. No, wait, technically I started the story in the real world in the morning, and set the time of the book a few hours before dawn. Which meant the real world was quite a few hours ahead of me.

"That, and Devin enjoys his beauty sleep."

Have you followed along in the story?

"Give me one second. Let me catch up."

It's mainly the stuff at the end of the tavern scene.

"Alright, let's see."

There was silence while I waited. I took off my glasses to rub my nose, trying to keep calm, but when the sky itself gasped in shock, it didn't help.

"I'm waking up Devin. Vince and Grace too. This changes everything. I will be back soon. Um... try not to do anything while I'm gone."

.... Sure.

I placed my glasses on my nose, leaning against the tavern, fingers in my hair, as I thought about my predicament. Additional code I never entered was now being incorporated into my story. If someone could alter the map without my knowledge, what else did they mess with? And if it was *him*, why would he target me? There's no way this could be him. It unnerved me how I couldn't sense the change in the world, nor did I sense my character's additional experiences with this new code.

My characters walked out of the tavern. Paldric noticed me and waved the others on before approaching. "Is everything alright?"

"Fine." I tried to smile. "Things are fine."

He leaned against the tavern next to me. "It shocked me, too, when I was a child and realized the cursed creatures of old were just banished to South Island and still around." I nodded, doing my best to not show how terrified I was. Despite his own parents' death, he was compassionate enough to make sure I was okay. "But don't worry. None of them escaped. Except maybe the dragon."

"I... I don't think the dragon came from the southern island," I said.

"It's called South Island."

Pain entered my smile. That island's name was abysmal. All my towns and villages used unique names: Omosa, Isinter, even Veniloria. Now this island in the southern portion of my map bore the name South Island. More proof I didn't create it.

"The dragon didn't come from South Island," I said again.

"Where else would it have come from?"

"Probably from—" I remembered my amnesia cover and needed to tread carefully. "Dragons hide in caves or mountains. And islands don't have those." Pretty sure islands had caves and mountains, but not in my story. The device took my words and coded it as hard rules for it to follow. Whoever this mysterious narrator was with their own evil island, they at least wouldn't have dragons. Dragons were epic, but only if I had control from the safety of my office, where they couldn't eat me.

Paldric straightened from the tavern. "We've got a day's lodging in the inn without charge. The innkeeper took pity on us and gave us lodging for the night."

"That is kind," I said, pretending it didn't happen in my original outline, too.

"It's across the street. Would you like to join us?"

"Of course." I straightened, brushing myself off as we crossed the dirt road. We approached the inn door before Paldric turned to me again.

"Alwin and I are going to South Island."

"To do what, exactly?" I asked, hiding my worry.

"Scout around. See what's going on. If South Island is getting stronger, we need to stop the cursed creatures before they escape and destroy the rest of us," Paldric said.

I froze at the door and gawked at my main character, programed to do the right thing even if it killed him. Especially if it tried to kill him. Life-or-death situations were more epic to read about. It was the same insane logic that made him want to locate the dragon in my original outline, but he had plot armor when I was in control. If I no longer had control, my main character didn't have plot armor anymore. "Paldric, you and Alwin are just two people. You don't know what's happening on that island. *I* don't know what's happening there."

Paldric focused on me, his voice quieter. "The peddler woman might be right that South Island is becoming a threat. We've got to stop them. South Island is near Dalehaven, and I hear they are a warrior people. They may already have the situation under control, but if not, we can volunteer our help to make sure the creatures are contained. I have no more family, and I will take on this quest. I have an obligation to make sure Veniloria is safe. We already saw what one creature could do to Omosa."

I rubbed my face before placing my hand on Paldric's shoulder. It was odd, considering I couldn't physically touch my characters when I had created them. "Let's wait on a decision until after a good night's rest."

Paldric nodded, opening the door. "Alright." It didn't matter. He already decided.

We walked in and talked with the innkeeper before I followed him to my room. They furnished us with some small rooms, and since there weren't a lot of guests, we each got our own. The innkeeper shut the door as I collapsed onto the bed and covered my face, trying not to panic.

Devin? Jim? Anyone?

"Devin is on his way." Jim's voice came from the rafters above me. **"He expertly hid the new code, but I know what to look for now. Just gathering it all together to help paint a clearer picture of what's going on."**

I straightened my glasses, trying not to freak out even though it was pointless. Jim could read my thoughts, which did not help me stay calm.

"Believe me, I'm freaking out too."

He. Jim said he, which was the last clue. "Do you know who did this?" I asked out loud, because I wanted to pretend we were having a normal conversation. Me and the rafters.

"Unfortunately, yes. It's the Rogue Narrator."

My brain froze to keep from reacting. Stories circulated about the Rogue to where he sounded more like a bogeyman. From what I heard, while a writer narrated their story, a character they didn't create would appear and slowly destroy the novel, ruining the original outline and killing the main characters for... reasons. No one even knew why this guy did what he did. As the narrator tried to salvage it, they watched their creations suffer and die instead.

"The Rogue's only got into a handful of stories, but I assure you, he's no bogeyman."

The Rogue Narrator was targeting me for some sick reason. But wait, no one accidentally stumbled into their story while the Rogue had control, right?

"Yours is the first. And the last, if I have any say. We're trying to track down how this device came to you. The Rogue must have slipped it in and deleted many of the failsafe functions once you placed your code in."

So, somehow, I need to protect my creations from these new characters without employing my God-like powers until the Guardians uncover how to get me out of a device the Rogue Narrator somehow slipped to me?

"That... sums it up great."

My fingers dragged across my face. "Any advice?"

"Once the other Guardians get here, we'll start planning. We know you don't want to stay there, so getting you out is still our top priority."

I nodded because they expected me to, not because I felt like it. Whatever was happening on South Island made me nervous. This turned into more than surviving a fantasy story. I needed to protect my characters, because I could not have their lives ruined. Alwin, Paldric, now Milla. The Rogue used psychological attacks. He knew each of them inside and out because he read their character codes. He would tear them apart slowly in front of my eyes. The man had to be sick in the head.

"The four of us are doing everything in our power to protect your characters, too. You're not alone in this."

My fingers interlocked behind my head as I paced the room. The Rogue's presence (and mine) ruined my original outline, and my characters were in grave danger. Given the choice, I'd rather stand by their side as they faced the Rogue's attacks instead of watching them in an office from a computer screen.

"No," Jim said. I glanced up, frowning. **"Once we know how you can return, you must get out. Unlimited power is too tempting."**

"This story is…" I didn't know how to explain it. When everything else in my life unraveled, this story remained my constant, giving me the hope I craved. Good guys triumphed over the dragon through an inseparable friendship and hard work, because I said so. It was the control I craved for in my life. To know the ending would be alright even while experiencing a divorce. Now my story fell apart as badly as the life waiting for me, and I had more control over this one.

"This is not a life, believe me. And it's not worth it. You can't play with ultimate power. It will consume you. The longer you stay, the more likely you are to destroy everything. I'm sitting here in a wing of the hospital dedicated to individuals in your situation. All of them doing anything they want while wasting away the rest of their lives. No matter how hard life is in the real world, don't give it up for a virtual one."

I said nothing. I tried to think about nothing, too, but it was impossible, since I'm sure Jim read about my attempt to think about nothing, which therefore meant he was reading about *something*.

"Devin, Grace, and Vince are here. We'll have a meeting then be in touch. Be careful."

The narrator device was hooked to two screens, one for written text, the other to play out the words as a movie. Which meant Jim not only saw my fake smile but also read how I did not feel any sincerity behind the grin I gave the rafters.

"I promise we'll work on getting you out. Try to sleep, Gunther."

I folded my arms and continued to pace. It's not time to sleep, considering I just ate a late lunch. Did I even need sleep anymore?

"You will get some sleep, because it's what normal people do. If you don't want to go mad with power, be normal," Devin said.

I closed one eye to look at the rafters. "Oh hi, Devin."

"Hello, and try not to worry. We'll work on this problem," Devin said.

I stopped pacing before falling onto the bed. It would make sense for me to feel tired before dinner, since I'd been up a couple hours before dawn. Sometimes I wish I could use my God-like powers to go right to sleep.

"Gunther—"

Don't worry Devin, I'll be normal.

Chapter Eight

I Put Important Things in Place

The sun barely peeked over the horizon and filled my room with so much light I cracked an eye open. I hadn't seen a sunrise in a long time, since I spent most mornings hung over and regretting my life choices.

My hand reached for my phone to check the time. When my fingers only brushed against glasses, I remembered where I was. Last night's sleep was rough, but with how much sunlight came through my curtainless windows, I couldn't sleep anymore.

"Good morning, Gunther," Devin said.

I sat up and put on my glasses. How long were you waiting for me?

"Not long. I'm about ready to go to sleep myself, so I'm glad I caught you before I did."

What time is it there?

"About ten in the morning. I only got a few hours of sleep last night, too."

The straw mattress was unfamiliar, but not the culprit of my poor sleep. I got out of bed, stretching. "Your lack of sleep is my fault, isn't it?"

"Don't worry, we're going to get you out."

My fingertips ran down my chin, feeling a noticeable lack of stubble, which was for the best. Shaving with a dagger sounded deadly. Oh, wait, I couldn't die. It didn't matter, this would still be nice. Since my beard grew in patches, I always kept myself clean-shaven so no one knew I couldn't grow one.

Which… now Devin knew. "Alright. What is your plan?"

"Despite this unsettling addition, you should still make one of your characters a gauge to help you know when you're closer to insanity. We've already written the code, so it won't hurt your percentage."

Pressure hit my mind, and I closed my eyes to sense the code. The device listed information about me like I was a character too, which was creepy, but I'd let it slide. The device quantified my sanity as best it could, then a character I chose would say whenever my percentage went up. Also, this character had access to whatever information they needed to keep my percentage low.

"Don't even try to reach fifty percent. People who willingly enter their stories take days to reach fifty, then hours to reach one hundred. Understand?"

"Yes." My characters were eating breakfast now, but I wanted to finish my conversation with Devin first. They might worry if they saw me talking to the ceiling.

"Jim mentioned your hesitancy about leaving your story once we find a way out. I know you care about your characters, so make the wise decision and leave once we find the solution. You can carry on the story once you're out."

"I understand your concern."

"I'd feel better if you gave verbal confirmation that you will leave once you can."

"I know you would." And I wasn't prepared to give that confirmation.

"Gunther—"

"Please. Just leave it be."

The ceiling sighed. I couldn't use the excuse of hunger to end the conversation, since I felt no urge to fill my stomach, most likely because of the IV they put into me in real life.

"Vince tasked Jim and me to uncover the Rogue's code within your story. We've collected all we could so far, and I'll transfer it to you now."

Once again, a pressure appeared in my head as I absorbed the code. Simply put, a dangerous power grew in South Island (still hated the name). Thousands of trolls, goblins, and cursed shadow soldiers lived on this island. It was like the Rogue picked these three evil races out of a hat. The Rogue, whoever he was, placed a dark wizard named Dark Wizard to lead the cursed creatures.

Dark Wizard? Seriously?

"We think he's trying not to leave anything unique, which might help us trace things back to him in real life. We still don't know who he is, just that he's a man."

Or maybe he doesn't write fantasy.

This Dark Wizard had a direct link to someone else's narration device, which meant a connection to the Rogue himself. The Dark Wizard knew I was a powerful individual, and I cared deeply for Paldric and Alwin.

"The Rogue's got a link to your story. Hidden behind data encrypted files that Jim is already trying to break into. We're going to figure out how he got the link, I assure you," Devin said.

Wait, so the Rogue can see everything happening right now?

"Yes." I could tell Devin hated to admit that. The unsettled feeling I had since seeing South Island on the map changed to panic. **"But he can only control his characters, so try to stay away from any of his creations."**

The Rogue had access to everything. Which meant he could read my thoughts, possibly even right now, just like Devin and Jim could. It brought me no comfort.

"Can't I simply… un-exist the Rogue's characters?" I asked.

"No, unfortunately. It cannot be unwritten as it's secured behind mountains of firewall. Even if you could, it would hurt your percentage too much."

I nodded, sorting through the code again as I sat down on the straw mattress. "Dark wizard. Trolls, goblins, shadow soldiers. Did the Rogue realize while creating them he's literally a villain?"

"All we know about him is he's some sort of hacker breaking into people's stories. We've tried catching him for years now, but he keeps slipping through our fingers."

The Rogue created a henchman for the Dark Wizard, too. A necromancer with his powers of regeneration, almost with a snap of the finger. It was a dangerous power. He already brought many of the trolls and goblins back. I wondered if reanimated creatures meant a zombified look, but it didn't make a physical difference to those on South Island, since the Dark Wizard already magically tortured them. The necromancer knew everything the Dark Wizard did, even though he didn't have a connection to the Rogue. Also, his name was just the necromancer. Not even capitalized.

As for the shadow soldiers, they were created by sacrificing a willing human under a dark ritual. The Dark Wizard was very skilled at manipulating people to do what he wanted.

"Is he going to alter my characters? Make them become shadow soldiers?" I asked.

"The Rogue tries to break the characters' will. It's how he..." Devin trailed off.

"Tortures me?"

He didn't reply right away. **"It's a sick game of his."**

I stretched again, trying not to reveal how unsettled I felt. This was more dangerous than a dragon. My mind flipped through the code, wondering what I could do on my end to track down the Rogue.

"Get out once you can. That's how you help."

"The Rogue and the Dark Wizard are connected, and if I get close enough, I can—"

"You will leave your story before you approach the Dark Wizard."

"All of this is way too coincidental for me to believe I accidentally slipped into my story with no way to get out. The Rogue was involved, and if my story proves 'successful' for him, more narrators will be in my situation. We need to stop him now." I paced, needing to do something.

"We've already limited distribution of new devices to ensure this never happens again."

I scrutinized the ceiling, still pacing. "Then tell me this. Is it plausible to track down the Rogue if I get near the Dark Wizard?"

The ceiling's silence felt like I was alone again until Devin started talking, his voice even, yet scared. **"You need to get out. Understand? Everyone you talk to in there is a figment of your creation as you lie here in a coma, surrounded by other power addicts.**

This, where I am, is real life. Where I interact with other independent humans with their own complex lives.”

So, that's a yes. If I get close enough to the Dark Wizard, I could discover who the Rogue is and stop him from torturing other narrators with his sick, twisted games. And if I succeed, it will keep my story from falling apart. Unless I failed again. But maybe I wouldn't.

“Do not, I repeat, do not develop a hero complex. We Guardians refuse to risk your sanity to catch the Rogue. The second we get the problem solved, you get out.”

Again, I said nothing as I remembered how my thoughts betrayed me, so I thought of other things. Like goats. Screaming goats. Those were funny. I closed my eyes, remembering one of my favorite screaming goat videos. I snorted at the thought of it. And then I thought about—

“I've given my warning. It might feel suffocating having your inner thoughts broadcasted for me to read, so know I'll try to give you a semblance of privacy,” Devin mumbled.

Will you feel obligated to call me out when I think about it? How I want to go after him? Figure out who he is?

The silence from the ceiling was the longest one since, and I waited patiently for Devin's answer. **“There is one more thing, for your safety, I must insist on.”**

“Which is?”

“You must give us a failsafe. If your percentage gets to forty-five, grant the Guardians the ability to ease the plot however we see fit.”

My honest thoughts, mainly because I couldn't hide them from Devin, were that I hated his failsafe. Would you write me out of my novel if it came to it?

“No. We don't do that anymore.”

"Anymore? What does that mean?"

Devin hesitated before he talked again, his voice much quieter. Not angry, not scared, but in pain. **"We tried it a few times. Tricked narrators into saying the code or creating codes to force them out before locking them away from their devices. They did everything possible to get back, all dying in the attempt. The addiction, the power, it's too much for them to survive. We have only seen success when the narrator gives up their world."**

I winced, turning away to hide my reaction, even though it was pointless. Maybe that privacy alone could spur me into getting out once it was available. "Have you tried creating those kinds of failsafe codes in my story?"

"Due to the accidental nature of your story, yes. We have. And they still don't work. It's like every failsafe we programed into the devices was removed."

I straightened my glasses to hide my unease about the Rogue being after me for some bizarre reason. "Let's bargain. You can have your failsafe if you help me discover who the Rogue is... and also not ask me to leave my story."

"Gunther—"

"Do you want your failsafe?"

Despite not seeing his face, I almost sensed him weighing the pros and cons. **"Here's the additional code for the failsafe. Check it over."**

The pressure returned in my head, and I closed my eyes to sift through the code. I made sure only Devin, Jim, Grace, and Vince could nudge the plot, which it did.

"And in exchange, you will not ask me to leave my story while we find out the Rogue's identity."

"We will help you stay sane, which does not involve going straight to the Dark Wizard to find out who the Rogue is."

"Of course, nothing that stupid."

He hesitated again. "Our top priority is getting you out. If such an opportunity arises, you will leave immediately. But…"

"How much do you want this failsafe?"

Devin groaned. "But if you need something to occupy your time, we can go about this in a safe and lawful manner, as much as possible, to discover the Rogue's identity. Agreed?"

"Agreed." I thought of something. "Why don't you stick that in the code itself? That way, even if you accidentally talk about me leaving my story, I won't hear it?"

Devin said nothing. Again, I could almost sense him weighing it out. "That's… an interesting thought."

It then hit me. All these codes were to keep me in check. Devin didn't want to create the code, because he desperately wanted me out. This was all formalities, but if I wanted to, if I *really* wanted to, I could prevent these conversations without a code. This was, after all, my world.

"If you tried something like that, it would hurt your per-centage, but here's the additional code I've added." He sounded hasty as he spoke, and the pressure on the back of my head loosened and traveled throughout my body. Already I saw how to change the code enough to void their failsafe. "Gunther, stop. Please. We are putting a safety net around you. If you don't want to go mad with power, you will keep it there. Are we clear?"

I nodded. "Clear."

"Good. Once you choose the character to keep yourself in check, I shall leave to get some sleep. Please, stay away from the

island. Do not go near the Dark Wizard. And do not get past forty-five percent."

I would only promise to keep my characters safe. Other than that, I couldn't predict what a madman with hacking skills could do.

Chapter Nine

I SECURE MY SAFETY NET

Milla knocked on my door.

"Hello!" she said in a singsong voice as I opened the door. "I heard you talking and thought Paldric was here. We've been looking for him."

"He's um..." I closed my eyes, sensing my main character in his grief. Paldric had a nightmare, like from the original outline, and he was out on a walk. "He's figuring things out."

Her own memories of the attack returned, and her face dropped. "Oh."

"Are you alright?" I looked at this little girl I met only yesterday.

She nodded, but the loneliness remained in her eyes. "The bed was soft. The nicest I ever slept on."

Bits of her past bubbled up. "Your family was poor?"

"My dad was a farmer. Said this year's crops weren't doing as well." Which meant they were poor enough an eight-year-old took notice when meals were smaller than usual.

"What are your plans now, Milla?"

"I want to stay with you and the others."

Though not nearly as developed as Paldric or Alwin, she sensed a familiarity about me. "I don't think that's safe. We're about to go on a dangerous journey." Despite telling Devin I wouldn't run straight for South Island to discover who the Rogue was, we could still accomplish this mission carefully.

"Very, *very* carefully," Devin added for good measure.

But I still didn't want an eight-year-old girl tagging along.

"Please, let me come." Her voice wavered in terror. Not sensible terror at nearing an island covered in cursed creatures, but because we might leave her behind. Curious, I reached out to sense why she felt this way.

None of her family remained. She didn't want to stay in a village where, according to her active imagination, another dragon would appear and destroy it, killing her this time. I was ready to assure her no other dragons existed when I paused. My feelings of protectiveness grew, and now the Rogue and the Dark Wizard knew it, too. It was my turn to feel the terror of leaving her behind. Not because of a dragon, but something else. The Rogue got to narrators by breaking their characters. If the stories were true, the Rogue was twisted enough to go after children.

When I saw those big brown eyes, I realized who I wanted to help me with my safety net. If Paldric and Alwin told me off, I might punch them in the face. With Milla, I could never intentionally hurt her.

I knelt to be at eye level. "This goes against my better judgment, but take this."

"Take what?" Milla asked.

My hand rested on her shoulder, transferring the code into her character.

"An interesting choice, but I'll accept it. Goodnight, Gunther."

Sleep well, Devin.

Milla stumbled back, blinking, then looked up at me. "You are at four percent."

I chewed on my tongue, taking this in. "Four percent?"

"Opening up the dragon, changing your clothes, not feeling tired after walking here half the day. It all adds up to four percent." She didn't understand what she said, but kept speaking anyway. "Though your conversation with God is fine. That didn't raise the percentage."

"Conversation with God?" I asked. Milla shrugged. With no concept of the narration device or the position Devin and I had, God was what made sense in her mind. "Can I get my percentage down?"

She frowned, then thought about it, sticking her tongue out and closing one eye. "A calm way of life. Meditation. Maybe take up gardening or something?"

I sighed before standing up. "Thanks, Milla. Tell me discreetly whenever it goes up and report to me before you go to sleep."

"Does this mean I'm coming with you?"

"Yes, it does." Milla squealed in excitement. "Come, let's find Alwin." I took her hand as we walked out of my room.

We descended the stairs right as Alwin strode through the door. My elf felt nervous even though no one else saw the emotion on his perfectly controlled face. "Have you seen Paldric?"

"He'll be back. He's taking a walk through the town, working through some grief," I said.

"Oh. You saw him leave?" Alwin asked.

"No, I was talking with Milla, but I—" Wait. Knowing other people's inner emotional turmoil when I'm not around them would be suspicious. "Yes. I did. See him. Leave," I said instead.

Alwin did not believe me. He even narrowed his eyes enough for Milla to pick up on the mistrust. "Have you had breakfast yet?" he asked.

"Not yet, no," I said.

"I'm hungry!" Milla said.

"I'll talk with the innkeeper's wife. They should still have some hot oats. You two slept in."

Once again, I reached for my phone to check the time before remembering it was gone. I sat down and Milla scooted over next to me, a wide smile at the prospect of joining us on our dangerous journey to South Island. Alwin returned with two bowls of hot oats and placed them down before sitting across from us, monitoring the door as he waited for Paldric. Even though they just met, Alwin felt a deep sense of loyalty to Paldric. After all, it was Paldric's great-grandfather who found him as a baby.

A woman passed, giving Alwin a second look before moving on. Alwin noticed, but didn't understand what it meant. One of his character traits was not understanding how attractive he was to humans. He knew from early on he was an elf, and there was nothing about humans he considered sexually attractive. That was my addition to elf lore. If an incredibly hot race of elves were sexually attracted to humans, humans wouldn't bother trying to mate with themselves. Wars would break out to win the favor of any elf who so much as looked their way. Making elves attracted to humans would have caused the entire world to be populated by half-elves. Humans fascinated Alwin, but the sexual aspect never made sense to him.

Paldric walked inside feeling deeply concerned, but trying to hide it. Since he wasn't an elf, his emotions were easier to see on his face. Milla finished eating her breakfast, still hungry, so I passed my bowl over to her. I didn't need nourishment. Milla took it without question and continued to eat.

"This information about South Island troubles me." Paldric sat down. He pushed the nightmare of his parents' death to the back of his mind. "If we don't want other villages to potentially suffer Omosa's fate, we need to figure out what's happening and go to Dalehaven to enlist their help. They know better than us what's been stirring in South Island the past few decades."

The dragon never came from South Island, but for someone with amnesia, I shouldn't know that much. I placed my elbows on the table as I went over my connection with the code again. I tried to sense the dark species living on the island.

"Don't. It will raise your percentage," Milla said.

I frowned, then turned to her. "What?"

"Only the Gods can understand the evil one's armies from the heavens above. If you try, the evil God will make it so difficult for you that you'll have to use your powers." Milla took another bite of hot oats after she finished talking. I glanced at Paldric and Alwin, who were looking at me, confused.

"What is she talking about?" Paldric asked.

I shrugged, making my facial expression too comical for them to think I was taking this seriously. We needed to change the subject before Alwin asked his questions. "If we do travel to South Island, we're going to need an army, more than the inhabitants of Dalehaven."

"We don't know that," Paldric said.

"Yes, we—" I froze, realizing the others didn't know what they were up against. "We know they… probably have a dragon." No, they didn't. My code made sure of it, but I had to pretend I didn't know. "That alone would take an army."

"South Island is on the other side of the world. We could try to gather an army as we go. We should start with the King and Queen. Make sure they understand what's going on and have them send their armies to the southern borders," Paldric said.

Getting help from the monarchy reminded me of my original outline, which was a good sign. And besides, the King and Queen had one of the three elf artifacts originally meant to defeat the dragon. If the artifacts could defeat Pavaldri, they would certainly help infiltrate South Island.

The innkeeper gave Paldric a bowl of hot oats. My main character smiled in thanks before scooping some with his spoon. "I've got some provisions from the townsfolk here. And Milla, there's a wonderful family who will take you—"

"No," both Milla and I said.

Paldric frowned, his gaze bouncing between me and Milla. "It's the safest for her to remain here. If even a portion of the myths about South Island are true, we can't risk her safety."

"I need her with me." Technically, I could transfer the gauge between characters if needed, but my thoughts from before were still sound. Of all the people sitting at this table, Milla was the one I wouldn't dare hurt. Her childlike innocence became my last line of defense. And if the Rogue Narrator's twisted rumors were true, I didn't want to leave her without my protection.

"I want to stay with Gunther. I want to see the King and Queen," Milla said.

Paldric and Alwin exchanged glances before my elf shrugged. "I hear the King's Court is a fine place to visit. She would be safer there, too."

My main character tapped a finger against the table. "Alright. Gunther? You will protect her with your life?"

"Absolutely."

"Fine, she can travel with us to King's court," Paldric said. Milla leapt from her chair and wrapped her arms around Paldric's middle. He patted her head, allowing himself to smile before remembering something else. "I don't have many provisions. Enough food for another day split amongst the four of us."

"I know the forest. I can hunt and forage well enough," Alwin said as Milla moved back to her seat next to me.

"My dad told me you were the best hunter," Paldric said. A stab of mental pain hit him at remembering his dad's last words.

"I've had a lot of practice." Alwin turned to the window to keep people from seeing the smallest hint of emotion on his face. Right. No one else knew he was an elf. Sometimes I forgot.

Paldric focused on eating his breakfast, so no one saw the quiet pain he felt, and Milla was just happy to come on this journey. She finished her second bowl and leaned back, satisfied.

"Alright. It's a three-day journey to King's Court." Paldric took his last bite. "I suggest we start."

Chapter Ten

WE LEAVE. EVENTUALLY. A LOT OF THINGS ARE INVOLVED.

We walked out of the inn to see the two horses. "We should barter one of them for a cart," Alwin said.

With two horses and four people, a cart was the logical choice despite my desperation to leave. Bartering took forever. The longer it lasted, the more I wanted to make a cart appear, but I didn't dare. That much power would dent my percentage, so I waited as the two men talked with villagers. The outline didn't account for me or Milla, and Alwin and Paldric were too kindhearted to make us walk.

For the sake of brevity, we eventually found a cart and left. The only power I used was the magic of narration and summary, where Alwin willingly gave away his horse for a cart.

Hours after deciding to leave, we finally entered the darker part of the forest, making the most of the delay. Milla climbed into the cart, but none of us men dared use it yet, waiting for the horse to get familiar with it.

"My horse can only handle so much weight, and I don't want to tire her. Milla isn't a burden, but us men should take turns walking on the side of the cart." Paldric hoped that by talking about it, someone would get in.

"Honestly, we should all be fine getting in the cart. Alwin's not that heavy," I said without thinking.

Alwin's gaze snapped in my direction, his eyes widening. His reaction caused Paldric to wonder if there was anything more he was missing. "What do you mean?"

"Uh... nothing." My mind raced. This was Alwin's secret to share, not mine. "I'll take the first turn inside the cart." Paldric stopped the horse as I climbed on, sitting next to Milla, who watched this fresh conversation.

Paldric studied Alwin, who met his gaze but said nothing. There was another beat of silence before Paldric shrugged. "I'm not too tired. I wouldn't mind walking."

Alwin said nothing and made no move to enter the cart. After spending half a day bartering, Milla and I were the only ones in it. Paldric got his horse walking again, and we moved deeper into the forest. The silence was deafening. The bugs were deafening, too. So I guess it wasn't really silent, but it sure felt awkward.

"Um, Alwin. I have a few questions for you, if you don't mind," Paldric said. My elf still said nothing. This was it. The conversation that would dissolve into a fight. I closed my eyes, bracing for it. "My father said you were a good friend of his."

"Yes. I helped..."

Raise Paldric's father. Like an older brother. That was the phrase he left unsaid.

"How old are you?" Paldric asked.

"Twenty-three," he said after a moment's hesitation.

The only sound was the horse's hooves on the dirt path. Milla frowned, her gaze shifting between the two men. Paldric folded his arms. "You're a year younger than I, yet Father talked about you like an old friend," Paldric said. Again, silence settled over the group. Alwin looked at his feet, studying out something in his mind before glancing at Paldric. Something not in the original outline at all.

"Alright. I will tell you the truth. Not only do I know your father, but I consider him and your grandfather to be my brothers. Your great-grandfather found me as a baby when your grandfather was three years old and helped raise me. We are brothers in every sense of the word. It is a curse to see so many of your family members die. I will outlive you, too, if the legends are correct. Growing up in your father's time, the vision has shifted from people seeing my race in awe to seeing them as evil, so I ran away when your grandfather died. When your father was a few months shy of his twenty-fifth year, and you were two. Your father is a master hunter himself, and tracked me down six years after I left, and we had been in secret communication since."

I stared at Alwin, then turned to catch Paldric's reaction. "You're an elf?"

"Yes."

Alwin wasn't supposed to be so blunt. Granted, they both had a new purpose. The dragon was dead, and now we headed to a new foe. Maybe they wouldn't fight about it. Paldric studied the elf before him, taking this information in. The fear of Alwin being the son his father would have preferred never crossed his mind. It was too early in their friendship for it.

Paldric turned his head enough to see the scars on Alwin's ears. Alwin touched them. "I did it myself. To keep me hidden."

"Why did they say nothing to me?" Paldric asked, purely out of curiosity instead of bitterness.

"Because elves abandoned us to the dark creatures of South Island," Milla said, frowning at Alwin. "Or so my father tells me. Used to tell me." I placed an arm around Milla as she once again grappled with her family being dead.

Alwin did not look at anyone. "I don't know what the other elves thought. I was a baby when your great-grandfather found me. They tried to find my birth parents, but the elves had left by that point."

"For the moon," Milla said.

Alwin shrugged. "For all I know, I am the last one."

The moon almost became a religious symbol until the elves fell out of favor in the eyes of the people. And no, they didn't go to the moon, but I refused to tell them the truth. Especially Alwin.

"Some of my townsfolk said they were snobbish, but my father never joined the conversations." Paldric stared ahead as he thought of his parents with this new information. "Maybe we humans are too afraid to live among people who live for centuries, even millenniums."

Alwin scuffed up his hair to hide the scars on his ears. "I just know I owe my life to your great-grandfather, and I owe who I am to your grandfather and father. My loyalty extends to you as well."

A lump formed in Paldric's throat at the reminder that all his family were now dead. "I shall try to be worthy of such loyalty."

"How old are you?" Milla asked in awe.

"One hundred and forty-six. Still quite young for an elf."

Practically a teenager, though teenager wasn't the word these medieval folk would say.

"We are traveling companions for the journey ahead, and I don't want secrets between us." Alwin turned his head to look at me. "Which is why I must ask. Who are you, Gunther?"

Everyone watched me as I sat in the cart, hugging my legs as I took in Alwin's gaze. "I don't know what you mean."

"You are not human, of that I am certain," Alwin said.

"That's right. When we met you, you were covered in dragon stomach fluid," Paldric said.

Milla's face twisted in disgust. "Ew."

"I mean… I think it's kind of awe-inspiring," I mumbled, not sure why I defended myself to an eight-year-old.

"Do you know who you are?" Paldric asked.

I reached into my characters' code to figure out how they would react. It was almost like seeing the future. It didn't take any of my power, since Milla didn't tug at my sleeve to tell me my percentage. As their narrator, I knew them better than they knew themselves, and I came to one conclusion. Paldric and Alwin, in the original outline, fought and almost destroyed their budding friendship because my elf kept his identity a secret for so long. The best course of action was to tell the truth now.

But I couldn't. Alwin, Paldric, and Milla could not know they were characters in a story: their entire lives made of narration code. They didn't understand the technology, let alone the spiraling existential crisis it would give them. So, I tried to be as truthful as possible, and Milla already gave me an idea.

"I am a… a God. Of sorts. Cast from… from the heavens. And I'm trying to find my way back."

Their stares made me wonder if this was the wrong approach. I hadn't developed a religion, so calling myself God might be an overload. The closest thing to religion was the elves and other mystical creatures of the past.

"A God?" Alwin asked.

"So, *you're* from the moon?" Milla asked right after.

I winced, hugging my legs closer to me. "It's the best way to describe it for you to understand. This world cannot cause me harm because I'm not of it. I can make things appear, but at a cost." My unease grew, not sure how much to reveal. "If I realize my full potential, I could destroy this world and recreate it to however I wish. So... so I'll use my powers as little as possible."

Paldric grabbed the horse and pulled him to a stop. "Pardon, but *what*?"

I sighed again. "I'm sorry. You wanted to know."

"I didn't expect an answer like that," Alwin said.

"It's true. I overheard him talking to another God this morning," Milla said.

My face twitched in pain as I tried to smile. "The other Gods are working on getting me out, so I don't destroy you all."

Alwin and Paldric stared at me, alarmed, while Milla simply sat there. I sighed. "If you give me a minute, I could sort through your history and personality quirks that no one but me would know in order for you to believe me. Honestly, Paldric already believes me, which is true to his character. He always trusts strangers a little too easily. Alwin would need a bit more convincing. Let me think..."

"Do you know where the elves went?" Alwin asked.

I winced, knowing he would ask that, but I didn't want him to get too obsessed with this mission he formed in his mind to get back to his own kind.

"So, my compulsion to tell you that you're at four percent is..." Milla started to say.

"To keep me in check. If I reach one hundred, then…"

"Then we all die," Paldric said.

"Then everything dies." The finality of it brought an air of somberness to my characters. "I'm trying not to reach fifty."

I practically told the group I was a walking time bomb. I understood the fear on Alwin's face, and the worry in Milla's. Paldric, however, had none of that, which made me study him closer. Shouldn't he be afraid?

Prompted by my stare, Paldric spoke. "I don't believe you'll get there, Gunther. If that is indeed your real name."

"My real name is too dangerous. I forced myself to forget it," I said. Why was he so trusting?

"It's a two-edged sword, is it not?" Paldric asked.

"My powers?"

"Yes. I'm certain it's a hard burden to carry, wanting to protect us, but knowing if you use too much, it will cause harm." Paldric eased his horse forward again. "A complicated situation."

The cart and my characters moved forward. "But… you're not afraid?" I asked.

Paldric shrugged. "Should I be?"

I let out a breath. This was weird. Yes, Paldric always trusted people, but that was when I had control over the world. Now it was dangerous. His happy-go-lucky attitude made me worry.

A feeling hit my chest. The best way to describe it was dread. It came out of nowhere. Alwin's neutral look dropped to a frown as he looked around. "You feel it too?" I asked.

He nodded, turning to study the forest. "I've never felt this before."

It was a dark dread. I leaned against the cart as I flipped through my understanding of this world. The birds, animals, and insects didn't make a noise. With a pounding heart, I realized the forest had been eerily silent for a while.

A scream cut through the silence, and Paldric pulled out his sword in response. Alwin already disappeared into the forest, following the sound. Once the initial shock was done, I covered my face and groaned. I had hoped we skipped this scene entirely. I almost felt excited about this journey with my three characters. Now we had to rescue *this* woman.

Chapter Eleven

TARA, MUCH LIKE THIS CHAPTER TITLE, WAS NOT WELL THOUGHT OUT

The small cart wall dug into my lower back as Paldric raced after Alwin toward the woman's screams. Despite the dread pressing my other senses, I kept the annoyance from my face. The horse felt skittish.

The air shifted, and I heard multiple arrows released from bows. I grabbed Milla and jumped off the cart, landing on the ground. I covered her with my body the best I could without crushing her as arrows bounced off me. The horse cried, and I saw too many arrows sticking out of her.

"No!" The horse was supposed to survive. Animals had their own plot armor in my stories. Not only did I hate it when animals died, but the horse, the last remaining memory of Omosa for Paldric, needed to live. Bad things happened, but not *this* bad. I hated these kinds of stories!

The cart rolled back, and I grabbed it to stop the momentum as the horse collapsed, dead.

Laughter surrounded us, and Milla hugged me, whimpering. Creatures who laughed after killing a horse couldn't be good.

"Your percentage is in danger of rising," Milla whispered. I scrambled to my feet, keeping a tight hold on the girl as the surrounding shadows twisted and morphed, forming into humanoid beings. Fear struck my heart. It looked like the Rogue didn't need to wait for us to go to South Island.

"Milla? Are you okay?"

"Oh-kay?" Despite her fear, the strange word confused her.

I did not have time to explain the modern word to her. "Do not let go of me. We've got to follow Alwin and Paldric. I have no weapon." Not one I could safely use, anyway.

She wrapped her arms around my neck before I sprinted through the trees. The soldiers followed me through the thick shadows in the dark part of the forest.

As we got to Tara, the least developed character I ever wrote, her screams grew louder. I hoped we could avoid her and stick with the dynamic from my first draft, where the main characters were just Paldric and Alwin. Besides, the group was full enough with me and Milla now.

"Help me!" Tara's pitch grated against my ears. "Please! Help!"

Paldric and Alwin fought the inhumanly fast shadow soldiers. It was supposed to be bandits in my original outline. How did these cursed creatures get here? There were at least four shadow soldiers, and four more cropped up after following me and Milla. They were thin with pale skin, but where the shadows naturally fell on their face, it was stark black.

A few turned toward me, their wooden bows raised, with gleaming sharp arrows pointed right at us. They must have carried the bows with them through the forest. The others had swords and knives. The weapons glowed with a purple light, and I didn't like it. I hugged Milla tighter and turned to protect her.

"Stop it!" Tara screamed, tied to a tree.

Alwin struck a few down as the other soldiers sunk into the depths to dodge the blade. Paldric shouted in exertion as he stabbed one of them through the stomach.

One appeared next to me. His eyes were pale as he stared right at me, the dread they seemed to create striking my heart again. I grabbed his wrist to keep him from stabbing Milla and sensed his code. Touching him meant I didn't need to use my God powers to sense the enemy or, more importantly, to know how to destroy him. Like any regular man, stabbing them would be fatal, but I had no sword.

They were in the dark part of the forest because they thrived on shadows. Even though it was noon, the forest was thick.

The shadow soldier tried to stab me multiple times, and I attempted to dodge his knife because I forgot I couldn't die. It would be cool to say I never got hit, but it would also be a lie. The soldier's knife got me more than once, but bounced off. I was more focused on making sure he never stabbed Milla.

Alwin thrust a knife into the shadow soldier's throat, and a spurt of incorporeal blood would have hit me in the face. The blood was composed of shadow, and the soldier writhed, the humanoid part of him disintegrating before blending back into the shadows of the trees. Alwin stood there with his dagger still in the area where the soldier's throat once was, panting. "What were you thinking, bringing Milla here?"

"There were four other shadow soldiers back at the cart. I have no weapons."

Alwin sighed, then checked his knife to see if he needed to wipe off any blood, but there was none. Paldric finished with another soldier as the others fled into the shadows.

I set Milla down, holding her as she found her footing. "They've already escaped South Island?" she asked.

"Not all of them." I wiped the sweat from my face.

"How do you know?" Milla asked.

"The co—" No, wait, I couldn't say code. It wouldn't make sense. "I just know they haven't left yet. I touched his arm and... sensed it."

Paldric sheathed his sword. "They must travel in small packs. We can't tell where they are until they're right there."

Milla pointed to me and Alwin. "You two sensed them."

"Not quick enough to change anything," I said. Paldric walked over to Tara who, despite being tied to a tree and screaming during the attack, waited for us to notice her now.

"Thank you, good sir." She sounded exhausted and scared.

Paldric worked on untying the knot. "It's no trouble at all, ma'am."

Maybe Tara was not as horrible as my outline suggested. Maybe somehow, magically, it wouldn't be obvious a male wrote her. I straightened my glasses and looked the other way.

Esme demanded a female in the main character group, so I stuck her in. I'm also certain how I wrote this character is the reason Esme became my ex-wife. Maybe not *the* reason, but she mentioned multiple times how misogynistic I was while crafting Tara. In the core of my being, as I saw Tara tied to the tree with a few buttons on the top of her dress undone, her brown hair somehow falling flawlessly around her shoulders, I knew this was offensive to a large population of women. Tara's very existence would get my name smeared on many sites of eye rolling women everywhere. But according to Esme, my original idea of Tara was even worse.

I didn't realize how much Esme and I fought over my story. She rarely read fantasy, and the main reason was because of the lack of proper female representation. Early in our relationship, I tried to follow her advice, but no matter what I did, it was wrong. Fierce female warrior? Just a man with boobs. Pretty good fighter and also Paldric's love interest? Only exists to be the love interest with no arch outside the male gaze. Have her introduced as she is being saved by Paldric? Stupid damsel in distress. The thing was, I knew I couldn't write female characters. It was why I didn't *have* any in my first draft, but that was a sin, too, according to Esme. She sat me down and lectured me about proper male to female ratios in stories, about all the vile, evil tropes women had to suffer at the hands of incompetent male writers like me.

So again, I suggested my original outline where there *were* no female characters. The argument dissolved into screaming about how women needed to exist in books because that's how it was in real life, and I needed to use the Bechdel test. That if I failed the simple Bechdel test, clearly I was a misogynist. But when I added a small scene where Tara and a named female store keeper gave her directions, Esme screamed at me about this being the trope of the sexy lamps where women can't just sit there looking pretty just to give information, or else I was misogynistic, too. Esme collected a long list of ways a man could write wrong, despite never narrating a book herself. She also informed me I hit ninety-five percent of them.

But Esme and I were divorced now. Why did I bother putting Tara in the story? I tried to remember my motivations, but the clearest memory of that night was the bottle of hard liquor next to me while I was putting Tara's code in the computer. As the night progressed, I got more hammered. I must have interviewed her, too, because the next day, the computer stated Tara's character code was finished, and I moved on.

Once Paldric finished untying Tara, she took a dainty step forward. She rubbed her delicate wrists that only had a hint of red on them, despite being tied for a while and pulling herself against the tree. Her face was perfectly made up, her hair not at all disheveled. In fact, the only thing that was disheveled were the buttons of her dress that revealed a fan service I didn't remember requesting. "Thank you, kind gentlemen." Her voice sounded like she'd burst into song at any moment.

Esme was right. I can't write women. No one tell Esme this.

Paldric headed toward her. "Are you alright, ma'am?"

"Oh, good sir! You're hurt! I must patch you up!" All our gazes fell on Paldric, who had a minor cut on his arm. "I may not know many things, but I know how to patch a man!" Her smile brightened.

I covered my mouth to keep in a groan. Curse that hard liquor. This woman was an insult to everyone. Tara grabbed her pack, leaning against the side of the tree.

"Remove your shirt, and I will have you mended in no time!"

Paldric's face fell as he took a few steps back. "Um, what?"

Being blackout drunk, I didn't recall which Tara ended up in the actual story, but apparently it was Tara, the romantic subplot, and *only* the romantic subplot. No warrior, no value in anything else but fulfilling a check box of tropes more common in a romcom. Now I would watch my abysmal romantic subplot play before my eyes. I should have never created Tara. This is what I get for trying to please my ex-wife.

A barely put together female character who was now trying to take off my main character's shirt in order to patch his forearms.

Paldric kept backing away, frowning. "It's just on my arm. I don't... it's not appropriate. Just patch my arm."

She kept trying to lift his shirt. "It's how it's always been done!"

"It's unnecessary."

"Don't worry, gentle sir! I shall not peek! This is how I must repay you for saving my life!"

"I am a misogynistic pig." My fingers still gripped my mouth, but the words got out.

Alwin's scarred ears perked up, and he turned to me. "What was that?"

"Nothing."

Paldric gripped the hem of his shirt, backing away. "Please, ma'am. It would... distress me to take off my shirt. Just... just use your skill to work around it."

Tara's already wide eyes widened more in fear. "I would never want to do anything to cause a man distress. I will not take off your shirt."

A part of me resented Tara's character. She was here because of Esme. Tara turned to smile at me as she wrapped Paldric's arm, and I saw her code I created while drunk. Age twenty-three. Female. Loves Paldric. Has some healing skills. And that's it. I needed to develop her, because this new threat with the Dark Wizard was real, and he could use Tara somehow. With how underwritten she was, she was practically a blank slate. The Rogue must know this too. Why else were there shadow soldiers instead of bandits? The reality of the situation chilled me.

Which meant I would have to develop the woman I felt was a symbol of my failed marriage. Or at least a symbol of me trying far too hard to please my ex-wife.

Tara finished tying the bandage, and Paldric covered it with his sleeve. "Thank you."

"Oh, sir! You have another one! Do you need me to check it?"

Paldric looked confused until she touched the bandage around his hand. "No, don't worry. That one happened a while ago. Do you have family nearby?"

She frowned, cocking her head to one side. "Family? I don't understand."

"You know. Brothers and sisters. Parents. A village or town? Where are you from?" Tara smiled, acting as though he hadn't asked a bunch of questions he expected her to answer. When she gave no answers, Paldric thought of something else. "Do you have a name?"

"Tara."

"That's a beautiful name."

She giggled, and it took every ounce of strength to keep me from slapping my forehead. I walked forward, clearing my throat. "Um, Tara, hello."

She looked at me, her blue eyes wide as she smiled. Her hair was still perfectly done, her teeth too white, her innocence far too uncomfortable coming from a woman in her twenties. I was too afraid to make her look grungy, which meant she also looked perfect, which was unnatural. Everything about Tara was unnatural. "Hello, good sir. Do you have any patching you need me to take care of?"

"No, no." I pushed my glasses up the bridge of my nose. "I'm fine."

Tara kept her wide eyes on me as I touched her shoulder. I didn't know where to add depth. There was too much to work on, and I felt overwhelmed.

"I will do what I can to serve you, sir."

"Alright, let's just..." This shouldn't take any power to add some depth. I tried to take out her love for Paldric, since it was the reason she acted this way, but the code couldn't change that drastically without the use of my God-like power. I had to develop her the same way I did Milla. Milla was a girl, too. I could do this. "Do you have a family?"

"I don't know, sir. A woman must need a family to be born, but I've never given it much thought."

"Let's think about it, then." I kept my eyes on her. "Who's your family?"

"I don't know, sir."

"Why don't you know?" I tried not to sound impatient. There was an audience to this, and I was getting flustered.

"Because you don't know. And if you don't know, I won't know." Again, her high, song voice hurt my ears.

It was a level of clarity I didn't expect from her, but she was right. I wanted her to figure herself out on her own, but she still needed some basic foundation. "Please tell me who your parents are."

She placed her hands behind her, rocking on the balls of her feet like she was Milla's age, except she still had that ridiculous fan service I refused to look at. "I need you to tell me who my parents are."

"That's..." I closed my eyes to stop myself from glaring. Although I did this with all my other characters, it was her phrasing that irked me. I almost heard Esme screaming how Tara didn't need a man to tell her what to do. And yet she was livid at my first draft warrior Tara, who absolutely refused to let a man tell her what to do. Esme often confused me. "Fine. You're an orphan," I said so the others couldn't hear.

"Thank you, good sir." She walked over to Paldric. "My name is Tara, and I am an orphan. Whatever that means."

"It means your parents are dead," I said.

"My parents are dead," Tara parroted.

Alwin appeared by my side, frowning. "So... we're all orphans."

The groan I kept locked away broke out so loud a flock of birds took flight. Paldric and Milla had just become orphans. Alwin never knew his parents. And Tara, the last character I made, albeit reluctantly, was now also an orphan. There were too many orphans in this epic fantasy novel.

I started walking back to the dirt road, my hands deep in my pockets. "Let's head for the King's Court. With no horse and cart, we'll have to walk the whole way."

Chapter Twelve

WE WALK A LOT

We eased the poor horse to the side of the road and covered her with rocks and leaves. I was the most distressed about the poor creature. Everyone else mourned her, but for me, she was a symbol of how little control I had over this story.

Tara walked next to Paldric as we left for King's Court. She listened to his every word. Paldric talked about some of his hunting trips with his father, but he admitted how boring they were and tried to change the subject. Not being an expert hunter was part of Paldric's insecurities, since he came from a family of hunters. He tried asking her about her past, but she had no past to talk about. With Paldric not wanting to talk about his hunting trips, and Tara having nothing to say, the conversation soon fizzled, and they walked in silence. Maybe I should have coded more background for Tara, but I wanted to wait until there wasn't an audience.

Alwin and Milla walked behind them, striking up their own conversation, and I was in the back, minding my own business. I never felt tired, because my physical body wasn't actually here. It was a strange sensation, but I didn't mind. My feet never got sore, and I didn't trip over fallen roots like Tara did. A lot. Always grabbing Paldric's arm to catch herself before giggling. They always returned to a silence I couldn't tell was comfortable or awkward.

We stopped for camp well before the sun set, since we didn't have enough to eat and Alwin needed to hunt. Our progress to King's Court was slow, considering we spent half a day bartering for a horse and cart before said horse ended up dead not half a mile outside the town.

I poked the fire with a stick, resting my fist against my chin as I watched my characters interacting with each other. Alwin slipped into the forest to do some hunting. Milla sat by the fire, worried, as Tara and Paldric sat in a silence that definitely grew awkward. Paldric said something, and Tara giggled. He had a frown on his face. "So... are you?"

"Am I what?"

Paldric lifted his arm with the bandage she wrapped that afternoon. "Do you want to look at the cut again?"

She giggled again. "I'd love to. Do you want to remove your shirt?"

"Um, no."

Tara shrugged, then moved closer to check his wound, which was a scratch now.

I turned to see Milla next to me. She chewed her bottom lip. "Will they be back? The shadow people that tried to kill us?"

Worry etched her youthful face. If it wasn't absolutely necessary, I would have left her in Isinter. The fight returned to my memory, where I did little else but dodge those soldiers to keep them from hurting her, but I had no skills in combat. "They wouldn't dare come here."

"Promise?"

Lying to her was impossible. Not only was she my gauge, but also an eight-year-old girl. "We will all do our best to protect you. Every single one of us." I said it with confidence until I heard Tara giggling again and I realized maybe not all of us could protect her.

Milla nodded, not comforted, but understood the truthfulness of my words. And I knew my characters would do their best to keep her safe, even if Tara wasn't as big of a help. "You're still at four percent even after the fight."

That, at least, was good news. "Thanks, Milla."

Alwin walked back with some rabbits and an assortment of berries. He handed the berries to Milla and Tara before going behind a rock to clean and skin the animals.

Paldric stared at the fire in a trance before I moved over and sat next to him. He straightened. "Hello."

"Hi." The sun set, but the trees made it already feel like night. "You okay?" Paldric frowned, confused at the modern word. "Um, are you fine?"

"I'm well enough." He broke a small stick and threw it into the fire.

"Sorry about your horse. I know how important she was to you. How much she reminded you of home."

Paldric turned his head, studying me. "Could you have stopped the dragon? Being God, after all?"

I frowned at the fire, listening to it pop. "Not without cracking." That was a safe enough answer. I didn't want anyone to know I had drafted it from the beginning. Or how the dragon was the main driving plot of the story. At least in my old outline, anyway.

"And you cracking would kill us all?" I said nothing to Paldric's question, uncomfortable to admit how dangerous I was to my characters. We watched Alwin come around with the meat before placing it above the fire to cook. "What's your thoughts about Tara?" Paldric asked.

My eyes shot toward Tara, saw her bright, hopeful face as she complimented Alwin on his skills at cooking. "I... have no thoughts. You?"

Paldric said nothing, but studied her face. I saw the code coming out. There wasn't much, except the end was clear about their relationship. Love, marriage, babies, the entire package, no matter how underdeveloped Tara's character was. "It was kind of her to listen to me today. Helped me keep my mind off things."

My main character was no soldier. He was an unskilled hunter who would never achieve his father's legacy, try as he might. The battle today played on his insecurities, and I had to help. "We're safe. We all survived. You got a minor cut, which Tara expertly patched up." Paldric smiled, touching the bandage that Tara had retied around his arm, using valuable oils to mend the skin.

Healing was one of the few instances of remaining magic in Veniloria. The healers passed down knowledge of the herbs or flowers to concoct the salves and oils to heal the body. Healers picked plants in the moonlight, as it was magical, hence the belief the elves went there. It was a brilliant piece of lore that Tara's character explored, but Alwin was an actual elf and knew it better. He didn't need the moonlight to help enhance the plants.

I looked back at dinner cooking on the fire, then saw Paldric lost in his own thoughts. A bit of me shone through Paldric, back when I was twenty-three. Back then, I created him to be a year older than me, as I hoped it would only take a year to narrate. Instead, it took nine years, but it was better this way. I needed to iron out more world building.

Life was different when I was twenty-three. Esme was supportive of my goals and had read a few chapters of a different project and loved it, so I shelved this one to work on the one she loved. She made her thoughts clear about how much she disliked the fantasy genre, but at least back then she didn't make me feel like an adult child for loving it.

And I loved to make her happy. Both of us were in college. Esme rarely listened to her mother. We were in love. We were going to conquer the world.

And now things were different. In the corrosive way, the "quirks" we discovered in each other became irritants. The rosy glasses came off. We got older, entering the daily grind of life. There was no adventure for us, no metaphorical dragon to slay for her. No life-or-death situation forcing us to give last confessions of love before everything magically became better and our affection grew stronger. We should have done those things regardless, but we didn't. We simply existed. Got married to satisfy everyone else but ourselves. Waited for the adventure to come to us in our mundane lives. I wrote about it instead, and she criticized my need for escapism, driving the wedge further between us. And now she was gone, and I found myself smack dab in the middle of the adventure I hoped to share with Esme back when I, too, was twenty-four.

I saw Paldric; the sadness mingled with the ever present hope in his eyes. He was the hero, after all. Even when hope was but a flicker, he could keep it alive. A hero never lost his optimism. He was twenty-four and on the cusp of adventure. If Paldric was in my place, could he have made a mundane life work with Esme? Because that was the difference between us, wasn't it? I lost my hope. He never would. At least, I was pretty sure Paldric never would. With this unknown plot, I didn't know. Maybe life would hit him as hard as it hit me.

Alwin walked over with the cooked meat, smiling as he handed it to us. "Is there enough for everyone?" I asked.

My elf nodded. "There is, yes."

I settled in to eat my cooked rabbit, which I never tried before. Since I had no frame of reference, the meat tasted exactly like chicken.

"I'm sorry about your situation, but I am glad we found you," Paldric said before taking a bite.

"Yeah." I looked back at the fire. "Me going insane is an uncomfortable thought, but thanks for being so welcoming."

"Oh, you are far too harsh on yourself. You have done so much good already. You've kept Milla safe, and you trusted Alwin and I enough with your secret."

I glanced at Tara, not necessarily sure I trusted *her*. I couldn't even trust myself enough to develop her character further.

"Do you... do you like Tara?"

"Nope." I almost cut Paldric's question off in my eagerness to assure him. "She is all yours."

"Well, I mean, I don't think I'd... I wasn't asking to..."

I gave my main character a look, because I knew his code. Even though a decomposing plate possessed more character than Tara, I set the device in motion. They would end up together, however awkward and cringy it would be.

"What is in this?" Tara asked Milla.

"Um, rabbit?" Milla wondered why the woman didn't realize this, since everyone saw Alwin returning with the rabbits.

"It has such an interesting flavor." Tara took another bite.

Milla tore a chunk of rabbit with her teeth, talking with her mouth full. "I really like rabbit."

Ha! Bechdel test passed! It didn't cure Tara's horrible characterization, but at least I could say it passed.

"Was this rabbit a girl or b—"

"You know what, Paldric?" I said, loud enough to cut Tara off so Alwin wouldn't answer her and ruin my moment. "Why don't you talk with Tara?"

Paldric was confused, but wouldn't pass up the chance to talk to her. Milla was happy when Paldric didn't dismiss her and instead sat on the other side, talking with them both.

Alwin took Paldric's spot next to me, settling down as he popped a few berries in his mouth, watching them. "I'm unfamiliar with human customs. Are those two in love?"

"Uh..." I watched Tara beaming at Paldric as he and Milla talked. "It's forced, but... yes?"

Alwin shook his head as Tara gave a loud laugh at something Paldric said. "I don't think I'll ever understand human relationships."

I hesitated again before sighing. "Me either."

Tara leaned forward, elbows on her knees, acting like Paldric's story was the only nutrients she needed. It was then that I realized she still hadn't buttoned herself up from the kidnapping attempt. Tara was more underdeveloped than Milla, clearly incapable of reacting on her own. Well, if I could develop Milla here, I would have to help Tara.

I tried catching her gaze, but she only had eyes for Paldric. My body leaned far to the left, confusing Alwin in the process before Tara noticed me.

"You are modest in dress, and can fix it yourself," I thought while staring right at her.

She felt confused before noticing the buttons undone on her dress. She fixed herself, blushing ever so slightly before again focusing on Paldric.

It might take the entire journey to deepen her, but this was a start. In my original outline, she didn't appear too much, and it didn't matter. But now I wasn't the only narrator here who could deepen someone's character, and I didn't want to find out what the Dark Wizard would do with her.

Chapter Thirteen

THE ROGUE HATES ME

We woke up the next morning and continued our journey. The forest wasn't nearly so dark, which comforted Milla. Once we got to King's Court, the King would give Paldric one of the three elf artifacts.

Oh, wait. The artifacts. Paldric and Alwin didn't know about them yet, but I did. Which meant the Rogue Narrator did, too. The three artifacts helped defeat the dragon in the original outline. The armor, sword, and shield, the last remaining artifacts of the elves, were scattered to three different places. No one knew how to use them, but Alwin would, once he touched them and filled them with his energizing magic. In fact, once Alwin filled the artifacts with magic, it would make sense that they would be extremely effective against cursed creatures.

Extremely. Effective.

The device coded my words into the basic laws of the world, and I smirked. Take that, Rogue.

I remained in the back, watching my characters interact with each other. Once again, I remembered I was in my story. As terrifying as it was, watching my characters interacting was still cool.

Milla walked over to me, rubbing her eyes.

"Tired?" I asked.

She nodded. I knelt to help her onto my back before catching up with the others. She rested her head against my shoulders. "You're at five percent, by the way."

"Five percent?" I frowned. "How'd I get to five percent?"

"You made the rabbit taste like chicken," she said. "And you woke up rested. And you're carrying me without feeling tired."

I let out a sigh. "Alright, well, thank you for telling me. How do I stop the percentage from spiking?"

Milla shrugged, then kept her head on my shoulder. The little girl was exhausted.

Devin? Do you know how to keep my percentage low?

The pause lasted long enough for me to realize Devin probably wasn't watching the story the entire time. He was a busy man. Devin, take your time. It's not like I'm going anywhere.

"It takes a moment to patch the code into my work computer," Devin said.

How long since I stumbled into my story? I spoke it in my head, because my characters didn't need to hear me talking to the air after telling them I might crack and destroy the world.

"You've been in your story for almost three days."

Three? Oh.

"You are to be commended, Gunther. Truly. You've lasted longer than seventy percent of the people who entered their stories."

I tried to take comfort in this, but my situation was different. I accidentally stumbled into my story, where others made the choice to enter it. They probably had a plan once they got to their own worlds.

"It's still quite impressive."

Thankfully, I wrote fantasy, and not horror. If this was a classic slasher novel, I would have changed everything to sunshine and daisies real quick.

Devin chuckled. **"You have a point."**

Was there any update on me leaving?

"Jim has been working non-stop with our device engineer to find a way. The device itself is normal, except you got sucked into your story. And it's taken out all the failsafe's we've used that could have gotten you out. It concerns us that we can't find out why."

I adjusted Milla to make sure the circulation to her legs wasn't getting cut off. She was content to keep her head resting against my shoulder.

"But back to your original question. The best way to make sure it doesn't rise too fast is accepting consequences," Devin said.

Accepting consequences? What do you mean?

"I mean, the reason this device is so addictive is because people can literally control the consequences of their actions."

Like robbing a bank and never getting caught?

When Devin finally answered, his voice was quieter. **"Even more. You don't have to follow the laws of nature in there. For example, you've walked for miles and you're not winded. You slept on the ground and didn't get sore. Milla is on your back and you're not exhausted."**

I ate rabbit, and it tasted like chicken.

"Which is why I suggested in the beginning to sleep, to keep yourself as normal as possible. You need to follow the laws of nature. I've also seen it happen in reverse. If someone does

something with their powers, taking the consequences of one's actions will decrease the percentage bar."

How can I feel the consequences now?

"There are ways. Though I will warn you if you do it now, it could hurt. After walking for hours, it can hit you all at once."

Could I die in this world? Take the consequences that way? Would I die in real life?

"No, not in real life, but... but it might jolt you back into this world. Huh, that's an interesting thought. We'd have to talk to a doctor about it, though, just to cover our bases."

I raised an eyebrow.

"Just to be safe, don't try it until I've discussed the idea with the other Guardians and a few doctors. I don't want to be wrong, and none of us want you to be braindead."

I'm liking this Rogue guy less and less. It seems like the Guardians just help narrators who have been targeted by the Rogue.

"There are other problems narrators face, but the Rogue has certainly given us job security."

Well, thank you. I appreciate your help.

"Since the Rogue entered one of my stories and I only got a little scathed, Vince always assigns me these situations."

I looked up at the sky. The Rogue targeted you?

"Yes. My story is, unfortunately, unpublishable, and it hurts that it happened this way, but I got out of the situation with my sanity intact. But it still takes a mental toll to watch your characters deviate from their original outline."

My eyes fell on my characters, Paldric walking with Tara again. She picked a berry from a bush and handed it to him with a smile. He went to take it before Alwin strode forward and snatched the berry, telling her it wasn't poisonous, but it would still destroy one's digestion for about a day. I couldn't help but smile. Not because it was a touching scene, but they were my characters, and I loved watching them interact.

Do you always work with narrators who have written themselves in stories, Devin?

There was a pause. Long enough, I thought Devin logged off. **"I do, yes."** There was pain in his voice. I didn't realize I stumbled on a sensitive subject.

I'm sorry for bringing it up.

"No, no, it's... doing this job, having these assignments. I know how dangerous these devices are. My brother wrote himself into his story about five years ago. I check on his story now and then but... but he's lost. I don't even recognize him anymore."

"I'm sorry," I whispered, feeling like it was the best way to portray my feelings, and even then, it didn't feel adequate. We all heard the tales from my narration classes at university. Stories about narrators so addicted to power they became monsters. Psychopaths. Gluttons. Living out their fantasies and becoming worse than the tyrants of history. But it must be so much worse to see it. To read horrible things people did, to disregard the consequences.

And then for it to be your own brother?

I almost ran into Paldric. He, Tara, and Alwin all stopped at the road, shocked to silence. Milla gasped. I walked past Paldric, deeper into the forest, but it wasn't a forest. Not anymore. It had been destroyed. Like a dragon had burned it down. There, way in the distance, I saw the crumbled remains of King's Court.

Chapter Fourteen

AND I HATE THE ROGUE

I let Milla go and knelt at the edge of the ash. "No, no, no." My fingers dug into the ground as I sensed how this happened. This was the monarchy, the government! How did we not get the message yet? Not even rumors?

A dragon. Pavaldri. The code appeared as I demanded it, and Milla frowned.

"Gunther—" she warned.

Before flying to an obscure little town where she sensed a hidden elf, she first burned the King's Court. The code was there, set from before the story even started. Burn as much of it as possible and leave no survivors.

"No." I scrambled to my feet and sprinted into the rubble.

"Gunther! Wait!" Paldric shouted, but he was already far behind. I still sensed the code surrounding me, taunting me. It had been a few days since the attack. The fire stopped at the river. The Dark Wizard's forces helped put the fire out to keep it all a secret. This was the job of the hundred goblins who followed the necromancer, to keep the destruction a secret so I wouldn't find out until now.

Never winded, I ran faster, terrified of what this meant for my story. For my characters. **"Gunther…"** Devin started to say.

I know. I'm sprinting and not winded. But I need to find the artifact.

"Don't start down this slope."

It wasn't smart to ignore him, but I needed to get the sword. I reached the smoldering ashes of the King's Court and searched through the broken rock to find the treasury room. The ash repelled from my glasses at my command so I could see. The gold and melted jewels were there, but I needed to find the artifact.

The secret floorboards were splintered and broken. I ran down the stairs, the place full of smoke. I shouldn't be alive here. With smoke filling every corner, my lungs continued to function as normal. No one else would be down here, despite the broken boards. No one would have entered to steal…

Shattered glass covered the secret room, the red pillow resting against the wall where someone tossed it. Not a sword in sight.

My knees collapsed on broken glass as I breathed in the smoke, staring at nothing.

"Gunther, careful. Get back to your characters." I saw a scroll in the broken glass, so I crept forward. **"Don't make excuses. This is a dangerous amount of power you just used. Get back to Milla. Get back to your friends."**

The scroll rolled open in my hands as I read the note.

I will have so much fun breaking you.

"Get out of there. Now."

The note slipped from my slack fingers as I backed away, nausea finally hitting me. Was that the Dark Wizard? Or the Rogue?

"The Dark Wizard through the Rogue. It's what he does."

My knees quivered as I stumbled up the stairs, my thoughts racing. The Dark Wizard had the sword. They must be gathering the shield strong enough to withstand a dragon's blast, and the armor able to protect a mortal body from dragon scales and claws. If the Dark Wizard got all three artifacts...

I touched the smoldering ground again, sensing the Rogue's code.

"Gunther, stop!"

He was going to kill them. Kill all my characters and force me to watch. Watch until I let them die, or go insane with newfound power and protect them, which would end up killing everyone, anyway. The Dark Wizard sent the necromancer to retrieve the shield from Vaywell, the port city, while he collected the armor from the dark forests near Dalehaven. The armor was almost a month's travel, and the Dark Wizard was three weeks closer. It took a week to reach Vaywell. The necromancer would get there a day sooner. There was a better chance of stopping the necromancer.

"You can't access the Rogue's code from there. You're using too much power!"

The Dark Wizard needed Alwin to activate the artifacts, so even if he got them, he couldn't unlock their full potential. It wasn't just Tara who needed protection now. I needed to protect my elf so the Dark Wizard wouldn't use him to activate the artifacts. With just one enhanced artifact, he could destroy my world.

I opened my eyes, appearing next to my characters at the line of the destruction, still on my knees.

"Gunther!" Milla wrapped her arms around my neck and gasped. "Don't! You're... you're at twelve percent! Don't do that again!"

My mind was a jumbled mess as I nodded, but it needed to calm down to think. I stood up, hugging Milla back, and then Paldric,

Alwin, and yes, even Tara. They said nothing, allowing themselves to be hugged.

"I'm reporting this to the other Guardians, but I'll monitor your story for the next little while. Please, bring that percentage down."

The shield is a week away.

"With any luck, we'll get you out by then."

To do what? Watch my characters get tortured and killed in real life instead of here by their side?

"In real life, you're not God, and won't be tempted to live out your wildest fantasies."

I closed my eyes, hugging all my characters tighter. They said nothing, and I knew why. They were terrified by my reaction, scared of what this meant. Something that shook a God to his core was bad, but me hugging them meant that for now I wasn't trying to kill them.

"New plan." Since they were all around me, I didn't have to talk too loud. "We leave for Vaywell and track down a shield before the necromancer can. If the Dark Wizard gets all three artifacts, he will become impossible to kill."

"What are these artifacts?" Paldric asked.

"Elvish." I looked at Alwin. "Do not, under any circumstances, get caught. Being the only elf left, your value to the evil men has now quadrupled. I cannot let any harm come to you. You... you are mine. All of you. We will get through this st—this journey. I can't let you die." I thought of the years I spent pouring my creativity into Alwin and Paldric. How they, at one point, were constantly on my mind as I went over their individual arcs. They would grow into something better until their teamwork could literally take down a dragon. This story was always there, even when my life got its darkest. It helped me through my divorce, and I could not let the Rogue destroy it, too. I'd have nothing left.

I'd make a new storyline, and though I didn't enjoy plotting on the go, it was better than doing nothing. Maybe the optimism of Paldric, of a twenty-three-year-old Gunther, would return. I needed to keep my cynicism under control. This had to succeed. The Rogue was in my story, and he needed to get out. And somehow, I had to do it without cracking.

We skirted around the destruction before heading toward Vaywell. My other characters watched in horror as they got closer to the ruins.

Paldric squirmed. "The King and Queen. Are they…"

"Pavaldri left no one alive." I didn't look at the rubble, keeping my face toward the road. "Incinerated as they slept."

"Everyone." Alwin sounded sick to his stomach. "Royalty, nobility, they're all dead. What's going to happen to Veniloria?"

I rubbed the back of my neck, trying to sort through my ideas, but I couldn't. This was a situation I'd have to put on the back burner. Right now, we needed to… to destroy the Dark Wizard? Get him out? Contain his evil horde? I honestly didn't know, but once the Rogue got out of my story, I could focus on rebuilding the monarchy. Actually, the Lord and Lady of Vaywell were next in line for the throne. As long as the necromancer didn't slaughter them when they arrived. Or the entire country didn't collapse in anarchy when they eventually heard about King's Court.

My pace quickened. We had a week to get to Vaywell. A week to make sure my twelve percent dropped as low as possible.

Alwin took a turn with Milla on his back, staying near me. "I wanted to check if you were alright."

"Yeah, um... I've been better."

"Is there any way I can assist you?" Alwin asked.

I glanced at him, then at Milla. "I'm at twelve percent, and I need to lower it before we meet the necromancer in Vaywell. Do either of you have ideas?"

"Distract yourself by doing something calm, not something that might trigger you to mull about the situation," Milla said.

Alwin frowned, turning to give her a surprised look. "You know ways to help lower his numbers? Is it part of your ability?"

"Yep! Take your mind off the stress, Gunther. Being nervous about your situation might make you want to fix it with your powers, so find a hobby. Something not deadly. Like crochet." She blinked. "I don't know what that is."

The mental image of me crocheting a scarf as we made our way to Vaywell brought a tiny smile to my face. "I don't know, Milla. Crochet hooks are dangerous in the wrong hands."

Milla shrugged. "If it involves hooks, it's probably super violent and you should choose something else. Like scrapbooking? What's scrapbooking?"

I snorted. "That involves scissors."

She shook her head. "You Gods are so dangerous."

The smile grew, and I knew I did the right thing in saving Milla. Tara giggled, and I looked over to see her and Paldric. Again, he told a brief story, and the woman hung on his every word.

"Actually..." The smile dropped from my face. "I need to help Tara." I didn't know how to say develop her character without receiving strange looks. "Maybe I could focus on helping her. And Paldric."

"Help them do what?" Alwin asked.

I hesitated, and during the silence, Tara giggled again. Alwin watched, his head cocked to one side, frowning.

Milla's voice dropped. "Are we going to help them..."

Tara finished giggling, then sighed. Her girlish sigh made me uncomfortable. I didn't want to interact with Tara, but she needed my help. I didn't have any idea how to write a compelling female character. Perhaps I could write a few scenes with her and Paldric, and that would help her character grow.

"Pardon, but what exactly are we going to do?" Alwin asked.

I took a deep breath, then slowly let it out. "Write a romantic subplot." Only the dread of her falling into the Dark Wizard's hand compelled me to undertake this.

Chapter Fifteen

In Which I, a Divorcee, Writes a Romantic Subplot

I will not lie. This was a daunting distraction, and I needed it. I flipped through my mental list of romance tropes I accumulated over the years of being with a woman who forced me to watch every romance story ever written. Okay, not all, but it certainly felt like it. I did my duty and watched them, even though they were the same story with different beautiful people plugged into the formula. How hard could it be?

Forbidden love wouldn't work. Neither was enemies to lovers, since Tara was incapable of hating Paldric. Instalove was definitely there, which made me groan because I despise instalove stories. At least Paldric wouldn't be a jerk. That was another one I hated. Yes, I hated most of these tropes, but I had to choose something.

Paldric wasn't a jerk, and Tara was too innocent. According to the countless hours of romcoms I've digested, Tara would get kidnapped so Paldric could show his true feelings by saving her, but that couldn't happen right now.

We stopped for a quick lunch, Milla and I watching Paldric and Tara becoming friends. At least, I'm pretty sure they were becoming friends. The silence between them was comfortable now. It had to be, right?

Alwin sat next to me and began eating his lunch.

"Do either of you have ideas on how to help them fall in love?" I asked.

Glancing up from his lunch, Alwin studied Tara and Paldric. "Oh. Is *that* what we're doing?"

I frowned, looking at him. "Didn't you hear me before?"

He shrugged. "I asked, but you said something about a subplot? I don't know what that is."

My gaze shifted to Milla, who enjoyed her palm full of berries. Neither seemed interested in helping, though I doubted they knew how. An eight-year-old and an elf who didn't understand human relationships. It was all on me.

We came to an inn after a full day of walking, trading some of Alwin's perfectly hunted animals for a couple of rooms. I walked over to my characters after bartering, holding a tray of mugs.

"Great news!" I settled next to Alwin and placed a large mug of rum spiked ale in front of Paldric. "We've got two rooms for the venison. The meat impressed them that much."

Paldric took a sip of ale and winced. "Perfect. So Milla and Tara will take one room, and us three will share the other."

I started divvying up the other mugs. "Actually, I have a better plan. The innkeeper wanted to give us one room, but I bartered for two because I told him you and Tara were married. You two get your own room, and the three of us will take the other. Pretending to be married and there's only one bed!" I raised my mug to get a cheer, but my characters simply stared at me, blinking. Since no one responded, I tapped Paldric's mug with my own.

Paldric barely glanced at Tara, his face reddening. "That is unethical. We *aren't* married."

"I know. You pretend."

My main character leaned forward as though trying to have a private conversation with me as Tara drank her ale. "Gunther, I will not defame her character in such a way. We are not married."

"Here's the thing you need to remember. You share the bed, but you do nothing. It's part of the... the tension."

"But I *am* doing something. I should not even share a bed to sleep. Don't you agree, Tara?" He turned toward her.

She didn't answer, downing her ale. The mug thunked back on the table as she wiped her chin. "I was so thirsty, forgive me." I frowned, then realized she wouldn't drink unless I told her to. This was her first drink of the day. I stared at her, trying not to worry as she caught my gaze.

"If you're thirsty, get a drink for yourself," I thought in my mind. She frowned, then glanced at the empty mug again. Did I do this level of basic characteristics with anyone else? Maybe I had, but this felt like a horrible reminder of how little depth Tara's character had.

Paldric tried sipping his ale, but again winced. "What's in this?"

"It's fine." I lifted my mug. "Just drink it." I sipped before choking, spitting it out. Paldric's face stilled, worried someone poisoned me. I must have used my powers to change the other ale into alcoholic drinks I was familiar with. Now that I wasn't changing the consequences, I tasted the medieval time period ale. I did not expect the watered down, almost sweet mixture with the barest hint of alcohol. Aware that Paldric was still watching, I gave a weak smile. "So good." I took another sip, prepared for the weak, warm alcohol to hit my stomach.

My main character looked alarmed before turning toward Alwin for help. Alwin's gaze bounced between the two of us before sniffing his ale.

"Are you having that?" Tara asked, pointing to Paldric's mug.

"Um, no."

Without another word, Tara picked it up. I felt a spike of alarm. "No, wait!" It was too late. Her character was developed enough to ignore me in pursuit of quenching her thirst.

She drained the entire thing before shivering. "There was definitely something in there." She handed the mug back to Paldric, who watched with horror.

I groaned, rubbing my forehead. Paldric was supposed to have the drunken confession of love, not Tara. If Tara got drunk and let all her feelings loose, Paldric might run. Modern romcom tropes were a lot harder to integrate into epic fantasies.

"Are we making good time?" Paldric asked Alwin.

"Yes. We got far enough to keep us on track."

"We still need to be wary." Paldric barely glanced in Milla's direction before focusing on Alwin again. "We have to watch for potential attacks."

"The news will travel about King's Court, and I don't know how the people will react," I said.

Tara reached over and patted Paldric's cheek. She had tears in her eyes. Alarm grew on his face. "Tara?"

"I just love you. I love you so much."

How could she *already* be this drunk? I took off my glasses and placed them on the table before covering my face in my palms. Paldric blinked a few times. "Pardon?"

"I love you. I love you so much. So much."

Alwin looked uncomfortable, bowing his head. The innkeeper arrived with a platter of food. "Venison from your own catch. That's some of the best meat I'd seen in a long while. Cheers to you."

Tara squished Paldric's cheeks. "I love food. I love inns. Paldric, I love you."

The innkeeper hesitated, unsure what to do with this strange scene, backing away slowly toward the kitchens.

I placed my glasses back on my nose and broke a loaf of bread in half. "Eat this as quickly as you can." I dropped it in front of Tara, because she somehow wrapped her arms around Paldric to where he couldn't move.

"If anything were to happen to you, I'd simply die. If you die, I die." Then she liked that so much she repeated it. A lot.

"Tara." I stared at her right in the eye and she stopped mumbling. "Eat the bread, please."

"But I love him, Gunther. I love him."

"And so, Tara, you'll eat the bread." I tried to put on my narrator's voice.

She did, sort of. She leaned over while still hugging Paldric and ate the bread, giggling the entire time. Paldric tried not to let the horror show on his face, and nausea grew in my stomach. This was an insult to all women. It's official. Writing romance sucks, and I never should have listened to Esme. In the need to be less misogynistic by adding a female character, I somehow made it worse. So much worse.

Already I could see Paldric rethinking his feelings for her. "I'll be back. I'll just take her to... to her room."

"To your room," I said, even though the desire to push them together swiftly ran out.

Paldric helped her to her feet. "I'll just let her and Milla sleep in their own room."

I didn't argue.

Milla frowned as she finished her roasted potatoes. "I'm not sure I want to sleep in there, either."

I grumbled, but said nothing as Paldric lifted her up to carry her to the room as she giggled uncontrollably.

⎯⎯⎯◆O◆⎯⎯⎯

The next morning, Tara sat at the table with a hangover. I watched her rubbing her head as she ate breakfast, and I couldn't help but feel bad. Last night was my fault because I ran straight for the romantic subplot, hoping it would somehow give her a personality. Right now, her personality amounted to a pretty face who loved a man. Despite the many, *many* memories of Esme instructing me to develop her like any other character, I was too terrified.

Imposter syndrome. That's what it was. Something about female characters terrified me because I didn't know what it was like to *be* a woman. It didn't help that my last relationship ended in flames.

But I had the formula and everything! Wasn't that how this worked? I put in my time watching hours upon hours of romcoms, all worthless.

We started out. Once again, I found myself wherever Tara wasn't, which meant she was with Paldric, and I was with Alwin and Milla. Paldric was hesitant to be around her, but part of his character required him to make sure she was alright. They walked in silence, and I sensed, just under the surface, Tara wanting to say something to Paldric.

"I don't know what came over me." She blurted it out before I could analyze it. "I'm sorry. It's, um..." She tucked her already perfect hair behind her ears. "I've honestly never done that before."

"It's alright." Paldric smiled. "It was kind of funny, after the fact."

Was something happening here?

"Yeah, it kind of was." Tara giggled, which still sounded girlish, and squashed whatever feelings Paldric let grow. I let out a breath, rubbing my face.

Alwin walked beside me, frowning. "You seem anxious. Is it about Paldric and Tara again?"

I said nothing, despite having a lot to say.

My elf patted my shoulder. "Don't worry. They've only known each other a couple of days."

My hands lowered, pointing at them. "That's the problem. This is instalove. They should already have the marriage proposal by now."

Alwin frowned, then studied my face. "I don't think that's how this works."

"That's exactly how instalove works." It came out harshly, judging by the worried looks on Alwin and Milla's faces. I sighed again. "Sorry. I've... I've been easing into the consequences of my actions. The effects of traveling caught up with me, and I woke up sore today. And I'm just tired. Straw mattresses are not what I'm used to." Milla watched me like I spoke a language she didn't, though she tried hard to understand.

I saw an opportunity and threw my hands out to stop Alwin and Milla. There was a break in the trees, and Paldric pointed to a butterfly flitting through the air. I didn't let Alwin or Milla move, both giving me worried looks. Paldric and Tara spoke quietly to not startle the butterfly as it got closer. The butterfly landed on Tara because... symbolic? Of purity and virginity and what not? At least, I was pretty sure Tara was a virgin. It seemed plausible, since she only had eyes for Paldric since... her very existence. She spent twenty-three years just thinking about Paldric.

Not only do I suck at titles, I also suck at writing women.

Paldric and Tara watched the butterfly lift off her shoulder and fly away. Paldric chuckled, then smiled at her.

"Aaaaand..." I waited, anticipating. Their code clearly stated they loved each other, and despite my best efforts to mess everything up, they were having a moment meant to express emotion, but Paldric did nothing. In fact, he turned to keep walking when I raised my hand, pointing at the two of them. "Kiss."

Paldric turned on command and grabbed the back of Tara's head, kissing her. I tried to smile, to make this seem like a natural occurrence.

"I don't..." Alwin folded his arms and adjusted the weight on the balls of his feet. "I don't understand what's happening here."

"Gunther is trying too hard to make them love each other," Milla said.

"Romantic subplot. I'm writing this stupid romantic subplot to distract me, and it's got to work. This is natural. This is completely one hundred percent natural. Look at them." Which they did. Paldric and Tara still kissed under the filtering sunlight of the trees.

Milla tugged my pant leg. "You're at thirteen percent."

I sighed, dropping my hand and Paldric instantly let go of Tara, taking a step back, his eyes wide. "Sorry. I'm so sorry. I... I don't know what came over me. Please forgive me."

"So..." Alwin studied them closer. "Not natural?"

Milla turned her childlike eyes toward me. "Despite the dangers of crochet and scrapbooking, maybe you should pick those up instead."

I kept my mouth shut and moved forward, figuring I could lead the way. Exhaustion hit me, the aches in my legs burning from walk-ing, and we still had five and a half more days of this. My characters followed dutifully behind me. Paldric stayed far away from Tara, and Tara... well, I don't know what she thought of this whole thing. Milla was right. I needed to give up this stupid subplot and do the thing I'd avoided. Tara needed depth.

Chapter Sixteen

I Talk with Tara

We stopped for lunch, the four of them chatting, laughing, and exchanging jokes. Despite the underlining awkwardness of it all, Tara and Paldric soon laughed away their kiss. I sat on the opposite side, eating my rabbit, trying not to stew in my own insecurities and anger. In a way, it was better they excluded me. I wasn't supposed to be here.

Once lunch was done, we followed Alwin on the path. Tara approached from behind, smiling as always. "Hello." I said nothing, glancing at her before facing the dirt road. "Alwin said it might be a good idea if I talk to you. He thinks I can help somehow, and I am only here to serve."

It took a lot to keep myself from wincing. "Isn't there *anything* that tells you that was a weird thing to say?"

"I don't understand." She genuinely didn't.

My focus remained on placing one foot in front of the other. "I just don't know how to help you. And I'm afraid if I tried, I'll screw it up. Again."

"No, no, *I* want to help *you*. It is my nature to serve men," Tara said.

"Please... stop saying things like that."

Confusion etched into her perfectly made-up face. "Like what? Helping men? So... I shouldn't help men?"

Her character code opened, and I needed to be careful about my next words, or she really would stop trying to help men. "I would like you to sound as though you're written by a woman. That's all."

Tara frowned, cocking her head to one side. "I don't know what you mean. What is this 'written by a woman' phrase you said?"

I rubbed the bridge of my nose, my glasses rising as I did so. Tara's very existence was proof I didn't understand women.

Just do what you did with Milla. With Paldric. With Alwin. Trust the process.

We kept walking as I dropped my hand. "So, Tara, what are your life goals?"

"I want to marry Paldric and have his children."

I looked at the sky above me. Esme wouldn't read this. Of that, I was certain. If I could develop Tara without the fear of Esme's judgmental gaze, it might work. "Do you have any other goals that... that don't revolve around men?"

She frowned. "I don't understand the question."

The character code was still up and waiting, ready to listen to my words, so I placed a hand on her shoulder and repeated my question. "What goals do you have that don't revolve around men?"

What I said confused her. "Is that even po—"

"Yes, it's possible. What is something you like to do?"

Something changed in her. I saw it, subtle as it was. The realization hit that she could think or do something for herself first. "I enjoy healing. It brings me satisfaction knowing someone's injuries were eased because of the care I gave them. But... but that doesn't resolve your issue about making goals that don't revolve around men. I want to heal anyone who's hurt. Men or women."

"It's... um." I squinted at the forest as this entered into her character code. "Yeah, it works fine. Is there anything else?"

She shrugged. "I don't know. Why don't you ask me something?"

It wasn't as dependent as before, but it still made me uncomfortable. What with her being slightly more developed, I had to ask her about this, but it still made me squirm. "How was the kiss with Paldric?"

She frowned, mulling over my question. "Paldric seemed embarrassed by the whole thing."

Something about her answer made me uncomfortable, but I couldn't put my finger on it. I stared as far as I could past the dirt road, when I realized she hadn't answered my question at all. "My question wasn't about Paldric's reaction to it. I want to know what *you* thought about it."

Tara again gave me a strange look before she realized what I meant. "I...." She trailed off, frowning. A breakthrough happened. Her eyebrows furrowed together as she formed her own opinion on it. "I liked it. If it happened again, I wouldn't mind, but only if he's comfortable with it. But it embarrassed him, so... I think it won't happen again. And it makes me... sad."

Semi-breakthrough. She still pined for him, but at least we had something. "You can initiate it, you know. You don't have to wait for him to make the first move," I said.

"I can?" She sounded like a child finding out how to work the TV.

Her character code popped up. I placed my hand on her shoulder. Paldric was near, and I didn't want to tip him off, so I used my narrator's voice in my mind. *"Make moves on the main character to help him know you're interested."* I released my hand, smiling. That should help with the romantic subplot. They could figure things out themselves.

"I'm sure you want to—" Before I could finish, Alwin grabbed my collar and pulled me away. "Alwin, what—" An arrow buried into the tree trunk too close for comfort. I gasped. For being an all-powerful God, how did that surprise me?

Paldric grabbed Tara, bringing her closer to him as another three arrows hit the trees. Paldric and Alwin both had their swords out, and Milla ran into my arms. I held her tight.

"What are they?" Tara asked.

As I shifted focus, I understood why they surprised me. I couldn't sense them until they were right there. "Goblins."

"The next town is not far. We can make it if we run," Alwin said.

Milla buried her head in my shoulder as we took off. There were screeches and cries behind us as the goblins gave themselves away. It was much harder to run now that I could feel my aches and also the added weight of an eight-year-old girl.

Dying right now was not an option. Not until Devin told me it was safe, and despite killing her in my original outline, I refused to let Milla die now. Not just because she was my gauge, but because I'd gotten to know her, and put forth energy to deepen her character. This little girl was mine, and she wouldn't die unless I said so.

I did my best to protect Milla as we ran on the dirt road through the forest. Alwin ran ahead, making sure we were safe, and Paldric ran behind with his own sword out.

The burning sensation in my legs grew as the arrows became less.

"Is that smoke?" Paldric asked, out of breath.

My heart sank. Goblins weren't in my original outline, and neither was smoke billowing from the town of Reykir.

We ran toward the edge of Reykir to see buildings on fire. People fought in the streets, but they weren't fighting goblins. They fought each other. The news about King's Court arrived, and I could no longer push it to the back burner. Milla whimpered.

"What happened here?" Alwin's voice trembled, meaning he was terrified, but his elf nature only let that small break show through.

My narration ability reached out, sensing what happened off screen. "Anarchy." I didn't want to set Milla down, as this chaos was as threatening as the goblins behind us, but adrenaline ran its course and I was exhausted. Milla stayed within my shadow. "This is Reykir. One ruled by a strict Lord who visited King's Court often. None of the people liked him, and the King and Queen's death caused them to break. Pavaldri didn't kill him, the people did. They are fighting for power over the lord's manor."

Alwin glanced behind him at the forest. "There are goblins coming. They'll kill the people if they don't kill each other first. Then the goblins will take over instead."

Paldric leapt onto a cart, cupping his hands to his mouth. "Goblins!" Those nearest him paused as the others continued to fight against themselves. "There are goblins in the forest!" More people grew quiet at this, giving him a cautious gaze. "There is a group of goblins who chased us into your town. Please! We need your help to get rid of them!"

I raised an eyebrow, glancing at the townsfolk. Stuff like this only worked in stories. I may have enough control over my story to make it believable. Books had their own sort of logic, so something completely out of the blue, like an entire town putting aside their differences to fight a common enemy, would only make sense if it was a story. Poorly written, but still.

"Prove it!" someone shouted.

Paldric seemed prepared for that. He pulled out an arrow with a jagged arrowhead with a black staff and black feathers from inside his cloak and dropped it to the ground. "They are close. They followed us here, and if you're fighting amongst each other, then they will overtake you easily." He stood taller, his voice stronger. "Please, help us kill the goblins before they get your women and children."

Hero speech. Paldric was trying to be a hero. I winced at how uncomfortable it was, but I could help it along. Being the narrator, I could try to get some more people to believe him, since a small speech wouldn't solve this deep issue of mistrust amongst everyone.

"I have not seen a goblin in this forest for four hundred years!" someone shouted.

There shouldn't have been a goblin ever, but apparently the Rogue wove his evil creatures into my histories just like everything else he'd done.

Alwin leapt up on the cart with Paldric, holding a thick piece of wood next to him. Another black arrow buried into the wood, and there was a loud, unhuman cry of war coming from the forest, far too close to the town. I had to work fast if the entire town would band together.

"Don't be afraid, good people of Reykir!" Paldric ignored the arrow that almost caused his death. His focus was on uniting the town. A hero thing, certainly, but the arrow? Why was he unconcerned about the arrow? "Times may be uncertain, but I know you, people of Veniloria! We cannot let these evil creatures kill our women and children, and for that, let us put aside our differences! Unite to vanquish a common foe!" Paldric said, unsheathing his sword.

The cheers rose, and I frowned. I did nothing. No altering their character, no easing of the anger, it just worked. I glanced at the townsfolk, seeing them prepare for battle, and I frowned. Paldric's optimism would in no way completely change people's minds like this. Maybe the people feared the goblins more. That had to be it.

Alwin grabbed his bow and arrow as I hugged Milla again, turning my back to the forest as a dozen arrows rained down on the town. There were shrieks of surprise as I sensed the townsfolk understand death was near.

"Gather your weapons! Face the enemy!" Paldric shouted.

The arrows stopped, and I passed Milla over to Tara. "Both of you find somewhere safe."

She nodded, taking Milla's hand and running deeper into the chaos of town. I grabbed a jagged piece of wood and moved forward with the men. Maybe Milla should have remained with me, but I was both the safest and the least safest person right now.

"Thirteen percent," I mumbled as the goblins ran toward the town. "I will keep myself at thirteen percent."

The goblins were nasty creatures, with pale skin fit for a corpse and rows of sharp teeth. Their hair was black and slimy. They were once as tall as men, but their backs and legs were bent at odd angles, like someone broke them in multiple places and the creatures magically learned to walk again. They shrieked at each other as they moved forward in a frenzy toward the light, holding their swords. Not that they feared the light, but their berserker rage kicked in whenever they were in danger, and they always felt in danger in the light. What they lacked in coordination, they gained in generating fear in their enemies.

I moved forward with my plank of wood, taking comfort in knowing they couldn't kill me, and tried not to let that be an ego boost. Paldric's hero speech gave the townsfolk little time to prepare, but on the plus side, they already had their weapons out.

The goblins started attacking, and Alwin, Paldric, and I tried to stop the first onslaught as the townsfolk organized themselves. I rammed my plank of wood into one of the goblin's head, dark purple matter getting everywhere. I didn't tap into the code to discover what it was.

My plank of wood snapped after the third goblin, so I stole a sword from one of the dead ones and kept going. I felt as bad killing these things as I would a gnarly spider in my parent's basement.

Little. I cared little. Maybe the thought was dangerous, but I didn't focus on it.

The battle was just getting heated. Then it ended. This scouting party had less than thirty goblins, but that berserker rage made it feel like we faced seventy-five.

Alwin shouldered his bow. "I'll go make sure there aren't anymore in the forest."

Paldric was out of breath, but turned to the elf, frightened. "I can't let you go in alone. What if you get caught?"

My elf gave my main character a look which was as close as he would get to saying, "That's cute," before disappearing into the forest.

I refused to sense him with my narration powers. If I tracked Alwin, the Rogue would know where he was, and Alwin *not* getting caught was the key to making sure the Dark Wizard wasn't powerful enough to release his horde into my world.

I Make a Grave Error

We rounded up the goblin bodies to burn them, and Paldric did his best to keep everyone optimistic. I watched, conflicted, as Paldric talked to a group of men. "It's important to put aside your differences. There's a greater enemy out there, but never forget today. You came together to defeat it, and that kind of strength will help Veniloria stop the creatures of South Island."

The men cheered as I frowned. Now that we took care of the threat, my thoughts returned to Paldric. Was he even that good of a character? He was twenty-four years old. Not a young, stupid idiot, but he also never made decisions which shook his world view and left him with devastating consequences. He helped his father with the fur business, and that was it. The most painful part was how I remember thinking Paldric was everything when I was twenty-three. But now? If I'd written a wooden main character, what did that say about the rest of the book?

Paldric walked over to me, smiling, his eyes bright with optimism. I wracked my brain for anything this man had done that might have shaken him to his core. He had lost his family. He hadn't been there when the dragon killed his parents. This journey *was* his moment to learn. And yet, despite being a new orphan, he was so incredibly optimistic. Was this even relatable? Was Paldric too good of a character? Or was he just another generic, run of the mill humble man from humble beginnings chosen to defeat a dragon? Paldric survived because I was in charge of the antagonist, but now? How badly would the Dark Wizard destroy us?

"Hello, Gunther!" Paldric patted me on the back. "We've all but secured our stay in the inn. They just need help to rebuild some of it." He surveyed the town, still smiling. "A few buildings need help, but look! The people want to put aside their hate!"

He patted me on the back again before following a group toward the inn. I watched, saying nothing. Had nine years changed me that much? Had my romantic relationship and subsequent dissolving of it cause me to break? Or did I just need to admit Paldric wasn't that well written? Maybe it wasn't his optimism I didn't believe in, but that I, personally, could never believably write a character like this, just like I couldn't write a woman.

I walked to another group holding a flat plank of wood steady. Alwin appeared on the other side of me, nodding. No more goblins. For now, at least.

Everyone celebrated in the inn, and I tried not to be cynical. After defeating about thirty goblins, would the townsfolk remember they still had no lord and return to each other's throats? How long before temptation trickled back in? If I thought about it, I could figure it out, but I couldn't bring myself to do it.

I sipped more ale before wincing again at the sweetened, weak alcohol that wasn't even carbonated. It was a small step up from water. Maybe.

Paldric and Alwin had an entire crowd around them. I set my mug down before heading toward the back of the inn.

"Gunther!" Milla ran over to me.

I paused my step. "Hello."

"Where are you going?"

"It's been a long day. I think I'll hit the sack early."

Milla looked confused. "You're going to what?"

"Hit the…" Right. Non-fantasy lingo might not translate well. "I'm turning in early. Sleeping. I'm going to sleep."

"You're at thirteen percent."

"Oh, good. Still stayed the same."

She nodded before rushing off to Tara, who was listening to every word Paldric said. I headed up the stairs and went to my room. I walked in and closed the door, sighing. With a small kick of my feet, my boots came off. I sat on the straw mattress, once again reaching into my pocket to find my phone and check the time before remembering I was in an epic fantasy. If I experienced cell phone withdrawals, I couldn't tell. We had been way busier trying to survive, so I hadn't stopped to think about it. Now that I was thinking about it, I missed it. Had anyone tried to call? Was anyone in the real world worried about me? Was I a huge story? Or did they already move on from the narrator who stumbled into his story to the next sensational headline?

The aches and pains caught up to me. At thirteen percent, I let them hurt. Hopefully, my muscles wouldn't be too stiff tomorrow. I probably logged in a lot of steps today. No, wait, I didn't. I was unconscious on a hospital bed, hooked up to the device and whatever else to keep me alive.

I must have nodded off, because when the knock came, my eyes snapped open. The stars twinkled in the sky as I stood up, straightening my glasses that I forgot to take off. I walked to the door and opened it to see Tara holding a lit lantern.

"Hello." Her musically inclined voice seemed odd at an hour that I knew was still late. She walked in, placing the lantern on the desk.

"Is everyone else asleep?"

She lit the other lantern to give more light. "Yes."

"Can I help you with anything?"

"Yes." She walked over to close the door.

"Alright, what—"

She cut me off by wrapping her arms around my neck and kissing me. My brain took a few seconds to comprehend what was happening. I struggled to unfold my arms before I grabbed her shoulders, forcing her away. "What are you doing?"

"Making moves on the main character." She leaned in to kiss me again, so I backed away. She kept coming closer, so I did the only thing I could think of and grabbed her forehead to keep her at arm's length.

"Tara, I'm not—" I stopped, taking in what she meant. This was a first-person narrative, through *my* perspective. Which, according to basic rules of narration.... "I didn't mean *me*. I meant Paldric. He's *clearly* the hero."

"I go where I am commanded." She pushed my arm aside and kissed me. I didn't realize how close I was to the wall until the force of her knocked me against it. She kept kissing me as I tried to grab her face to stop her. It was getting hard to breathe, and not because of any sexual tension between us, but because she squeezed me and meshed her face into mine. She grabbed my glasses to keep them from hitting her face, and I tried to grab them back while simultaneously trying to break her grip.

"Tara!" I tried to say in the miniscule breaks between kisses. "Stop... it! You... must..." I grabbed her head and pulled her away. "You must listen to me. Stop!"

Tara finally did, but she still had her arms wrapped around me. I tried to peel her off. "I understand now. You have the power to do anything." I never thought I'd miss her sing-song voice, but I would have given anything to hear it instead of the seductive one she had now.

"Forget what I told you."

"I can't. Not without you using your powers."

I winced, knowing she was right. A change in the character code that big needed my God powers. "Alright, well, I'll just have to talk you down and dilute the code somehow." I moved away from the wall to give myself some room to peel her off me.

"Are you certain?" she whispered in my ear. "Don't you realize what you have in me? I could be anything for you. I could even be your ex-wife, Esme."

My arms froze as I grew nauseous. "How do you know about my ex-wife? I never told you that."

"You gave me all the information I needed when you asked me to make moves on you."

"On Paldric. I'd like to emphasize, this was for Pa—"

"To know what you want so I can *be* what you want. Change me into Esme. Do it."

My heart pounded in my chest as I got her off me, backing away from her. "No."

"All your arguments you had with her, you were right every time. She should have listened to you. That's what you want to hear, isn't it?"

"That's not... you can't possibly know all our arguments."

"It doesn't matter. You were still right every single time." Tara tried to hug me again, and I backed away. She tried to take my glasses off again, but I pinned her wrists together, not trusting her to get any closer.

"This is ridiculous. You honestly think this is what I want from my ex-wife? From you?"

"I know what you want, Gunther. How to make the moves on you. You are an all-powerful God. You can do whatever you want."

Of course I made a stupid mistake like this. She tried to kiss me again, but I still held her wrists and wrestled her back. "You cannot exist only as a sexual object. You must believe this deep in your core. Don't you?" I tried to get the character code open again, but the device firmly shut it.

"It's what you want me to be for Paldric, isn't it? What does it matter that it's for you, too?"

"Stop it!" I couldn't help but snap.

"You don't have to follow the rules of actual life." Her voice grew even more seductive, and the hairs on my arms stood straight up. This wasn't working. The velvety tone, the way she somehow moaned with her words. This was totally, completely, absolutely not working on me right now. "You can even make my breasts grow so large they rip through my dress. I know you want to. Do it, Gunther."

"Tara—"

"I can be whatever you want me to be. Don't you realize what you can do with someone like me?"

"Yes, I realize perfectly what will happen. I will go insane," I said through gritted teeth. "You honestly think I'm just building you as the perfect sex partner? You think I would be that degrading to women? I will be the first to admit I cannot create a female character, but a bland character is better than a harmful, stereotypical one." There was a ripping sound. I frowned, then glanced down to see...

I snapped my gaze back at her face, and just her face. "I didn't do that."

Tara smirked. "Yes, you did."

I stared into her eyes, my mind racing. Okay, I admit there was the smallest part of my brain that didn't develop past middle school, which gave in and wondered if I could grow her boobs to rip through her dress, but I didn't want to admit it right after my speech of assuring her she isn't a sexual object. I cleared my throat, glancing at the ceiling, refusing to acknowledge there was a partially naked woman in front of me. The woman whose wrists I was holding to keep her from coming straight at me. The woman with the biggest boobs I ever saw.

Briefly glimpsed them. I was definitely not looking anymore.

"Gunther!" It was Devin. He sounded out of breath like he ran a mile, but also exhausted, like he just woke up. **"Don't. Whatever it is, don't!"**

I wondered how Devin showed up, since I never said his name. Then again, he mentioned before that he could program his phone to alert him if I'd said his name. There were probably other words he'd secretly coded into his phone to alert him for situations like this.

Here's the deal, Devin, I realize what this might look like, and there's a perfectly logical and idiotic reason you're seeing this.

She broke from my grip, leaping onto me as she wrapped her legs around my waist. She grabbed my face, kissing me. I freaked out as I felt *everything*. We slammed against the wall again, but if it hurt her, she didn't show it.

"Focus, Gunther. I need you to stop kissing her."

I've tried! Honest, I have.

"Come on, this is bad. You can't do this. Not now, not ever."

Oh, no. Oh, her lips. I think… they're getting softer. And her tongue! What is she…

"You're the one doing this, Gunther!"

Nothing else is going to happen, Devin. Don't worry.

"Okay, but I need you to stop."

I will. I definitely will.

"Now, Gunther." There was a beat of silence where auto narration took over, mentioning how I didn't respond because it was getting difficult to focus. **"Gunther?"**

We're just kissing. That's all we're doing.

"Then explain to me why your shirt is off."

Is it?

"Absolutely no turning into an unreliable narrator. I can see you too. You realize this, right?"

Yes, you can, and… and it's… important to…

Devin gave a disgruntled hiss. **"I'm doing this for your own good. Grace? Are you patched in?"**

"I am, yes," a female voice said. It was enough to make me pause, to open my eyes and glance at the ceiling as Tara kissed my neck. I hadn't met Grace, but knew she was the age of my grandmother. The kind who would bring you a meal if you were sick. Knit a sweater. Offer you a place to stay if you were homeless. Her grandmotherly voice projected through my story while I was shirtless, kissing a woman with…

It was like my own grandmother watched, so yes, it put a damper on things.

"If you won't listen to me, you will listen to Grace. Are we clear?" Devin asked.

"I've read enough, Gunther. You may use your power to erase the code. I give you permission. Do it now," she said in her oh-so grandmotherly voice.

I did everything in my power to not describe Tara kissing me and where exactly my mind was going while she did it. I braced myself against the wall, trying to stop, but this was swiftly becoming the best make-out session I've ever had. The last time I kissed a woman was—

"Erase the code, dear. This is sexual assault. You must stop this."

Sexual assault? No, it isn't. We're not even… nothing like that is…. If anything, this was all her idea. The very definition of consensual.

"As God, you can choose who gives consent, and therefore no one really does. You are not erasing the code you gave her accidentally, therefore you are letting this happen against her will. I'm sorry, but you cannot keep doing this if you want to stay sane."

It was difficult to describe what was happening, but we were definitely not having sex.

Which is when the door flew open.

"Hey Gunther? You're at forty-seven per—" Milla stopped as she saw the sight in front of her, her mouth falling open.

Chapter Eighteen

I Force Myself to Face Some Consequences

Tara gasped as I let her go. She kept her back to Milla, giggling as she grabbed the blankets off the bed to cover her torn dress.

My eyes widened, my hands against the wall. "What are you doing here?"

Milla's mouth still hung open. She didn't want to stare, but she couldn't think of another option. Her outline was blurry, and I scrambled for my glasses on the floor. Forty-seven percent. This entire ordeal (which was just a long make-out session, and it definitely wasn't sex) cost me over thirty percent of my sanity. I'd hate to know what would have happened if we actually had sex. I placed my glasses back on my nose.

I frowned, straightening. What was Milla doing here? The code came to me, and I realized this was all Devin. While I explained away my actions to Grace, he waited for the instant I hit forty-five percent and woke Milla up, playing on her obligation to tell me when I reached a dangerous percentage.

No, wait. Not just Milla. I heard footsteps coming down the hall before Alwin and Paldric walked in.

"Did anyone else hear something?" Paldric asked before stopping dead in his tracks, his face showing every single negative emotion before it simply shut down.

You know what? At least I still had pants on. Because we definitely did not have sex.

"Yeah. Because Grace slowed you down," Devin said.

Alwin was not smiling and glanced at Paldric. From their perspective, with its medieval rules of chastity, I had done something worthy of being thrown in a dungeon somewhere. It didn't help that Tara still giggled.

This is a lovely predicament. Clever move, Devin.

"You're welcome."

I chewed on the tip of my tongue as I got my thoughts organized. "This might be... difficult to understand..."

"If you want your percentage to lower, I strongly encourage you to take every consequence coming your way. You are dangerously close to fifty percent. Do not shy away from what's about to happen," Devin said.

I sighed, rubbing my forehead before touching Tara's shoulder. Paldric's eyes narrowed at my movement, but I only erased the accidental code. I also shrank her boobs, as awkward as that was to admit, even in my head. She stopped giggling, her eyes widening as she covered herself all the way to her neck. She looked at me, horror in her eyes as fear hit her. Like waking up from a dream she vividly remembered, and realizing it was a nightmare. Then to understand it happened in real life. She became a different person with the code, and was now back, bland as she was. Except there was another addition to her code that naturally formed. Not only did she love Paldric, but she felt horrified by what I forced her to do.

Oh, I am such a misogynistic pig.

"Forty-eight percent," Milla said. Alwin stared at Milla in alarm. Paldric's glare darkened.

"Alright, yes, thank you, Milla." My mind came back to the situation. Forty-eight percent. Could I return from this?

"Yes, dear. Don't do it again. Do what you can to drop the percentage. The longer you wait, the harder it will be to drop it," Grace said.

But how do I accept the consequences?

"The way it happens in the real world. Apologize, then accept whatever ramifications this causes without trying to erase them," Devin said.

Alwin took Milla's shoulder and ushered her out the door, closing it to keep her on the other side.

"Look, Paldric." I unfolded my arms and headed toward him. "I realize what this might look like, and I'm—"

He punched me in the face. Alwin's eyes widened. The skin on my cheek broke and my vision swam as my glasses flew across the room. Tara screamed in surprise. My cheek throbbed in pain. What happened? I thought I was invulnerable.

"You're accepting the consequences, and not having invulnerability is part of it," Devin said.

I glanced at Paldric. It surprised him that his punch drew blood, but it didn't lessen his anger toward me one bit.

"Whatever you did, keep doing it!" Milla said from the other side of the door. "He felt the consequences, so it brought him down a whole three percent!"

Paldric raised his fist again. "Gladly." He punched me, and I almost lost my balance, certain one of my teeth came loose.

"Stop it!" Tara screamed.

"Paldric!" I managed to say, backing toward the wall. "I didn't... we never had sex..."

"That's not an apology, Gunther," Grace said.

He punched me again, and I fell, prepared for a severe beating, before Alwin grabbed Paldric and dragged him away. I remained on my back, holding my face.

"You are going to kill him," Alwin said.

Paldric tried to break out of his grasp. "No, I'm not. He can't die."

"Then take a moment to consider if you want to anger someone who can't die."

Paldric glared at Alwin before breaking free of his grip to back away, facing the wall as he tried to calm down. I kept a groan in, still holding my cheek like it would take the pain away. I mean, I knew how to make the pain disappear, but I wouldn't.

"Good man," Grace said.

Milla's spoke from behind the door. "He's settled at thirty-eight percent."

A whole ten percent for my little beating. That, at least, was good news. Still dangerously high, but it was something.

Tara spun around and marched out the door, holding back a sob as she slammed it behind her. I winced. No matter how I justified it during the moment, Grace was right. This was all my fault. When my mistaken code presented itself, I didn't fix it fast enough. Then I almost blew my entire sanity on a moment that lasted maybe ten minutes.

"The device truly is that dangerous. I would like to commend you on your humility. Wait for when you're back in the real

world before trying to have any sort of relationship, dear. Don't do it again. If you do, I will be back." It felt like being chastised by my grandmother, and I didn't know how to respond. **"Even good people can fall at the temptation of so much power. Keep your chin up. We will get you out."**

I nodded before climbing to my feet, leaning against the wall. Paldric faced me while I was talking with Grace, and I didn't know how long he glared at me. His entire profile was blurry, but I could still tell he was livid.

"I was an idiot." There was pain in my mouth as I spoke. I rubbed my chin before realizing my lip was bleeding. "It was all my fault. Don't blame Tara for this."

My main character tried to say something. He was too angry to get his jumbled thoughts together, but he wanted to strangle me to see if he could kill a God. I might have killed the bright, hopeful, optimistic outlook he had. Paldric strode toward the door, the vexation oozing from his body as he slammed the door harder than Tara had. I winced, knowing I could make everyone forget this encounter, but that would be avoiding the consequences.

Milla peeked her head inside as Alwin went to collect my glasses. "Thirty-seven. You're now at thirty-seven percent."

My fingers touched my face, trying to find any other injuries I didn't know about. "Thank you, Milla."

She nodded, then left for her room. Alwin grabbed my shirt and tossed it to me before placing my glasses in my hand. "For all our sakes, please take up crochet."

I sighed as Alwin left, then put on my shirt before placing my glasses back on my nose. Once again, my fingers tenderly touched my injuries as I walked over to the lanterns, blowing them out. I sat on the side of my bed in total darkness, burying my head tenderly in my hands. My blankets were in Tara's room, but I would let her have those.

"Find a balance, Gunther. Be hard on yourself to never do this again, but pat yourself on the back for accomplishing something few have done in your position," Devin said.

Few? Only a few?

"Don't misinterpret my meaning. You were wrong to do what you did, but you also stopped. I don't envy the uphill climb you now need to make to rebuild the trust of your characters, but I'm relieved you have a climb to make."

I nodded before taking a deep breath and settling into bed, looking at the ceiling. "So, I can't even kiss in my story?"

"Let's just say I've never seen a person stay sane after altering someone to be who they want physically, no matter the level of intimacy. Passions are too high. Yes, people who write themselves in their stories may not be the best to get a conclusive analysis, but I also refuse to study this further. Just stay away from it."

"Alright." I didn't mean to sound like I was in pain; it just came out that way. But Devin was right. I couldn't do this again. I was a hot-blooded male, and I felt awful about how this hurt Tara. "How does it look, trying to get me out?" I needed a change of subject.

"We've all combed through the code about a dozen times each. None of us have found anything. We have a few theories. One, as mentioned before, is dying in this world. If you're in a battle, call my name and we'll be here to guide you through it. To see if your death could bring you out. Don't try it without our help, just in case something goes wrong."

Even though my story was a highly realistic simulation, the thought of dying still filled me with existential dread. Especially considering

Devin *still* mentioned something could go wrong. With death. It did not bring me comfort.

"We don't like it either. The other idea Vince had was doing a sequel."

I couldn't help but speak out loud. "Sorry, a what?"

"A sequel. We're all uncomfortable about the idea, even Vince, but if you hit a certain word count, we can condense the data and move it to a new device. The new device would have the failsafe and let you write yourself out of your story."

My eyes traced the rafters. "And it will be safer than dying?"

"Theoretically. The problem is you'll be in your story for a long time. There's a certain word count you need to hit before we think about a sequel."

That's true. Epic fantasies run at least a hundred thousand words, which I don't even know how long that would equate to real word narration.

"Luckily, we don't have to follow what's usual for an epic fantasy. Eighty thousand words will suffice," Devin said.

"What am I at now?"

"You are at..." there was a pause as Devin most likely scrolled through whatever data he needed. **"About thirty-six thousand, two hundred words."** He chuckled. **"You could try beefing up your descriptions."**

I tried to smile, looking up at the ceiling. Looking at the dark wood rafters. With the off whitish walls. Tying in with the dark wood floors.

Descriptions can be hard.

"Something tells me you'll get in a battle before the end of the novel. We'll try letting you die first," Devin said.

"Great." I curled up, ready to sleep without blankets tonight. I would not ask for them back. "As long as the group doesn't kick me out first."

"I don't blame them if they do, but then again, they might not."

I was a danger to everyone around me. Not only because of the Rogue, but because I needed to keep my sanity in check. Maybe it would be better if they left me behind.

Chapter Nineteen

AND EVEN MORE CONSEQUENCES

The sun peeked over the horizon, though no one would see it directly because of the thick forest. The sky was a beautiful blue, with little white clouds. Sunlight filtered in through the window, illuminating my room. The birds chirped, and a few people were already outside, bustling about.

Was that enough description? Maybe. Let's see, I had sights and a few sounds. That was two of the senses. Smell.

The air was anything but fresh, which was odd, considering I associated fresh with morning time. Then I remembered the battle last night, and how we burned those goblin bodies. Whatever was in their dark purple blood and corpse-like flesh, it lingered in the air. I couldn't tell what they were cooking for breakfast. Probably some sort of oatmeal. Between the stench of the bodies and the IV in real life, I had no appetite.

Right. Now feel.

I was getting used to the straw mattress, even though my sleep last night was rough. It wasn't just because I didn't have a blanket. I straightened my clothes that still felt like my university tee and shorts. I turned off, so to speak, the texture of my modern clothes, to feel the scratchy shirt and the far simple thread of my pants. These felt way too easy to tear.

There. That should give almost two hundred words of description. Was I worried about death? Absolutely. I'd much rather try reaching a sequel instead of dying, even if it meant staying here longer than expected.

When I opened the door, I found Paldric already there. I sucked air through my teeth as I tried not to imagine him beating me again. Alwin was nowhere in sight to stop him, so it was a possibility. I waited, watching him with a cautious gaze. The ghost of anger remained on his face. He checked on Tara last night. The two talked about whether to run to the next town, but Tara was too afraid. Which ended in her sobbing into his shirt and him promising he would kill me if I tried to do that again. Paldric spent most of the night tossing and turning. Yet here he was, at my door, holding a bottle from Tara's pack.

"Look, Paldric. What happened last night was—"

"If you truly love her. Then I would suggest—"

"No," I said, maybe too fast. I didn't want to admit how horribly underwritten Tara was, and I listened to the wrong head last night. "It will never happen again. And if I do this again, then... then yes, kill me like you promised her last night." I folded my arms, not looking at him.

Paldric frowned. It did not scare him that I knew about their conversation. More affirmed how dangerous I could get if I ever made it past fifty percent. I knew everything, and them running away wouldn't help.

"So, we've got to make sure you don't crack?"

"If you still want me in the group. I understand if you don't."

Paldric gave the smallest of smiles before holding out the bottle to me. I took it, frowning as I read the label. "Witch hazel?"

"It keeps the wounds from getting infected." Paldric pulled out a rag from his pocket and placed it on top of the bottle. I stared at it, then I looked at him, wondering again if Tara wasn't the only underwritten character in this novel. Him getting angry and beating the crap out of me was relatable. This? I didn't understand this.

"Has anyone told you that you are too trusting? And optimistic? And you need a healthy dose of cynicism in order to survive this world?"

Paldric smiled, the anger gone from his face. "I truly believe you want to do better, Gunther. You care about this world, and you care about us. Yes, your mistakes come with more dangerous ramifications, but I don't believe I should treat you any less." I stared at him. The choices were we leave as a group, or I get left behind. This was mostly why he was tossing and turning so much last night. Once I hit fifty percent, it didn't matter where the group was. I would still find them and make them do whatever I wanted. But Paldric got it in his head that being kind would somehow keep me from cracking. Maybe he was right. Or maybe he was a standard hero who didn't realize how dangerous I was because he always needed to err on the side of kindness.

I sighed before attempting to uncork the bottle. "You're such a hero. Do you know that?"

Paldric chuckled before taking the bottle again and uncorking it for me. "Just trying to rectify my own mistakes last night."

"Nope. Don't you dare apologize for that. I deserved that and more." Paldric soaked some of the witch hazel on the rag before handing it to me.

"Maybe you did, but I should apologize anyway. I'm just grateful Alwin was there to stop me, or I might have made you crack."

I placed the rag against the cut on my lip, wincing. It was a cold tingle, but it felt nice. I didn't know what my face looked like, but it couldn't have been pretty. "And Paldric, if Milla ever says I'm past forty-five percent again, you have my permission to hit me. Especially if it makes the percentage go down. Hit me as much as you can until it levels out."

Paldric nodded, a grim look on his face. "I will."

Alwin climbed the stairs, panting, and both of us turned. Alwin appeared on the landing, splattered with dark purple blood, with one side of his face swollen. My eyes widened as I dropped the rag from my lip. "What happened?"

My elf wiped his forehead with his arm, smearing goblin blood across his face. "Two goblins tried kidnapping me just now." He said it as though this was an everyday occurrence. "They weren't successful."

Nausea grew in my stomach. Seeing Alwin covered in goblin blood reminded me again how little control I had over my story right now. And how goblins snuck up on me. While I talked with Paldric, Alwin struggled for his life and I didn't even notice.

Alwin paused, then his gaze shot toward a room down the hall. "Tara." As soon as he said it, she screamed at the top of her lungs. We raced down the hall to her room. I threw open the door next to Tara's room to find Milla, looking frightened. She sprinted into my arms and I held her before peeking into the other room. The goblin hissed at Paldric and Alwin while placing his jagged sword against Tara's throat. He stood on the bed to be as tall as her, considering he was so bent and broken. Alwin aimed his bow at the goblin.

"Don't try it, young elf. There are thousands of me, but one Tara. I am replaceable. She is not."

The chip in Paldric's sword looked threatening as he pointed it at the goblin. "What do you want with her?"

The goblin laughed again, though it sounded more like a hiss. "I will not answer to you, foolish boy."

"What are your intentions with Tara?" I used my best narrator voice, staying in the doorway to protect Milla.

"We were unsuccessful with the elf," the goblin couldn't help but say. "So, we will take the lady to draw you out and steal the elf that way. Tara is far weaker. More susceptible to our Dark Wizard's suggestions. We would make her one of us before having her seduce the elf to draw him out alone." The goblin clamped his mouth shut. Tara closed her eyes, tears running down her cheeks.

"Alwin is incapable of being seduced. Not by Tara, at least," I said.

The goblin's mouth trembled as it opened. "There are other ways besides love to seduce a person. And considering Tara is a malleable character, the Dark Wizard will be successful in turning her to our side."

I winced as the goblin said character. My other characters shouldn't get a hint they were in the story. Milla shivered in my arms, her hands covering her ears.

Tara slammed her heel against the goblin's foot, and he gasped.

"Drop, Tara," Alwin said.

She tried, but the goblin had a firm grip on her waist. It was enough for Alwin, though, as he shot the goblin between the eyes. Paldric strode forward, grabbing Tara and pulling her away from the slackening grip. My elf appeared by the goblin's side, a dagger to the creature's throat. "He's dead."

I crept into the room. "It would have surprised me if he wasn't."

Paldric held Tara's arms. "Are you alright?" She nodded, her fingers shaking as she touched her head, feeling the goblin's blood there. "That was a dangerous thing you did, but I'm glad you're safe."

Tara nodded again, her voice sounding breathless. "I didn't want to get kidnapped."

Another breakthrough! She acknowledged kidnapping was bad, and she didn't want to be a victim! She had a long way to go, but this start was promising. And considering she, in her state, was more valuable than Alwin, I needed to swallow my pride and make sure she got developed enough. If she even wanted to talk to me after last night.

Alwin sheathed his dagger. "I'll alert the innkeeper about what transpired."

I eased Milla down. "It would be best to eat our breakfast and leave quickly. The Dark Wizard wants all of us. Let's leave so this town can have the peace they need to rebuild."

They all nodded before we filed out of Tara's room.

Chapter Twenty

There's Probably a Montage of Us Walking, and I Hate It

Narration is hard. Being stuck in a story where narration falls on you is even harder. I tried describing every single flower on the path. Described how light filtered through the trees, and used it a lot. I described clouds lazily floating through the afternoon sky, morphing with the wind. I talked about the different trees and foliage, not caring that the dry descriptions belonged more in a high school biology book. For two days, I used this distraction. The crisp autumn turned warmer the closer we got to Vaywell, the always sunny port city. The aches and pains finally dulled on their own as I got stronger. I celebrated the minor victories as, after two days, Milla reported I dropped to thirty-one percent.

According to Alwin, we would get to Vaywell in another two days. Still behind the necromancer and his army, but since he didn't turn his creatures around to attack us, the shield was clearly his top priority. It was a relief to see no other towns get hit. The necromancer tried to be as secretive as possible. As secret as someone could after destroying the King's Court and attacking the town next to it with a scouting party of goblins.

That night, Devin and I chatted while I paced in my new room in the Needy Nymph Inn.

"Not reaching Vaywell in time shouldn't be a concern. I should have enough narration to dive into the sequel soon."

"What are you talking about?" Devin asked.

I took a long drink from my cup of water. I had mumbled through most of the journey the past two days, and my throat was sore. "Isn't there enough words?"

Devin paused. **"Um, I'm not exactly sure how to tell you this..."**

My heart dropped to my stomach. "What?"

"The device only picks up your narration if something interesting is happening. I'm pretty sure... yep. Your narration for the past two days amounted to a little over two hundred words of summary."

I swallowed, which should have felt nice on my raw throat, but it emphasized the uselessness of pushing it. I tried to place my cup of water down as gently as possible, but it wasn't gentle. "Two days? Of non-stop muttering? And it only amounts to... to *that*!" I tried to sound like I wasn't about to lose my temper.

Devin sighed. **"I'm sorry. When a narrator writes themselves in a story, the device takes over as editor and only picks up the narration if you're in a scene of action or character development.**

Since you've been walking for the past two days, it found nothing of interest. So it summarized instead."

"But what about the other narrators in my position? If the device is this selective, how do you keep tabs on them?"

"The narrators in the hospital don't bother walking to places, and... well, they are always doing things the device considers character development or action." I frowned, not liking his answer. **"It is the nature of the beast. You have written an epic fantasy, after all."**

I groaned, leaning against my bed, feeling my will to continue drain out of me. "Two days." My hoarse voice served as a reminder. "Two days of narration. All worthless."

"No, not completely worthless." I sensed him scrolling through the word section of the computer. **"Look at this. You're down to thirty-one percent in two days. That is fantastic news. And this conversation is being recorded, too."**

I sighed, hanging my head in dismay. "Fine. Do you want to help pad my word count?"

"Uh, sure?"

We talked about random things until we settled on our university experiences. We both got a Narration degree, and only one university specialized in those. Devin might have gone ten years earlier than I, but the legendary creamery never changed.

"That was the best ice cream I ever tried. I almost can't have ice cream anymore, because I remember what it was like there."

"Absolutely. Mint ice cream always tastes like toothpaste, but the creamery there just *worked*." The exhaustion hit me as I leaned against the wall my bed was up against. This wasn't helping my throat at all, but I needed more words. "I wish I could go back. Do you know why the Guardian Headquarters are so far from the university? You'd think they'd be closer together."

Devin then explained the long history of the narration device. No one expected the device to get as big as it had. It completely revolutionized the entertainment industry. A narrator built the story, created the plots, characters, everything, then narrated the story to be the audiobook. The word part became a bound book. The movie portion became the movie. Others took the unedited movie and slashed it to two, two-and-a-half-hours. Or the purists could watch the entire thing unedited. A narrator knew they reached popularity when professionals created a soundtrack, since music was the only thing the device couldn't do.

A year after the accidental discovery of the device, it exploded in popularity. They soon discovered the dangers, too. The government shut down production of the narration device because of the deadly accident between the scientists who first wrote themselves into their own story. They were the first to discover such an ability, and it cost them their sanity. The government founded the Guardians as part of a specialized branch to help control the powerful devices soon after, and the distribution of the devices resumed. The Guardians required people to obtain a narration degree before someone could touch a device, which became the duty of one university on the other side of the country.

"The university is happy to hand out degrees, and the city is happy to host the Guardians, too. We know the device is as deadly as ever, so we are careful to not shake things up too much."

"Huh." I folded my arms. "Well, that's super interesting. And thank you for padding my story with more words."

Devin hesitated again. **"Actually..."**

My heart sank. "No..."

"The narration device summarized it, both what I said and about the creamery. It was kind of pointless, after all. And info dumpy."

I hit my head softly against the wall a few times, trying not to get angry again. "This has been at least a two-hour conversation."

"All summed up in—" again I sensed Devin scrolling through the words, **"Eight hundred and... forty-two. Forty-three. Forty-four. Forty-five."**

"And yet I hiked through Veniloria for two days and this two-hour conversation accumulated more words."

"The device knows when something will happen. Or characters will develop. It's a genius invention."

"Character development?" I looked at the ceiling. "Is that me being developed right now?"

"You are, technically, now a character in this story."

A headache formed, so I took off my glasses. The inn was quiet, everyone sleeping peacefully except me. I should sleep, but I wanted to milk this conversation for every word.

"There's got to be a better method."

I understood what he meant. This conversation was being recorded, but listening to Devin count the words this conversation accumulated wouldn't be the most riveting book.

"Nine hundred and sixty-nine. Nine hundred and... seventy-three. Nine hundred and... seventy-seven," Devin mumbled for my benefit.

"Maybe that will put me to sleep." I grabbed my blankets and settled in for the night.

"If you don't want to die, we can choose another way. None of us will force you to do something you're uncomfortable with."

I stared at the ceiling, my eyes heavy with the desire to sleep. "Something going wrong with my death terrifies me. I don't want to actually die in the real world."

"We'd make sure that would never happen. You are barely halfway with your word count. I don't know how you'll last another forty-thousand words in this story. Let us know if you find yourself in another battle soon, and more importantly, whether you want to try dying."

The device focused on this conversation because this was where my character discovered I couldn't rely on word count. The character part of me in this vast story realized I spent the last two days avoiding my problems and needed to face them. Despite kicking myself repeatedly, I still hadn't talked with Tara and developed her character. I would rather mumble about the way the light hit a flower than talk to her after what I did. If I was being honest, I wanted to end the story before we all got to Vaywell. This story needed to end way before then so my characters could be safe.

"And if not? If you end up in Vaywell?"

Then this story needed to end well, and not...

"It will end well. Be like Paldric. Stay optimistic."

Yeah, well, I'm pretty sure Paldric only has a little more depth than Tara. There is no way someone can stay this optimistic all the time. Paldric must know, deep down in his core, that someone up there guided his actions and made sure everyone stayed safe. But me being here must remind him that it couldn't work like that anymore.

"Try being optimistic. You can do it," Devin said.

"It should all work out fine." I tried out this strange phrase to see if I believed it.

"There you go! And, hey! It looks like we're reaching the end of another chapter!"

I cracked an eye open. "Chapters? I haven't even thought about those."

"The device is breaking it down for you. You don't need to worry about them."

Both awe and unease came over me. "Fair enough. How many are there?"

"You are coming to the end of your twentieth chapter."

"Hmm. That's not bad." A realization hit me. "Do I have to name the chapter headings?"

"The device took care of that, too. It takes your overall emotions and does its best to name them how it assumes you would name them."

"As long as it's the device and not me. I would hate to rename those stupid chapter headings." Devin snorted, and I frowned. "What?"

"That's literally the name of your third chapter." I couldn't help it and smiled. Maybe I should feel unsettled that the device knew me this well, but it was kind of funny. I'd save the existential dread for a later time. Tonight, I was too exhausted. **"Good night, Gunther."**

I settled into my straw mattress, feeling some stalks poking at me. "Good night, Devin."

On to chapter twenty-one!

I Create a Clever Chapter Heading that Draws ALL the Attention!

The conversation with a certain man in the Guardians put a spring in my step. Maybe I wasn't nearly as optimistic as Paldric, but today, when he smiled at me, it was easier to smile back. Which then my body reminded me of my still healing fat lip, so I stopped smiling, but Paldric got the picture.

Despite my good mood, I still felt exhausted from my late chat with Guardian guy. My cup of water rested in my palms, and I contemplated how much percentage it would take to change it into a steaming cup of coffee. I failed to develop coffee in this world. Why I didn't add it to my story was an oversight on my part. I didn't have my phone to look it up, but I was pretty sure coffee already existed in the medieval period.

"The longer you think about it, the more the percentage will spike once you give in," Milla said.

I tore my gaze from my water. "Sorry?"

She shrugged. "I don't know. Just thought I'd say that."

The frown tugged at my healing lip again, but I considered what she said. "So if I stew about it days before changing my water into coffee, my percentage will get hit harder than if I change it now?"

She gave a look of genuine confusion, then realization crossed her face. "If you casually change it to coffee, it might not be as big of a spike, but it's still a tick. You'll be in danger of excusing your actions, and will reach forty percent again before you know it."

I sighed, draining the last of my water. "So, it's easier to... not?"

Milla shrugged. "You know better than I do."

"Where am I at, anyway?"

"Thirty percent. Good job." She patted my arm. She didn't understand why, but she hoped it made me feel better.

"Thanks." I patted her hand back.

"What's coffee?" she asked before taking a large bite of oatmeal.

I rubbed my head. "Something I'm seriously considering might be worth half a percent right now."

We finished and left the inn. We stepped outside to see Alwin teaching Tara the sword, and I raised an eyebrow.

Paldric walked up to us. "Are we ready to go?"

Their fight captivated me. "Whenever they are." Alwin went slowly with Tara. He held his sword with one hand while Tara held hers with both. It looked heavy. She noticed me and Milla and the sword tip touched the ground.

"Thanks, Alwin. May we practice more tomorrow morning?" She handed the sword back to him.

"Of course!" Alwin sheathed his two swords. "I can't promise you'll be a master swordswoman, but it should be enough to keep you protected."

Tara nodded, rubbing her arm.

I approached her. "Learning the sword?"

She looked at me, and her smile dropped. "Yes. I asked Alwin to help me learn, since we're tracking a group of cursed creatures with a necromancer as their leader."

Paldric's eyes bore a hole into my skull as I nodded. "That's smart. And proactive." She was making her own little breakthroughs, which was a relief to me. I was happy she took the initiative, but I knew I couldn't just abandon her to discovering her personality.

She said nothing, folding her arms and finding every excuse not to look at me. Clearly, the two days of us avoiding each other hadn't made it easier. Alwin joined Paldric in watching me.

"Could we talk?" I asked.

She still didn't look at me. "As long as you start by apologizing."

I winced. Had I not apologized yet? "Of course. An apology that's borderline groveling." A microscope could have caught Tara's smile, but at least her eyes noticeably softened. Alwin kept bouncing his gaze between the two of us before taking Milla's hand and leading our little group. Paldric was behind us, making sure I noticed his hand on the hilt of his sword. I nodded at him, agreeing with his position as we followed Alwin. "I'm sorry, Tara. Sorry about what happened. Sorry it's taken me so long to talk to you. I'm sorry I did not apologize right after it happened."

Tara said nothing, her arms folded as she looked at the town we passed through so she wouldn't have to look at me. "Apology acknowledged."

Yeah, that's the best I could hope for. I sighed, staring ahead. At least she was developing a character. If she was her usual bland self from before, she would have accepted my apology without another thought. The temptation returned about making everyone forget it had ever happened, but it would be too dangerous.

The problem was, I needed to help deepen her character so the Dark Wizard couldn't get her. It wouldn't take long for the Dark Wizard to turn her against me. I couldn't abandon her to do this herself, but this conversation was no doubt painful. Not pulling teeth painful. More like I had already pulled out her teeth, and I needed to acknowledge I wasn't a dentist as she writhed on the floor in pain.

"Are you comfortable with me being in the group?" I asked.

She didn't look at me, instead glancing at Paldric for security, who still gripped the hilt of his sword, listening to every word we said. "Paldric and I had a lengthy talk after what happened." I didn't want to tell her I already knew. "I don't know how I feel about you. What happened terrified me, but only after the fact. You changed my personality to fit what you wanted. It was me, but it wasn't."

I watched her out of the corner of my eye. This device was so dangerous because of things like this. It took me believing Tara was just a character, not on the same level as me, and I could do whatever I wanted to her. I held up the proverbial mirror and had the discussion with myself. Since everyone here were figments of my imagination brought to life by a scarily accurate simulation device, no one in this world was on my same level. But when it came down to it, despite whether my characters were real, there would undoubtably be a moral erosion of my character if I decided they didn't matter. Even if science proclaimed my characters weren't real, the erosion would still happen, and that was what I needed to avoid. To do that, I had to believe they were the same as me.

"What the Dark Wizard could do to you has me worried." I glanced at the sky through the canopy of trees. "His ability to... to manipulate you worries me." I did not know how else to word it. Saying she was an underdeveloped character in a story wouldn't work.

"I'm training myself as best I can to not get kidnapped," she said.

"An excellent start." I didn't mean it as a joke, but she smiled all the same.

"Do I really need your help to protect myself from the Dark Wizard's manipulation?" Tara asked.

Her question intimidated me, despite my efforts to not feel that way. I tried to approach it as if one of my male characters asked me instead. "It's vital I make sure you're on the right track. To understand what's going on and correct it if I need to."

She made a face at me, and I could have sworn I heard Esme in her words. "And if I don't want you in charge of correcting what I do?" Her character code popped up, sensing this conversation as important character development.

This was dangerous ground I found myself on. I organized my thoughts, because I couldn't be wrong about this. "I realize the position this puts you in, as I understand your disgust and fear of me right now." She stayed glaring at me, far more terrified than she let on. "Tara?"

She shook her head. "You talk about the dangers of the Dark Wizard manipulating me, but two days ago, it was *you* who manipulated *me*."

There are moments where a character says a phrase so defining that it surprises me, and it happened right now. But this time, it cut my soul. I slowed to a stop. Paldric stopped to stay near us, and Alwin and Milla moved enough so the little girl wouldn't overhear, but the elf would. Tara waited, trying to keep her face steady, but she was afraid she insulted me to the point I might crack.

"I manipulated you. You're right." Paldric watched me closely. "I... I changed your personality to fit what I wanted."

I saw it in her eyes. She didn't have to tell me. If the Dark Wizard was the bad guy, and the bad guy wanted to manipulate her, but the "good guy" already did it...

"You think I'm a villain, don't you?"

Gunther is a potential villain.

It slid so fast into her character code. Potential. Not a full-blown villain, but still incredibly dangerous if she ever ended up in the Dark Wizard's hands. I again resisted the urge to make her forget about what happened two days ago.

She looked away. "I would rather do this on my own."

I shifted on the balls of my feet. Making her forget it happened was wrong, but the Dark Wizard would absolutely use her anger and fear.

"Sorry, Tara, but I need to help. It's my only request. You can make whatever boundaries you need to help you feel safe." Right now, she had a few things on her character list besides seeing me as a potential villain. Loves Paldric. Hates me. Learning the sword. Doesn't want to be kidnapped anymore.

Tara stared at me, the distrust so clear even Milla noticed. She tested my promise. "If Paldric keeps his sword pointed at your throat the entire time we're talking?"

"If that's what makes you feel safe."

Paldric pulled out his sword, walking forward. Tara held out a hand. "No, Paldric. Not... not that drastic." Tara might have just said it to test my resolve, but Paldric absolutely would have placed his sword against my throat if she asked.

"You could even have Alwin hide in the trees with a bow and arrow, ready to assassinate me at whatever command you choose." I gave my equally absurd suggestion, prepared to commit if she agreed. Tara watched me with narrow eyes. "I realize I violated your trust, and I don't expect to get it back. At all. But this is something we've got to do to keep us safe. Not just me, but Paldric, Alwin, and Milla, too. If the Dark Wizard succeeds, it's not just me he'll try to destroy. It's also them."

She frowned, then glanced at the other three characters. Her code about me appeared, the device rewording it while keeping its core theme. I reached out to sense it.

I care more about the others than Gunther, but listening to him is in my best interest to keep the others safe. In my eyes, Gunther is an anti-hero with villainous tendencies, and I cannot trust him without the others near.

Alright, well, better than seeing me as a potential villain, even if being called an anti-hero does sting my law-abiding soul.

She started walking again. I followed her, and she purposefully didn't meet my gaze. "I shall see you at lunch, where we will talk in front of Paldric, Alwin, and Milla. If you are too uncomfortable to say something in front of them, then you will not say it to me. We will do this today, and I will decide if anything needs to be altered for tomorrow's lunch visit. It will only be at lunch, and you will not talk to me any other time unless I talk to you first. Are we clear?"

"Perfectly."

"Good." We kept walking. The silence was still prickly, but we finally broke it. Tara tucked some hair behind her ear, and I noticed that the curls in her hair were getting flat, and the make-up wasn't so caked on. After a morning sword training with Alwin, it made sense, but a small part of me smiled. She didn't look nearly as perfect, and it was a lovely thing to see. She turned to talk to me, and my smile dropped. "I'm going to walk with Paldric now."

I nodded. "I'm sorry again, Tara. It never should have happened."

"No. It should not have happened. Yet it did. And I'm glad you understand how incredibly wary I am of you." She slowed until she was with Paldric. I let her, sensing Paldric reaching over and taking her hand. She squeezed it back, and he let go of the hilt of his sword.

This was the first conversation I had with her where I didn't feel like Esme was breathing down my neck. Granted, I assured her I was wrong, because I *was* wrong. If Tara understood the word misogynistic pig, she would have called me that. If I wasn't careful, she might become a femme fatale, but with how flat her curls were, we might avoid it. The femme fatale always looked perfect, too.

Alwin stopped, almost frozen. I sensed the code created by the Rogue, but couldn't decipher it without using my God powers. Alwin's head jerked, looking at something to the side of us as he handed Milla to me.

Something lumbered through the forest as Milla nestled into my shoulder. A creature just woke up. Something enormous.

Alwin already had his sword out. Paldric moved forward, frowning. None of us dared speak. The creature got close, and we instinctively moved off the road to hide from its path. We hid behind trees right as a ten-foot troll limped onto the road. Milla gasped, and I covered her mouth. The troll didn't seem to notice, as his swollen foot took most of his attention.

He was an ugly, moss green troll, with teeth so big he couldn't close his mouth properly, causing him to drool everywhere. He started limping down the road when he froze and sniffed. I held onto Milla as tightly as I could, terrified.

The troll turned toward the trees we were hiding behind and roared.

Devin? Jim? Grace? Vince? I think I found a way to die.

Chapter Twenty-Two

I Try to Die

The troll must have broken his ankle, which is why the necromancer left him behind. Broken or not, it still frightened everyone to see a large troll lumbering right to us.

Devin? Anyone?

Three arrows appeared on his massive back before I realized Alwin put them there. He somehow climbed a tree without me noticing. The troll was very distracting.

"Yep, that troll should work nicely," Devin said.

I thought so, too.

"Pass Milla off to someone else," another man said. The only other person I hadn't met was the chairman, Vince. This must be him. **"We'll want little damage to the other characters."**

Milla was crying and spending a lot of energy pretending like she wasn't. I didn't dare set her down. I moved toward Tara. "Take Milla. Get out of here. I'll distract the troll."

"What?" Tara asked.

"I don't want Milla here with me when I distract the troll. Get somewhere safe. Paldric and Alwin will find you afterwards."

She nodded, taking Milla. The thing roared again, hitting the tree next to us with his mountain-like shoulder. We screamed as it splintered. I covered them both as best I could before pushing them away, ordering them to run. I picked up a piece of splintered wood and threw it at the troll. The thing didn't notice.

"Lessen your invincibility enough to die, but not instantly," Devin said.

I panted, picking up another splinter of wood and threw it. "Huh?"

"Die, but not all at once. Make sure it's slow so we can monitor what's happening. Sudden death might be dangerous," Vince said.

"Great. Slow and miserable is the aim, then." I hated everything about this as my adrenaline pushed me forward.

Paldric watched me run past. "Gunther! What are you doing?"

I stumbled onto the road toward death, waving my arms and shouting. The troll was smart enough to notice me. He stomped on his good leg and snorted when he walked on his bad one. A part of me felt bad for the troll with the twisted ankle. When it roared with a dozen arrows sticking out of his shoulders, the empathy left. The troll clasped his two hands together before swinging it forward. I closed my eyes, bracing for the impact.

It came. The wind sailed through my hair before a boulder appeared, smacking my head. In the sky above me, all four Guardians groaned in sympathy. I cracked an eye open. "Am I dead?"

"No. You made a knee jerk reaction and protected yourself. The boulder didn't last, though," Devin said.

I sat up, rubbing my head, which helped me realize I felt nothing at all. Especially considering my head turned the boulder into pebbles. No headache, no nothing, though I took out a few trees on the way. The troll screamed far in the background. He punched me far.

I grabbed my glasses, sticking them back on before scrambling to my feet and sprinting back to the troll. My glasses didn't have a crack on them. Maybe they were as invulnerable as me.

My head demanded that it should hurt. It messed with my vision, but I held my head, running back to the troll.

"Jim, do you have that code?" Devin asked.

"Finished now. Gunther? This might help," Jim said.

A weight returned to my mind, and I examined the code. Gradual decline of health until death. Safe word, "tacky", for me or any Guardian to say if something felt wrong. I kept running, feeling the exhaustion get to me. This troll threw me far.

"Gunther? Do you accept the code?" Grace asked.

I wanted to. I really did. My hesitancy came because we were discussing my death, and basic instincts demanded I keep myself safe, simulated or not. Don't die. Embrace invincibility. But this device was dangerous. My characters needed me to not be here. *Tara* needed me to not be here. It would be easier to develop her character if I left.

"I accept the code." The heaviness in my head disappeared throughout my body. I thought I let myself feel the exhaustion before, but this drain was different. I stumbled, the sharp pain in my side making it difficult to breathe. Just running toward the troll might kill me. Once I got to the road, I hollered to trick myself into being braver.

The troll didn't notice, as Paldric was now in the middle of the road diverting the troll's attention to keep it from finding Alwin in the trees. I grabbed another piece of wood before leaping, my arms wrapping around the troll's waist as I tried to pierce his skin with the broken wood. A few splinters got into my hands, a mild annoyance, before I slipped.

"Gunther! What are you doing?" Paldric shouted.

The troll tried to smack me like I was an annoying fly before he grabbed my leg. He brought me closer to his face to see me. His clumsy, large fingers mashed my femur into unusable splinters.

Nope. Hate that. The wave of nausea hit as I felt the pain of a crushed leg. Are you sure this was gradual?

"Try not to think about it too hard," Jim said.

Right. Try not to think about death. The thing all mortals contemplate. I'll just shut that portion of my brain off.

I hung upside down in the air, too close to the troll's reeking breath of rotten fish and bad eggs. My glasses tumbled from my head, but it was better to see a blurry outline instead of the sharp image of his ugly mug. He sniffed me, and I tried not to vomit. I screamed in pain as the troll mushed my leg to a pulp.

"You are the worst, Jim," I said through the scream. It slipped out, even though I didn't need to say it out loud. "I hate you so much. Why was this a good idea?" I had to stop, because I was about to vomit, but hopefully Jim got the picture.

"Perfectly. If it helps you get through the pain, you can scream at me," Jim said.

What did this guy do? Seriously. Why was he so good? Life so put together. Jim would never be in a position where he was hanging upside down from a troll's grip, barely conscious as the troll... licked? Was the troll licking me?

"Oh, come on!" I tried to wipe the spit from my face as my leg was officially mush. My hair dripped in slobber before the troll grabbed my waist again, trying to crush me. And it worked. My leg was useless, and my ribs cracked under the pressure. Blood drained from my face before I vomited. I was still upside down, so whatever didn't hit the ground traveled up my face and into my nose. Chunks of partially digested oatmeal stuck so far back, I felt it in my brain.

Those descriptions are for you, Jim. Just so you understand how much this hurts. I hate you. I hate you so much. Who thought this was a good idea? Who ran the tests before putting this into place? I coughed, trying to get more vomit out, dangling upside down in the air.

The troll grunted, then nibbled my hair.

I hope karma gets you, Jim. I'd scream this at the top of my lungs, but I didn't want to smell this troll's breath anymore.

"Gunther!" I vaguely heard Paldric screaming to get my attention. The pain was too much. My head cracked between the troll's teeth, and beautiful, beautiful darkness waited for me.

This meant the pain would leave, right?

Right?

Something appeared in the distance. It was blurry, and difficult to see, considering I didn't have my glasses on and still caught glimpses of the inside of the troll's mouth. The grinding of the troll's teeth, coupled with the eerie silence of this new world, messed with my senses.

No, not silence. A humming. Was it humming? No.

Screaming.

Was I dissolving?

"Tacky!" Grace screamed.

All at once, I was back in the troll's mouth. My leg reformed, my ribs snapping back into place, my skull magically melded together.

"Grace?" Vince asked.

"Limbo." Her voice trembled. **"That was limbo."**

Vince swore under his breath. I tried to shake off the shock. Despite everything in my body going back to normal, the memory of pain lingered.

And, of course, the vomit so deep inside my nose I could smell either it or the troll's breath. Neither one was a good option.

"Get rid of the troll, and don't die." Vince sounded grim. The plan to kill me failed.

I tried to wake my brain back up. I wasn't in pain, that was just memories, though the creature still pinned me, gnawing on my head to eat my brain. The thing's grip was impossible for someone like me to break. Not without using powers.

"Don't," literally every Guardian said.

I know.

"Gunther!" Alwin shouted close to me. Was he standing on the troll's head? I said nothing to him, as I was still bathing in the troll's saliva, pinned to his mouth and getting my hair styled by his teeth.

The troll bellowed. Alwin, like with the dragon, dug his sword deep into the troll's eye. The troll squeezed me like a stress ball, and I did nothing but close my eyes before I tumbled out of the mouth, hitting a tree and stripping it of all its branches, landing hard on the ground. Alwin leapt for the trees as Paldric sprinted out of the way. The troll landed, the ground shaking under the impact as I continued to stare at the sky, processing what happened.

"Gunther?" Grace asked.

Why did I hear screaming in limbo? I thought... I thought that's where the stories got shredded. Like a big paper shredder of digital code. If no characters were whole enough to do the screaming, then who...

"There are too many things we don't understand about limbo. We don't want more stories ending up there. We must find another way to get you out."

I made no reaction. Somehow, this discovery sickened me. Maybe not as much as the memory of a mushed leg, but since both happened at the same time, it didn't help in the slightest.

Alwin and Paldric both appeared in my vision. "Gunther!" Paldric was out of breath. "Are you alright?"

The trees above me looked pleasant enough. I wanted to lie here and do nothing. Paldric went to give me my glasses, but when I didn't take them, he placed them on my nose. Alwin lifted my pant leg covered in blood to see a normal leg underneath. He looked confused, then lifted my torn shirt with a large blood stain to see not a scratch on my body.

Paldric snapped his fingers in front of my face. "Gunther?"

"I'm alive." I didn't know how I felt about that phrase leaving my mouth. No, I didn't want to be dead, but it would've been nice to leave my story. "Alive and well. No thanks to Jim."

Paldric and Alwin exchanged worried glances.

"If it helps you process your shock, I'll accept this failure as mine," Jim said.

"It's probably the first failure to your name, isn't it?" I asked the sky.

Devin snorted, which was enough information to go by.

"Gunther?" My main character was terrified.

I lifted my hands, and Alwin and Paldric helped me up. My leg wouldn't respond, and I almost took Paldric out as it refused to stand on its own. A part of me still remembered the crushing pain, the mush, the splintered femur, and it was impossible for my brain to understand it was fine now. I leaned on Paldric as I walked on it, bracing myself for the pain my brain was certain I would feel, but it more felt like my leg was asleep.

Paldric helped steady me. "Alwin, find the girls. We've got to keep going."

Alwin studied my face before nodding. "Rest here, I'll find them."

My main character walked me away from the troll. I limped, even though I was fine. My mind wrestled with the screaming I'd heard. I tried to forget it. Forget the pain. Here I was, walking. Fine. Everything was fine. I was here. Still in my story. Fine.

I got a good whiff of the troll's breath since I'd spent a long minute or two in the thing's mouth. I fell to my knees again and vomited. If I wasn't busy expelling the oatmeal I thought was already out of my system, I would have given the sky an obscene gesture.

I hate you, Jim.

Chapter Twenty-Three

THE AFTERMATH OF JIM'S FAILURE. YEP. JIM'S FAULT.

I closed my eyes, wiping my mouth with the back of my hand. Paldric eased me against a rock, concerned. "What did you do?"

Blood coated my clothes. Troll's breath soaked into my pores as I situated myself against the rock. "I tried to die."

"What?"

"I tried to die. Because it could have helped me get out of this st—land. And back among the Gods. But clearly it didn't work."

Paldric stared at me, shocked. "When were you going to tell us?"

"It was a spur-of-the-moment idea."

My main character glanced around, trying to figure out how much time he had to give me a lecture. His terror during the moment still lingered. "I don't wish to lecture a God about what he should do with his mortal life, but if we were surrounding your lifeless body right now, I promise it would devastate members of this party."

Paldric was right. I should have warned my characters about my plans. It was still difficult to get out of the observer's mindset. To watch them work together but expect to not be included. Especially after what happened to Tara.

I leaned my head against the rock, pointed my nose toward the fresh air, and breathed deeply. It was a low move to not tell them. And if I was successful? If they didn't know this was my plan all along and they realized a God died? "It didn't work, and I won't try it again. I'm sorry I didn't tell you."

The man almost placed a hand on my shoulder, but once he smelled me, he rethought the kind gesture. "Is there anything else we should know?"

There wasn't enough fresh air in this simulated world to cleanse the smell of rotting fish and spoiled eggs. Pretty sure the troll had a disease in his mouth. "I'll be in Veniloria for a while. I'll try hard not to crack."

Paldric smiled. "We'd appreciate it." I moved my foot, staring at my blood covered pant leg. I bent my leg and wiggled my toes, the pins and needles feeling ebbing away. "So that Jim person you talked to in the sky? Is he a fellow God?"

"Sure. We'll go with that." I bent my leg to my chest, feeling fine.

He gave me a curious look. "What do you mean?"

Jim was probably still listening.

"I am, yes."

And could read my thoughts, which wasn't my favorite. I couldn't tell Paldric the truth that Jim was a narrator who wrote mystery stories, from what I heard. And had a perfectly put together life. And probably did nothing wrong ever in his life. Maybe he was a nerd at school. Got bullied, his lunch money stolen.

"I was valedictorian. Maybe that makes me a nerd. No one bullied me, though. I was the student body president my senior year, and I'd like to think-"

"He's a lesser God," I blurted. Paldric frowned but paid attention, curious about the ways of the Gods. "You know, busy with menial tasks. The other Gods allowed him to help, but this is the only time I've heard from him. Lesser God."

Pretty sure the memory of my mushed leg made me blurt all that out. Sorry Jim. I only slightly meant it.

Jim chuckled in the sky. **"Understood, Gunther."**

Branches snapped, and Milla appeared out of the forest. She ran to hug me, but stopped dead in her tracks a few feet away, gagging. "What happened to you?"

I reached out to Alwin, who helped me to my feet. "The troll tried to eat me." I walked on unsteady legs, trying to remember they were whole.

Milla pinched her nose, backing away. "I'm glad you're alright." Her voice sounded nasally.

"Thanks, Milla. Should I wash off, or do we keep going?"

"Wash off," everyone said in unison.

Paldric got up, then wobbled, holding his side. For a split second, I thought he smelled me, but then I realized the truth. Paldric kept his own wounds expertly hidden while making sure I was fine, like he was some sort of hero.

"Paldric's hurt," I said.

Alwin turned to look at him. Tara was already there. Paldric kept a brave face. "I'm fine, really."

"Shut up and show us," I said.

Paldric looked at me, confused, as I let slip some more modern lingo. In his confusion, Alwin lifted his shirt to show what my side should have looked like after hitting a tree. A dark purple bruise almost covered one side of his rib cage, and he had multiple cuts and gashes.

I winced in sympathy. "Do you need me to heal you?"

Milla shook her head. "You're at thirty percent."

"Thirty? That's impressive, considering the fight we just had," I said.

She looked down, touching one finger to her forehead and closing an eye. "You dropped to twenty-seven percent while talking with Tara. You then added three more percent during your fight with the troll."

Paldric straightened his shirt. "I can manage. Honest."

"Gunther won't be back for a while. We might as well tend to it to keep infection at bay. And check for any broken bones," Alwin said.

"I can... I can do that. My..." Tara frowned as she realized something, playing with a curl in her hair that was no longer sitting right. "My father was the town healer, and I'd help with some of the less gruesome cuts and wounds until I was old enough to be his assistant. He told me stories about my mother to ease me out of my nausea when I saw worse breaks or cuts. Usually my mom helped him, but she died when I was born." She shrugged. This discovered part of her entered her code. "Not sure why you needed my life story, but there you are." She reached for her pack, rummaging around before pulling out a small bottle and rag.

Alwin turned to me. "There is a river near here. Do you need me to lead you to it?"

I paused, hearing the river, before shaking my head. "I'll follow the sound."

"Take this." Tara handed me a bottle. "For all our sakes."

Whatever it was, I assumed it neutralized the smell of rotten eggs and old fish.

"Be careful," Alwin said.

"I'll scream if I see another troll," I said.

Milla giggled as Paldric eased himself out of his shirt. Tara's eyes widened, freezing long enough for Paldric to notice. "Uh, would you... do you want me to keep my shirt on?"

"Bad." Tara still stared at his chest. "Bad. The wound looks bad, that's all."

As narrator of the story, I need to emphasize Tara already saw the wound, so it wouldn't startle her. She definitely tried to cover her surprise at seeing him shirtless for the first time.

Tara finally moved her gaze to his eyes, her cheeks burning. "I'll, uh, get to work."

Paldric hid his smile. "Thanks."

They stumbled on the classic romance trope of after-action patch up and did a far better job. Which I didn't mind. As proved before, I couldn't write a romantic subplot to save my life. Unfortunately, I could not stay and describe exactly what happened, as fish and rotting eggs lingered in the air, but I have a guess. Paldric probably gasped when the rag first touched his wound, and Tara muttered her apology. He, being the optimistic hero, would crack a lame joke about how he's felt worse, and Tara would smile. She would do an excellent job of cleaning and wrapping the wound, taking every opportunity to brush her fingers against his skin. And he would do that thing in romcoms, where he checked to see if she was looking before taking his sweet time admiring her face.

That's probably what happened. Yes, I created them, but romance was never a skill I professed to have, either literarily or in real life. But if they stumbled on this trope, I'm assuming it played out by the book.

I found the river and stepped into the frigid water. Even as the days got warmer, the water remained stubbornly cold. My teeth chattered as I washed the blood off my clothes as best I could. I figured I'd dry myself with my powers as soon as I washed off.

"I wouldn't suggest it," Devin said.

I'm not walking for another five miles in wet clothes. I may be invulnerable, but I'd rather not worry about chafing.

"You're at thirty percent. A frightfully high number."

The chafing will annoy me. I'll heal it, eventually. Might as well stop the cause of it.

The sky sighed again. **"Just know I do not support you using your powers."**

Yeah. Fine.

"We're about to have a meeting to review what happened and form another plan."

I got the bottle open and poured a little of it on my shirt and pants. "Do the Guardians always have meetings?"

"It's part of the job, yes."

Glad I wasn't one. Devin chuckled again, and I forgot he could read my thoughts.

"Being a Guardian isn't for everyone."

"I hope Jim doesn't think I hate him. It was painful, and… and I lash out when I'm in pain." I rubbed the strange stuff into my clothes.

"No hard feelings," Jim said.

My gaze shot to the sky as I panicked. I thought he had logged off. "Oh, come on! Isn't there some way for you to alert you're listening in?"

Jim laughed. **"Forgive me, Gunther. I shall make a note of that for future interactions."**

I mumbled. Not anything intelligent, but because it felt good. **"I am logging off now. I shall see you at the meeting, Devin."**

"See you in a few minutes, Jim."

Grabbing my glasses to keep them on my face, I plunged my head into the river. It was cold, but the troll licking me was too recent a memory as I came back up. I rubbed more of the clear liquid stuff in my hair, scrubbing it as best I could.

"Are you alright, Gunther?" Devin asked. I said nothing, focused on my scrubbing, making sure my face got as clean as possible. **"Do I need to remind you that you almost died? People don't bounce back from that."**

"I didn't just almost die, though. I also touched limbo."

"Which prompts me to ask again, are you alright?"

My head submerged in the water one last time. I felt like myself again instead of a delicious candy for a troll. My body shivered as I stood up to talk. "It's not something I want to experience again."

"And we'll ensure it never does."

That world was terrifying. The limbo world was for stories that narrators abandoned. After a month of not using the device, the story broke down and entered limbo. But my story didn't break down. I was dying, and somehow ended up there, my very essence starting to shred. I thought I was safe from limbo because I didn't belong in this story world. How was this possible?

"Another thing we will discuss in our meeting. We are here to get you answers. I promise," Devin said.

"Thank you."

"I'll be back to report. See you later, Gunther."

Devin logged off. Essence of troll lingered on me, so I took off my shirt, keeping hold of it, and dumped the rest of the bottle all over my torso. I would smell of troll for a while, but this could mute it as much as possible.

"I better log off too," Grace said out of nowhere.

The shock of hearing her voice made me jump before I eventually smiled. At least she let me know she was still there, as awkward as this was. "Is Vince still on too?"

"That poor man is too busy. You may not see him much, but you have been constantly on his mind since you entered your story. He's learning to live with little sleep too, the poor dear. He's only ten, fifteen years younger than me. I certainly couldn't keep up with your story."

I wrung out my shirt, feeling grim. I've been in here for a while. Has it been a week? It took a week to get to thirty percent, almost fifty. The only way to leave was through the sequel.

"If anyone can do it, you can, Gunther," Grace said.

I smiled, dipping into the frigid water again to wash the liquid off. Considering one of my characters sees me as an anti-hero, hearing Grace's compliment seemed weird, but I'd take it. "Thanks, Grace." It was well meaning, and of course she believed it because she had the same mentality as Paldric, though certainly more complex than him. Which was rare to have such optimism at an old age.

Not old. She couldn't be old. Young, even. And I shouldn't just assume she was a grandmother.

She laughed. **"I am, Gunther. Both old, and a proud grandma of four little grandchildren. So far, at least. I'm keeping my mouth shut around my children, but I would very much like more. I want you to meet them one day."**

"I'd like that."

"See you later, Gunther."

"Bye, Grace." I didn't lie to her. I wanted to leave my story, because a week in here was terrifying enough, but I did not trust the Rogue.

Suppressing shivers, I walked out of the river before willing my body and clothes to be dry. Once they were, I stuffed my shirt back on and straightened my glasses. The tears in the shirt sewed themselves back up without me asking them to. I really needed to get out of here.

Chapter Twenty-Four

I Question Paldric's Optimism

We crested the hill; the trees breaking for us to catch our first glimpse of Paerra below us, and dread filled my heart when I saw it in ashes. It was almost too much, and I grabbed the nearest tree to keep myself standing. My thoughts whirled together, even as it tried to shut down. I wanted to sleep in a bed tonight. A troll tried to eat me not that long ago. My legs ached from walking so much. Vaywell was getting closer. So was the necromancer.

"Gunther." Alwin's voice was quiet, a warning to not use my powers.

My mind shut down as I walked closer to the place that had once been a town. Destruction hung in the air, ash falling like gray snowflakes, the embers still glowing hot. I stumbled before falling to my knees, touching the ground, sensing in the code what happened here.

News reached them of King's Court. It took days to destroy this city. The inhabitants killed each other, and those who remained moved on. This town, this once hopeful, sunny town, destroyed itself because something outside the original outline came and messed with the balance. Destroying creation is what the Rogue does. And he succeeds at it.

Milla's eyes were wide as she came to my side. She tried hard not to show her panic. It had been a long day for her. She faced many moments that would terrify anyone, let alone an eight-year-old child. I remained on my knees, tears in my eyes.

"Was it the necromancer?" Paldric asked.

I said nothing, simply stared ahead. Alwin shook his head. "There's no goblin or troll footprints anywhere near here. They've been staying away from settlements and towns." Tara covered her mouth with her hands, her eyes wide. "There is no inn to stay here. We've got to keep going. Find a safe place to camp."

Paldric stared at the destruction. A dragon didn't hit this town, but it was the same result. Yet he still had the audacity to smile. "It'll be alright, Gunther."

My fingers curled, and I kept my eyes closed so no one could see me glare. Despite my mind that had shut down, Paldric's words had snapped it back to a dark reality. I had ignored the fact long enough, but this proved it.

"Paldric, you are..." I took a breath, the hurt bubbling inside. "So terribly written."

Paldric didn't expect this reaction from me, and it made little sense to him. "What?"

How could Paldric know? How could he pretend things would be okay when we literally sat at the edge of a burning town? This was a foreshadowing of his own character, right here in the town of Paerra. The Dark Wizard, the *Rogue*, was going to take him and torture him until he broke. Unless I crack and destroy the entire world to keep the

Dark Wizard from doing that. So many horrible things could happen, and Paldric tried to slap on the Band-Aid of optimism and move on.

"You have a stupid amount of optimism. No one thinks like you. You are so two dimensional." I kept my eyes closed to hide the tears forming. "And you're the main character. You are not relatable. You need to wake up and face reality or you're going to end up just like this town."

"Gunther..." Paldric sounded concerned.

"Look around you. Paerra is gone. This entire town has burned to the ground and there's nothing left. They were happy and hopeful, just like you. Get it together, face reality, and stop pretending everything is going to be alright."

"Gunther—"

I opened my eyes and got to my feet, glaring. "Optimism only thrives because of ignorance, so let me describe what happened here. They lost hope. *Paerra* lost hope. They, too, were stupidly optimistic, and they *lost* it! The attack on the monarch, the threat of the Dark Wizard looming, this sunny town collapsed. The same thing will happen to you. But something tells me you are so horribly written that if actual life ever hit you, you'd still waltz in a field of dead flowers pretending they're alive, but that attitude won't help any of us."

My exhaustion was dangerous. It wasn't just Milla that had a long day. I was sore, a troll almost killed me, and I almost got ripped to pieces by the limbo world. My percentage was getting far too high.

Milla whimpered, edging closer to Tara, who knelt down to whisper words of comfort. There were numerous threats all of us faced. Not just the necromancer and the Dark Wizard, but also the dead monarchy of Veniloria. Everyone loved them or was loyal enough to them. To have them gone? It was enough to... to burn one's town to the ground. And Paldric simply smiled through the whole thing because Tara now had more depth than he did.

Paldric's smile faltered as he stared back at me, worried I was cracking. But he couldn't let my reaction go without commenting on it. "If you are accusing me of not feeling sad enough, I assure you I do. These were my countrymen, even if I didn't know them."

I said nothing because there was no point. At twenty-four, Paldric simply didn't understand. How could he? I programed him to never lose hope, because that's how I saw heroes when I was his age. His hope may waver. There might even be times where it seems like he might lose it forever, but he wouldn't. Of course the good guys would win. Of course they would defeat the dragon.

But that wasn't the story anymore. It wasn't me in charge. The never-ending hope in Paldric I once deemed so admirable was now dangerous, and I finally saw him as the two-dimensional character he was.

My tears started to fall. I wanted to not feel, because then it wouldn't hurt when the Dark Wizard found us. When they started torturing my characters. I was going to fail again. Paerra wasn't just a foreshadowing of Paldric, it was a sign of what would happen to this entire story.

I blinked, feeling a panic attack coming on.

"Don't give up, Gunther. Don't you dare," Paldric said. The hope was never gone. It was plain to see in his eyes, even without my narration ability. "You are God. You should understand better than any—"

"Don't act shocked when people who lived drastically different lives than you end up not nearly as happy." My tone was sharp, trying to get the panic from my mind to my voice so it could escape that way.

Paldric frowned, staring at me like he could not comprehend such a mindset. The ignorant, two-dimensional man stood among the town's ashes and still kept the stupid hope that could never make him relatable. If he understood the full extent, then he would lose it, because that's what happened to Paerra. They understood their king and queen were gone, and they couldn't handle it anymore.

He stood to his full height, pointing at me. "Things might burn, yes, but growth always comes from the destr—"

"Oh, shut up!" The last thing I needed to hear was some wooden, artificial dialogue. "Save it for a motivational poster!"

Alwin moved forward, extending his two hands toward me and Paldric. "We've walked a long way, and this could shake anyone after what we went through. You both are exhausted. Let's keep going before it gets too dark to see. We've got to find a different place to camp."

I shook my head, walking away from both of them, passing Milla and Tara. I was exhausted, and Alwin was right. My percentage was too high to keep this conversation going.

The town sign was mangled and hanging by a hook as we passed it. They lost hope. Paldric might still lose hope too if he didn't change his blind optimism to a healthy cynicism. A part of me figured if I hated Paldric enough, it wouldn't hurt as badly when the Rogue broke him.

The night was quiet. Alwin found a camp right outside the main road, and we didn't light a fire. It was better to not alert anyone where we were, which meant dinner was mostly berries and fruit. It was silent. The kind everyone knew was uncomfortable, but no one wanted to breach it. I was terrified of what we'd find in Vaywell. The port city a blaze. Inhabitants murdered. The shield missing.

I broke the silence. "I'll take the first watch." My nerves wouldn't let me sleep, anyway. "The rest of you get some sleep."

No one argued. A lingering sense of doom hung over us from the conversation before, and all of them obeyed without question. We had little supplies, as we relied on inns, mostly. And with no fire, I honestly doubted anyone got any sleep. I watched for the first hour as the four of them got closer together to conserve body heat. Alwin had a small blanket he offered to Milla, but it wasn't enough. Milla was the first to cuddle up to Tara, who wrapped her arms around her to keep her close. Paldric joined soon after. He was on the other side of Milla, and placed his hand on Tara's shoulder, trying to shield the little girl from the cold. It took a good twenty minutes before Alwin caved and rolled closer to the other three. Even though we were close to Vaywell, the nights still got cold. I heard Milla's teeth chatter. They needed sleep. We all did. We would arrive in Vaywell tomorrow, and we needed rest to prepare for whatever state that port city was in.

I reached up, causing a bubble of warmth to surround us, to keep us warm until sunrise.

"Thirty-one percent," Milla whispered before drifting off to sleep.

Alwin stayed awake the longest, making sure I wouldn't crack before he, too, gave in and slept.

I brought my legs to my chest, hugging them tight, placing my forehead against my knees. Tomorrow would happen, whether or not I worried about it, but I couldn't help it. The anxiety got to me, and I couldn't sleep. The temptation to make some hard liquor appear was getting difficult to ignore. Despite my fight with Paldric, I saw the four of them still together, and knew I would crack before I let anyone hurt them.

"Gunther? Is now a good time to talk?" Devin asked.

I raised my head, preparing myself. I assumed this was about the meeting they had today.

"It is, yes."

I didn't dare speak out loud, since my characters were asleep.

"That's fine. I'll make this quick. We've formed a plan and... our meeting was..."

It's alright, Devin, just give it to me. I'm used to hearing bad news.

Devin sighed. **"Our best bet is the sequel, which isn't much of an option to begin with. It's a lot to ask of someone."**

I added it to the other bad news I'd received today. There was a threshold of how much I could react to, and after a while, I just quit reacting.

"Please don't go insane."

Don't go insane. Got it. Right after seeing a town brought to ashes; right after seeing death and destruction. After experiencing death and touching limbo. To have my poorly written character just disregard everything, knowing this was a sign from the Rogue about how much control he was gaining.

I looked at my characters, wondering if I wrote any of them that well. Maybe Esme was right. Maybe I wasn't that great at crafting novels.

"You never would have gotten a narration degree if you weren't good."

Sure. Except Professor Andrews and the other teachers were never shy about telling me how little they thought of it. Escapism. Pointless. No real merit.

"Gunther?" There was a distinct worry in Devin's voice.

We're headed for Vaywell. I don't know what to expect. Either seeing the port city in flames or coming face to face with the necromancer, I was at thirty-one percent. A measly nineteen percent kept me from fifty.

"When's the last time you got some sleep?"

I closed my eyes and leaned my head against a tree. I was desperately trying not to wallow, but it was difficult. This was my story. The last thing in my life going for me, and perhaps it wasn't even that great. I found myself once again realizing that if it failed, it would absolutely, one hundred percent, be my fault. And I also hated that Devin could read all this stuff. It honestly felt like writing in my journal and having someone reading over my shoulders.

"The other Guardians, including myself, are treating this case with the utmost respect. I hope you realize that."

I do.

It was difficult to put any sort of inflection in my voice, since this conversation was happening mostly in my head, but I pretended to act like I would take Devin's words to heart. Then I realized how much my words betrayed me anyway, because he was reading those thoughts right now.

Again, Devin sighed. **"Look, I need to sleep. I've already been awake for twenty-six hours. I'm not much help in my state. Just know the moment you hit Vaywell, at least one Guardian will follow along in your story. We will not leave you alone. Understand?"**

I nodded. I was worried about Vaywell, but I added it onto the list of things to worry about.

"You are not alone. We will get through this."

There are only so many phrases I can hear before I assume you're just scraping the barrel of feel-good quotes. Good night, Devin. You need to sleep.

He sighed with trepidation. **"Goodnight, Gunther."**

Chapter Twenty-Five

A Chat by the Firelight If We Had One, But We Don't, So We Talk in the Dark

I missed my phone. Missed the ability to know instantly what happened without me going insane. Some people believed knowing everything instantly caused problems in the real world, but information, either too much or too little, had always been a deadly tool. I could instantly know if Vaywell was still standing, but I needed to save that nineteen percent.

Alwin stirred, and I opened my eyes to see him sitting up. I didn't know how long ago my Guardian friend signed off. The exhaustion was such that I might have shut my eyes longer than usual, but my characters didn't need to know.

My elf eased away from Paldric and Milla before tiptoeing over to me. I kept a hand in my hair, listening for any sort of intruder, whether it be goblin, troll, or anarchist medieval townsfolk.

"I'll take the next watch. You need your rest." Alwin sat down next to me.

"I don't feel like I've been on watch that long," I said.

"I'm rested enough. Go get some sleep."

"You know lying to a God is pointless, right?" Even in the near darkness, I sensed his true feelings. He, like the others, was afraid I cracked. He wanted to make sure I rested so my anger wouldn't get a hold of me like when we entered Paerra.

Alwin brought his legs up, resting his arms on his knees like I had. He fell back on mirroring human behavior so people wouldn't know he was an elf. He wanted to ask a specific question, but he was still trying to make sure I wasn't dangerous yet.

"You want to know why I reacted the way I did?" I asked.

"Not everyone has the power to understand a person by looking at their face."

"You noticed that, huh?" I shifted my legs, and Alwin did the same without realizing it. I sighed, resting my head against the trunk of the tree. "I lost Paerra. The people were so happy. Paldric and Tara were supposed to have their first kiss there. The memories we shared would carry us through the trials of Vaywell. We were to get the rest we needed before embarking on this leg of our journey, but... but the Dark Wizard hit them where it hurt, and they fell. Their kindness wasn't there, and there was trauma and misery instead. And..."

Alwin raised an eyebrow. "You think that's what will happen to the five of us?"

"Yes." I rubbed my arms even though it wasn't cold. Maybe Alwin, too, wasn't well written. He just stood around looking pretty. If he was a girl, Esme would be screaming at me.

Alwin screwed his face up in confusion. "We won't, though."

"How can you be so certain?"

He looked over at my three sleeping characters. "I won't pretend to understand these people better than their creator, but if I had to choose who would lose hope first, it would be you."

I winced before looking away. "Thanks, Alwin."

"The prospect of immortality takes a toll. You see so much death. You make friends and then lose them to an old age you'll never taste for thousands of years."

The guilt trickled in, and I refused to look at Alwin. I wasn't a God. That much was painfully obvious. My elf lived far longer than I ever would. I was only five years older than Paldric. Five years, and it was clear life left me shaking. I didn't see worlds come and go. Just my marriage. That was traumatic enough.

"The moon and stars are beautiful tonight."

I glanced at Alwin, who was staring at the sky. Our camp had a break in the trees enough for us to see them glimmering. It reminded me of when my parents took me camping for the first time as a kid, and I saw the beauty of nature. The night sky that hid from me in the city finally revealed itself, and it astounded me. I didn't want to sleep. I simply stared up at the beautiful night sky in awe.

"They are," I said.

"Is it glorious, the heavens where you came from?"

I turned away from the sky, folding my arms in the comfortably warm bubble, glad it was too dark for Alwin to see my face. His question reminded me how little I developed the religion in this world.

I became their religion, but I was unqualified to answer his questions. "I guess."

Alwin gave me a confused look. "You guess? You fell from the heavens, and you can only guess they might be glorious?"

"It's hard to describe."

"Too difficult for my mortal mind to comprehend?"

"Sure." My pained smile grew. "We'll go with that."

I thought about the modern world, with its instant gratification. Instant connection, instant everything. The cars that could have taken us to Vaywell in less than a day, and the planes that could've shortened it to an hour. It would have blown Alwin's mind to hear about cars, let alone the other gadgets that became a staple.

"Do you, do Gods, have families?" Alwin asked.

"Yeah. I lived with my mom and dad, and I'm an only child. They're probably worried sick about me."

Alwin chuckled. "They act like the parents of this world."

I sensed the pain he hid. Alwin's smile dropped as he realized I knew what he meant. My practically immortal character, doomed to wonder about his parentage for the rest of his existence. I created him with this, but I simply couldn't imagine the quiet pain he suffered.

Alwin picked up a twig next to the tree and played with it because he saw humans do that sometimes. He glanced again at the moon. "What happened to them?" It was the question he wanted to ask the moment I revealed my God status. "Why am I the only one left?"

His loneliness, almost survivor's guilt, was very much a part of his character, and I never thought I'd be the one he'd seek comfort from. But maybe it shouldn't surprise me. I was a God in everyone's eyes. Someone expected to dispense wisdom and knowledge. I had been with them long enough, they shouldn't expect wisdom from me.

"The elves left. Left because they no longer cared about men and their trivialities." After how angry I got at Paldric when we entered Paerra, that sentence leaving my mouth stung a bit more than it should have. "After living for thousands of years correcting men's mistakes, they were done. They left to perfect a land to rule. And no, they didn't go to the moon. They were supposed to be the Gods. Not me."

"So... the elves gave up. My parents, too?"

I glanced at Alwin, then took a deep breath before slowly letting it out. I had a backstory all made for Alwin when I created him. He might as well know. "Your parents were part of the small rebellion who didn't want to leave. They came to care for humans. They even loved them. When they fought back against their fellow elves, they were killed. A few elves knew you were still alive, but didn't rescue you. It was a way to prove themselves right. That men are evil. That men would destroy you."

Alwin had tears in his eyes. He looked up at the moon. "So those elves are wrong. Men aren't evil. They saved me."

It wasn't for me to decide, so I said nothing. I, the narrator, would not give the answer so easily, because *I* didn't know the answer myself. Sure, Paldric's family was unnaturally good, but the rest of the world?

Whatever happened tomorrow, I at least answered Alwin's life long questions about his birth. A hundred and fifty years was a long time to wonder where one came from, and since my original outline was no longer functioning, I had to let him know.

It was late. My powers itched to be used so I didn't feel exhausted, but I had thirty-one percent to my name.

Alwin placed a hand on my shoulder. "Eternity is a long time. I'm certain you have seen many things that caused you despair, but I still think, since you are here and doing your best to keep us all alive, there is the smallest flicker of hope in you. And hope has a tendency to spread if you let it."

My eyes met Alwin's hazel ones, trying to understand what he meant. I wasn't an all-powerful being who saw the rise and fall of civilizations. I just went through a messy divorce, and I was ready to give up to not get hurt again. It made me more similar to the elves than I wanted to admit. If I was an eternal being, I would give up hope, regardless if it was right or wrong. I stood up, brushing myself off. "I'll take you up on your offer to get some sleep."

We wished each other good night before I walked over to my other characters. Milla slept on her stomach with Tara's hand on her back. Paldric slept peacefully, as though the rise and fall of civilizations would never stop his two-dimensional optimism.

I walked farther and eased myself to the ground, taking off my glasses and placing them carefully next to me. So many people counted on me to keep my hope when I didn't feel it, and Paerra town proved something to me. They lost hope and destroyed the town. If I lose my hope, I'd kill this entire story. I had to fake my optimism until it was real. But faking it until it became real was the advice I gave myself with my marriage.

My shoulder ached, and I worked on finding a comfortable place on the ground, trying to sleep so I would stop thinking about everything. I really missed straw mattresses.

Chapter Twenty-Six

Tara Gets Some More Character Development

My warm bubble burst, and the chilly morning air sliced into us. Being woken up because of the cold wasn't my favorite way to start a day. We were close enough to Vaywell that the frost was already disappearing, but I still missed having a warm fire and a blanket. Getting back to sleep would be impossible, so I got to my feet, shoving my boots on. "Now is as good a time as any to leave."

Alwin stood, making it look effortless. "It'll help warm us up faster. I'd still rather not light a fire."

Milla nodded, her teeth back to chattering. We ate breakfast as we walked, some berries and apples Paldric and Alwin found on the road. The farther we traveled, the more nervous I got.

We stopped for lunch, as berries and fruit could only last us so long. Alwin disappeared to hunt while Paldric lit a small fire.

Tara sat down next to me, brushing dirt off her skirt before watching Paldric light the fire. "Let's do this quickly."

I glanced up at her, confused, until I realized what she meant. Her character needed to deepen before we got to Vaywell, for her own safety, and everyone else's. We didn't get around to it yesterday because of me almost dying and then the outburst with Paldric, which meant we were already behind. "Right. Let's, um…"

Paldric finished lighting the fire before giving me a warning look. There was still a rift between us after I shouted at him in Paerra. And a rift between Tara and me after what happened days ago. I didn't know how to fix either, but developing Tara's character was a start.

I straightened my glasses. "So, your mother died when you were young?"

"While giving birth to me."

"And your father was a town healer?"

"Yes. He couldn't find the herb to save my mother in time. He lived with the regret the rest of his life. The same herb he tried on himself to cure his lifelong illness, but it didn't work." It was great information about her father, but not much about herself. She clearly didn't trust me. And, again, I didn't blame her, but it was difficult to develop her character if she didn't want to speak to me.

Alwin returned with a rabbit.

"That was quick," Paldric said.

"The rabbit was fat and old. A lucky find."

"Do you like rabbit?" I asked Tara.

She still didn't look at me. "It's fine."

I couldn't get the flow of development. I was still as awkward around her as when she was first introduced.

Perhaps I was too stressed about it. Esme nitpicked my female characters, demanding I write them how she wanted to, because she didn't trust me to do it right. Not only that, but she assured me of the virtual tar and feathering that would happen from all the women who believed the same. The thought of being roasted alive for how I wrote women caused me to freeze up and produce this bland, two-dimensional character who, adding insult to injury, didn't like me either.

The Bechdel test, the sexy lamp, warrior women who are men with boobs. All these tropes were there to shoot at someone like me, a straight male narrator, to prove I didn't know a thing about women. And they're right, I didn't. But because of the ammunition she pointed at me, I was too terrified to learn. To learn was to make mistakes, and as a straight male narrator, the worst sin I could commit was making a mistake while creating a female character.

But this book wasn't getting published. I was here, so no other woman besides Grace would see it. And Grace just wanted me out. She didn't care how I wrote Tara. So, I might as well make mistakes in a book no one would see.

"Are we done?" She still didn't look at me as Alwin finished cleaning and skinning the rabbit. He was impossibly fast, having mad skills that came with practice over the decades.

I took a drink from the waterskin. "I'd like to take a different approach, if that's alright with you."

Tara narrowed her eyes, inching away from me. "What would that include?"

"You not talking with me."

Her face softened, liking this idea a lot better. The most I'd learned from her was when she interacted with other characters.

"Alwin? Paldric can finish up for you. Do you want to help Tara train with the sword?"

My elf glanced up, his eyes jumping between the two of us. "Of course. As long as Tara doesn't mind."

"No, I'd love to." She stood up, walking over to him.

"Come with me and I'll go wash up. We'll be back while that cooks," Alwin said. He wanted her to come with him to make sure I did nothing she considered uncomfortable while he was away hunting. I was the member everyone allowed in, but had one major strike against me. Only underwritten Paldric would dare give me another chance. I let Tara and Alwin have their conversation. It was vital for her development for her to feel safe in the group.

Milla sat down next to me. "Thirty-one percent. In case you're wondering."

"Thank you, Milla." I watched as Paldric finished placing vegetables and meat in the stew. "Any idea how I could drop it during this walk?"

Milla shrugged. "Just don't use any powers. My mind isn't coming up with any ideas."

Despite the dejection I felt, I smiled at Milla to help her not feel scared. I couldn't drop my percentage anymore. It would remain at thirty-one and we hadn't even entered Vaywell yet. I didn't know how we were going to face a necromancer, especially if he took over the city.

Alwin and Tara returned, talking amongst each other. It was a strange sensation to know exactly what they were thinking. Tara took one of Alwin's swords and listened to him, placing her feet into position. He went slow, showing her the different blocks and parries, doing his best to teach her, since he had taught no one before. Tara took this in, listening to his every word.

"As you are smaller than the average soldier, you need to strike fast and deadly," Alwin said.

"So go for the arteries?" Tara asked.

"Yes. Do you know where they are?"

"My father taught me."

It was easy for her to realize if she knew how to heal a human, she would know how to kill one, too, which made her think. "I don't know about the anatomy of a goblin. Are they the same?"

Alwin hadn't thought of this either. "I'd like to think so. At least, with the goblins I've killed, that seems to be the case."

My elf went slow and steady, helping her block his blows. I was right. It was much easier to develop her character while talking with Alwin than with me. I watched things drop into her code, watched the trust building between her and Alwin, becoming a swordswoman.

Paldric watched, curious, with another emotion intermixed. My heart dropped. No, Paldric, don't get jealous. This will not be that kind of story. Alwin isn't interested in her. He may be an elf, which meant he was alluring in his own way, and yes, practically everyone gave him a second glance when they saw him, but he was an entirely different species.

But I understood. Alwin was literally a graceful, hot elf who didn't realize how much he turned heads. And an excellent bowman and swordsman and lived over a hundred years. It was difficult not to feel insecure around him.

Alwin stopped the session to correct Tara's posture and her grip on the sword, placing his arms around her as he did so. Paldric frowned, getting distracted as the soup in the pot burned on the bottom. I stood, walking over to him. This would not happen in my story. Not if I could help it.

Paldric glanced at me before he noticed how hot the soup was getting. "Sorry. It's interesting, no? He's great at fighting." He glanced at Alwin, and even Milla noticed the insecurity playing across his face. "I've never seen an elf fight." His laugh was small. "It's fascinating." He took out a spoon and tasted the soup. "Absolutely fascinating."

My stare was deadpan, and I struggled to not whack him over the side of the head. He'd already seen Alwin fight before. Paldric may be underdeveloped, but I refused to let him develop *this* aspect of him. "So help me, I will not let you get away with the miscommunication trope."

Paldric stared at me as though I spoke an unfamiliar language. He didn't forget our argument the night before, so he had a higher spike of concern when I started saying words he didn't understand. "Sorry?"

"Miscommunication. It's demeaning, and you're a man with a spine. Not only that, but I am working on making sure loving a man isn't Tara's only personality trait. She's learning the sword, because—" the information came to me as though it was part of her development all along, "—because though she's not exactly tired of being the one in charge of Milla, she's afraid all she's doing is taking the little girl to hide. If a goblin were to follow them, she wants to defend herself and Milla to the best of her ability. She knows she'll never be as good as Alwin in such a brief span of time, but she wants to defend herself." Tara and Alwin stopped training to look over at us. "Basic self-defense is something Tara needs, because she seems to get kidnapped a lot, for reasons she doesn't understand which... which is my fault. I'll be the first to admit that." I sighed, looking at the pot of stew, running a hand through my hair. "Maybe her personality only started with her loving you, but it has spread to Milla, and yes, to Alwin, but not in that way. She's finally learning something that isn't about you, so don't make it about you. She can have a male friend who doesn't feel sexually attracted to her. Though... though that doesn't mean he's a gay best friend, because he's not gay. He's... oh, wait. Alwin is totally asexual and aromantic. I just realized that. Does that still count as the gay best friend? I honestly don't know. Hopefully that's not problematic."

Paldric again gave me a terrified look, like I was devolving into lunacy. He looked at Milla for help, but she only shrugged. "Thirty-one percent."

"You're an odd one, Gunther," Alwin said.

I sighed, rubbing the bridge of my nose. "The miscommunication trope triggers me."

"Sorry, but what are you talking about?" Paldric asked.

"Alwin has no sexual desires for Tara." I dropped my hand. "He never has, he never will. She asked him to teach her the sword, and it would be wise to let her. We need another person on the team who knows the sword." I winced. "But Tara can tell you that herself. She doesn't need me to defend her."

"Right." Paldric looked embarrassed as he glanced at Tara. "Of course. I... I knew that."

"Good." I patted his shoulder. "Lunch ready?"

"Yes." Paldric glanced at Alwin and Tara. "If... if you two want to be done, that is."

Alwin sheathed his sword. "I'm starving."

My main character poured a bowl of stew and handed it to Tara. "I'm glad you're learning the sword."

"Thanks." She smelled the stew, waiting for it to cool. "And yes, Alwin is attractive, but just because he looks nice doesn't mean I want to..."

"Yeah," Paldric said as Tara struggled to find the right word. "Yeah, Alwin is... he's..."

They both turned to look at him. He gave Milla some stew before slurping down his own. He smacked his lips before noticing Paldric and Tara's attention on him. Once again, he was unaware they were talking about his good looks, even if he could hear them. Which also begged the question of if Paldric was bisexual or Alwin was simply that attractive. Did I even check my main character's sexuality when I created him? I could have sworn I did. Wait, this was another trope I had stumbled into. A man so hot other men wanted him.

Alwin finished his stew before filling his bowl again, and as a narrator I had to say how model-like he did it. "Hungry, Gunther?" my elf asked.

I completely forgot I wasn't an observer, but someone well established in the group. "Sure."

"He's fantastic at the sword," Paldric finished, looking back at Tara. "It'd be better you learn from him than from me."

"I'd still learn from him, even if you said no." This slightly rebellious nature entered her character code.

I took a bowl of stew from Alwin and began eating.

"Me saying no would be for selfish reasons, and you would be right to ignore me." Paldric stated what was already in his character.

Tara's smile fully appeared. Admiration for Paldric entered her code, which differed from her love, though it deepened that, too. She took a bite of stew. "Better get your own bowl, Paldric."

"I will. Thank you." He headed for the stew.

Tara took another bite, looking at me before swiftly averting her gaze. "I'm sorry we didn't get to what you wanted." Once again, her voice was more formal than with Paldric and Alwin.

I shook my head. "No, we got exactly what I hoped for." There was an awkward silence between the two of us before I remembered something. "You should check his wound. You forgot this morning."

Tara looked at Paldric, who started eating his soup. "Right. Thank you for reminding me." She headed toward Paldric, who leaned over to hear her say she needed to check his wounds before he handed Alwin his bowl. "Eat, first. It's alright."

"No, no. Go ahead." He slipped his shirt off. I held back the desire to roll my eyes. It really was stupid, but I would let Tara and Paldric do this for the rest of eternity if it meant I could avoid the miscommunication trope.

Tara glanced at me as though she knew why I did this before unwrapping the bandages to check Paldric's wound. It looked so much better than the day before. Those magical lotions really did work wonders.

I sat on the other side of the fire, away from my characters, frowning. Did it matter what kind of character development she had? The Dark Wizard would still use her mistrust to hurt us all, and I would blame no one but me.

Chapter Twenty-Seven

Vaywell, the Port City

We were close enough that if Vaywell was on fire, we'd have seen it already. Since there wasn't any smoke, I could at least cross it off my list of worries. From what we saw, Vaywell still stood strong.

It was a lovely city. Many people sailed here, and back in the day, elves, nymphs, and fairies frequented the place. Vaywell had a rich history, which is why the elves left one of their artifacts here, hidden behind obstacles. The challenges were a significant source of tension in my original outline, but I knew how to escape every single puzzle. I didn't care about the tension anymore. For now, I needed to make sure the shield was nowhere near the necromancer. If he brought the sword with him, maybe we could steal that, too.

I walked next to Alwin, terrified of what might happen, and therefore almost driving him off the road with how close I got to him. He grabbed my shoulder, easing me away from him. "Are you alright?"

"Fine." The gates of the city got closer. I sensed people going about their lives, not a care in the world. My anxiety spiked. "Just fine." Alwin didn't believe me. "I don't want you to get kidnapped," I said.

He was the only elf in this world, and we were headed straight for the enemy.

"Thank you for your concern, but the necromancer isn't here."

My gaze shifted to him, trying to pick out what he meant. "How can you be sure?"

Alwin slowed his walk so the other members of the party moved ahead to give us privacy. "I've been tracking the necromancer's army."

"Oh?" I was pleasantly surprised at Alwin's initiative.

"Well, tracking isn't quite the word. Those footprints are impossible to miss." Alwin pointed behind him. We were on a hill right next to the ocean. "Two nights ago, they arrived at the sea, then headed toward South Island, away from Vaywell."

I continued to study him. With the port city so close, why did they turn around? My question must have been clear on my face, because Alwin shrugged. "A troll's footprints are impossible to ignore. I promise, they aren't in Vaywell."

Why would the army head south when the elf artifact was here? It made no sense. "And the necromancer?"

"Either he is an incredibly skilled sorcerer to keep himself hidden from me, or he, too, left with his army."

This chat with Alwin didn't comfort me. Tara gasped, and my gaze jerked in her direction. "What is it? What's wrong?"

Her eyes were wide with wonder. "It's so beautiful!"

I looked up and realized what she meant. We had entered villages and towns, but this port city didn't just boast of the different magic races. The grand archway, intricately carved with depictions of the different creatures, felt as though one traveled into another realm, leaving behind the dirt road and entering one of cobblestone. It was a gorgeous city, set on a steep hillside. There were houses all over the place, and some of them looked as though only magic held them up.

The sound of the sea crashing against the beach was melodic, like its own sort of heartbeat.

We entered the city, and I watched people go about their lives. Saw them greet us with smiles and waves. They were friendly. Too friendly. The necromancer should be here. This was the welcome they should have given Tara, Alwin, and Paldric in my original outline. All smiles. Cheerful people. But we weren't in my original outline anymore.

We walked the streets, seeing the large number of people finishing up their day's work and content to head home and live their lives. A dragon destroyed King's Court, and the necromancer should already be here. Why weren't they scared?

"We have little money for an inn. Does Alwin need to go hunting again?" Paldric asked.

"We should talk to the Lord and Lady of Vaywell. Clearly they don't know the King's Court is in ruins," I said.

Tara turned to look at me. "What do you mean?"

"These people are too happy." Paldric narrowed his eyes at my words. "What?"

"Too happy? Really, Gunther?" The sting from the night before lingered in Paldric's words.

"It would be smart to check in on the Lord and Lady. Gunther has a point. Maybe they don't know," Alwin said.

Paldric shrugged. "Alright. We'll ask around."

We followed the cobblestone road and headed toward the lighthouse on the steep hill. It might have been a mountain, except it wasn't nearly as large as the mountains I knew. We approached the gate of a large manor house, surrounded by shrubbery, as a guard approached.

"What business do you have with the Lord and Lady of Vaywell?"

Paldric stepped forward while the rest of us paused. "We come to bring news, if they hadn't already heard of it, of the destruction of King's Court."

The guard narrowed his eyes. "Of course they've heard of it."

"Has the rest of the town heard the news?" I asked before I could stop myself.

Paldric placed his hand on my arm and eased me toward the back of the group. "What my friend means is we watched the news of King's Court hurt many towns, even caused one town to collapse. We are therefore impressed the Lord and Lady have kept this one so full of good cheer." I tightened my smile and said nothing. "If we can do anything to keep this town in such good spirits, we humbly offer our services."

The guard nodded. "Of course. We heard the news about Paerra and have welcomed any refugees. Vaywell has always been known as a city who welcomed anyone. The Lord and Lady of Vaywell are eager to meet newcomers to our city. I shall introduce you to them."

My tight smile turned into a frown. The Lord and Lady of Vaywell did not like meeting newcomers. They were practically hermits except to their own citizens of Vaywell, where they were open and friendly. They didn't even enjoy going to King's Court. This had to be a trap. "Would it be offensive if we asked them to meet us outside?" I asked. It was a pointless question. Yes, it would offend them, but I was terrified.

The guard again looked at me, his eyes not as friendly. "An odd request."

It was Alwin's turn to grab my arm. "We don't want to offend the Lord and Lady of—"

"It is... such a beautiful day." I knew I was making up excuses. And I knew the guard knew. This guard in my original outline had little personality, but my apparent distrust made him push back.

"Is this some sort of trap?" the guard asked.

I shrugged. "Don't know. Is it?"

Alwin physically moved me behind him. "We do not wish to offend the good rulers of Vaywell. We will do what they ask." He said the words slow enough for me to not construe any other meaning.

"I *know* the good rulers of Vaywell." I kept my voice down, staring at the guard's eyes to make sure he couldn't hear. "This is odd." 'Odd' was a small portion of how I felt. The necromancer should be here already. Days before us. Why did the army go the other way? Why didn't the necromancer greet us with Lord Adrijian and Lady Ana as his new slaves and the city ransacked and destroyed? The thing I feared didn't happen, so somehow these bright faces we saw were more sinister than I wanted to admit.

"You will meet the good lord and lady in their home. If you behave, you might even get a dinner invitation. They are hospitable, if you are kind in return." The guard didn't hide his contempt for me.

"We humbly accept." Paldric said it fast before I could add anything.

The guard smiled, meaning his lips turned upward and he might have shown a few teeth, but he kept his warning look pointed at me. "Follow me, please."

Our group nodded, following the soldier. I grabbed Alwin and Paldric, moving them toward the back.

"Gunther, what—"

"Shh," I said to cut Paldric off, glancing at the guard. "I don't trust this."

Paldric frowned, annoyed. "I want you to know I am listening, because you are an all-powerful God, but we can't start making accusations and alienating people."

"Just keep your eyes open."

"For what?" Alwin asked.

"Anything. Sleep with a blade under your pillow, Alwin. Paldric, never let Tara out of your sight. I don't like any of this."

Paldric sighed, giving me another annoyed look. "Fine, but please let Alwin, Tara, or I take over diplomatic measures, so you don't end up offending all of Vaywell."

I matched his annoyed look, adding a frown of my own. "Fine."

Chapter Twenty-Eight

I Feel Cynical

We entered the fine manor house of the Lord and Lady of Vaywell, the artwork of nymphs, elves, and fairies from the ancient days on display. Paldric, Tara, Alwin, and Milla looked at the art display in awe while my eyes shot in every direction, trying to find the shadows to guess where the necromancer might hide. Shadow soldiers would follow shadows, right? I closed my eyes and accessed the code Devin gave me a long time ago about shadow soldiers. They could travel through shadows, but only on dark days or at night. They can go especially far with no moon in the sky. Since it was daytime, and the shadows weren't moving in strange ways, they couldn't be here.

"Hello!" a cheerful voice said. "Welcome to the manor house! I am Klement, personal servant of the Lord and Lady of Vaywell."

This, at least, was according to my outline.

"Klement, hello. I am Paldric, and these are my friends, Tara, Alwin, Milla, and Gunther." Paldric didn't say my name with the same feeling as the other three.

"You have traveled far, yes?" Klement asked.

Paldric nodded. "We went to King's Court, but..."

The servant's smile dropped, as did his gaze. "It is horrible what happened. Our scholars have combed the libraries of old and have narrowed down the dragon's lair."

"Oh, so news hasn't reached this far?" Paldric asked.

Klement watched, hesitant. "What news?"

"The dragon is dead. Alwin and I have already defeated it."

The personal servant let out a breath of pure relief. "Oh! This is wonderful! We didn't know how to destroy a dragon! I must tell Lord Adrijian at once! Come! They will want to celebrate!"

I followed, my eyes peeled for anything out of the ordinary. According to my original outline, we weren't supposed to meet the Lord and Lady of Vaywell until a large info dump told us where the dragon's lair was, as well as realizing the sword the King was supposed to give Paldric could defeat the dragon. But we didn't have the sword. The necromancer or Dark Wizard had it. And the shield, hopefully, was still here.

Klement threw open the doors of the throne room and we walked in. When trying to find something suspicious, I asked myself why Lord Adrijian and Lady Ana waited on their thrones for us to come see them. I would have suspected sinister intentions, except this is how I introduced them in my original outline.

"My Lord and Lady." Klement bowed low. "These people bring news of the death of the terrible dragon that destroyed King's Court."

Lord Adrijian stood, his eyes wide. "Is it true!"

"It is, sir." Alwin bowed, and everyone else followed his lead. "I plunged the sword into the beast's eye myself."

Lady Ana smiled. "This is most joyous news! We must have a celebration. You have defeated the beast!"

I watched in distrust as the large manor house became a madhouse of organization. Vaywell always had feasts, because they enjoyed celebrating with food. I wouldn't fault them for that.

We sat down for a feast, and I stayed quiet. The citizens demanded the story, and Alwin and Paldric obliged. They did not tire from telling it, and Tara smiled as she listened to them. Alwin got to a point in the story telling where he wanted me to add information, but I gave a quick shake of my head. I wanted to stay out of this as much as possible in case I needed to do some sleuthing.

I had my elbows on the table, wondering if this was a breach of social etiquette during the medieval period.

"Maybe you worry too much," Milla said.

I glanced at the girl, who was working her way through a large plate of roasted potatoes. "Someone's got to."

City folk filled the large table, enjoying a banquet the Lord and Lady of Vaywell prepared so graciously. But something was off. Devin? Am I right to be suspicious?

As I waited for the answer, I pawed my potatoes with my fork, watching my characters tell the story.

"I don't like it, no," Jim said.

Oh. Hi Jim. Is Devin asleep?

"Most likely. When I took over at eight, he looked dead on his feet."

How old is he? Thirty-eight? Thirty-nine?

"Forty-one."

Well, he certainly needs his rest. This situation hasn't exactly been a vacation for anyone involved.

"He's happy to help, and so am I."

I put aside my jealousy of Jim, because I will be the first to admit it was childish. And I needed his help to figure out what was going on.

"Well, thank you, Gunther. That is kind of you."

Put it aside for now. Sometimes it's hard to see a guy a year younger have his life in such order. Seriously, a Guardian? Already?

"Been a couple of years, but yes."

Youngest ever? I think that's what I remember the headlines saying when Vince hired you.

"Yes, but this story isn't about me. This is about you. A story about you getting out."

I snorted, then hid it with a cough as Milla gave me a strange look. You're humble, too, apparently.

"The necromancer absolutely should be in Vaywell, meaning the Rogue must have done something."

Is there a way to find out?

"The Rogue's MO is to place his own characters in other narrators' stories. I have a feeling some of his creations might be in this city, blending in with the other inhabitants. Characters who are loyal to him and, therefore, the Dark Wizard."

"Gunther?" Milla asked. I looked down at her. She pointed to where Paldric and Alwin were talking. "Shouldn't you be part of that? You killed the dragon too, didn't you? That's what Paldric told me. You're more responsible for weakening it than Paldric or Alwin," Milla said.

I looked over again at my characters. "No. That's information I'd rather not spread. The people here don't need to know who I am."

Milla frowned, but nodded. "I guess."

Jim, can you check the code and see if there's anyone here I didn't create?

"Yes. It shouldn't take long."

I'd feel better if I knew what I was up against.

"Let me start that now."

Easing back into my narrator role was simple. As soon as I finished my dinner, I stayed against the wall as music played and an impromptu dance began. Alwin had far more women asking him to dance, which he obliged to, but didn't understand why. Paldric and Tara even took a turn around the dance floor, smiling and laughing. I watched the servants, the city folk, looking into their eyes and sensing their code. All of them were characters I created. Simple, yes, but mine. Servant: in charge of cleaning up after a feast. Servant: keep the wine filled. Soldier: guard the Lord and Lady of Vaywell. Front gate guard: monitor me because he doesn't like me. But I knew my touch. I created this guard who ended up not liking me.

It was getting late. Jim ran into a snag and needed to look through the code individually, but in his mind, it was proof a Rogue character was here.

The city folk had conversations filled with joy and relief that the threat was finally gone. There was still much to rebuild, but at least there wasn't a fear of something tearing it down again. They were content, and I was distraught. They shouldn't be this happy. Where was the necromancer?

The party ended, and we shuffled off to our rooms. It was so much nicer than an inn, but I couldn't trust it.

"Jim? How's the search?" I asked, pacing my room.

There was a pause, and I placed my hands behind my head, my eyes staying on the door.

"I've checked more than half the inhabitants of this city. All of them have your distinct creation mark, so they are all yours, but it would be easy to hide one character among thousands."

I winced. "Sorry. Will this take you long?"

"I have the time," Jim said.

"Isn't there a way to find the alien character if they don't have my distinct creation?"

"I've tried that already. The Rogue is too good at creating these people. I agree with you, Gunther. There is no way the necromancer hasn't entered Vaywell. Even if it were to happen off screen for you, I'm also searching for any character who saw the necromancer. Or even a goblin, or a troll. No one has seen them."

Jim's dedication strangely touched me. All this, even after I admitted to my characters he was a lesser God.

"I'm a Guardian, Gunther. I swore to help people in any situation dealing with the narration device, no matter what they think of me."

"You have the personality of a hero, you know."

"Meh. Supportive side character at most."

I smiled, my eyes still at the door. "Those are always the fan favorite characters, anyway."

Jim chuckled. **"Well thanks. I'll always be here when the hero needs an extra push."**

"Paldric won't hear you."

"I was talking about you."

I rolled my eyes. "I'm not the hero, either. Just because it's in first person, doesn't mean it's me. I'm more... more the bitter old mentor character." The revelation made me pause, mulling it over before groaning. "I'm a mentor character in a fantasy novel. I might as well dig my grave now."

Jim's laugh was loud. I shook my head, smiling as I tried to force myself out of the unease I felt.

He was still chortling. **"Grace will take over for me in a few hours. I'll get back to searching through the code."**

"Thanks Jim."

I went back to pacing, trying to figure out why the necromancer wasn't here with his army. I knew little about the Rogue, since he kept himself secret in the real world. It was difficult to know how to predict the actions of a man I didn't know, but I had to try. If I were a villain, what would I do? They kind of act the same. Capture the hero, make long, boring villain monologues before waiting for the last possible moment to kill the hero before ultimately failing.

That's what a villain would do if *I* wrote them. What if an actual, evil person were to write like their evil self? Was I being harsh against the Rogue? Maybe. But a mysterious man entered my story, forced me into it, destroyed my outline and threatened my characters. So much of it sounded like a typical mustache twirling villain, but the Rogue behind the villains? Whoever he was, he didn't care if my characters lived or died. He didn't play by my rules, and that was all I could predict.

This Dark Wizard and his necromancer buddy had, according to the histories of Veniloria, simply waited on South Island, growing in power. Except for the occasional troll and goblin attack in this book, they didn't show themselves. They wanted to stay a secret as long as possible. Pavaldri destroyed King's Court, and they remained away, waiting for the world to fall with the monarchy. With the added benefit of the Rogue Narrator knowing what would happen in the original outline, the thing that made the most sense was for the necromancer to steal the shield and quietly get out before anyone noticed.

I lowered my hands, my fingers turning to ice.

Chapter Twenty-Nine

LET'S DISCUSS WRITING TECHNIQUES!

In medias res. In the middle of the action. It's a way to start one's story, in this case, mine. Even without me waking up in the middle of action, I still fully intended to use in medias res as the introduction to my story. Big, scary dragon destroying a town? Classic. Plenty of action. Plenty of suspense. Gives the reader a good heart rate boost before I use softer scenes to feed them information. Like introducing my characters to set up the emotional weight needed for further action. Gives a taste for what's coming, and maybe the reader can excuse the occasional info dumps.

Why info dumps? Shouldn't one avoid them every time, one might ask? Moderation, I say. I have written and am narrating an epic fantasy. To build a vastly different world than my own, I cannot help but explain what's going on so the reader doesn't get lost, and there is no other way but dumping information. A skilled narrator would do it so well the reader wouldn't even notice they were gleefully absorbing world building. This, however, is not one of those times. Being in this book helped me reconsider my skill as a narrator. As with all art, I hope to get better. I doubt this book will ever get published, but hopefully readers would trust me enough to understand this dry information I am giving them has a purpose. As we are nearing the end of book one, hopefully the reader will excuse me for this wall of text they are about to read.

For the sake of brevity, let's call the reader Jim, as he's the only one reading this right now. Jim is reading this mountain of text (if he's not distracted with his search through the code), and therefore gets turned off by paragraphs of information. On the second screen, he'll see where I am, but doesn't know where it is, as I won't describe it.

"Um, Gunther?" Jim asked.

And my musings will reveal no information either, because Vaywell is a vast city. And as I shall not confirm where I am, no one else can, either. This is terrible. As a narrator, you shouldn't do this. We refer to this as talking heads, as there is no description that grounds the reader to the setting. But it is necessary for survival, so I will continue and hope the reader, Jim, forgives me.

"What are you—"

You want to know a super fun word? Epizeuxis. Cue flashback on the second screen to further mask where I am.

"Gunther, wait!"

Professor Andrews, one of the top narration instructors in the country, spelled out the word epizeuxis on the whiteboard in my class, along with a lot of other literary devices, and I couldn't figure out how to say it. The word caught my attention, though. Was it because Esme loved scrabble at the time? Yes. And this beautiful word fell into my lap.

"What is happening? Are you using your powers?"

Even after Professor Andrews said it multiple times, I couldn't figure out how to say it. Which is ironic, considering what epizeuxis is. I still had to look up the pronunciation when I got home and practiced it in front of the mirror. Epizeuxis. The repetition of words to help drive home a point. I will never, never, never tell you where I am. Epizeuxis. Epizeuxis. Epizeuxis. Epi — okay, it's hard to say over and over again.

"Switch back now. What was that shark creature? Are you alright?"

Was that intentional? To have a word difficult to say over and over again, and for it to mean the repetition of a word. Do you want to know another funny word to say? Anadiplosis. Repetition of a word or phrase. Get it? Because I said, "over and over", over and over again?

"Gunther!"

I know. It's not funny because I had to explain the joke. Phew! Next lesson should be word fatigue. An editor would *hate* that paragraph there.

"Did you survive the shark?"

Obviously. The mythical Siludontia was a few obstacles ago. I'm fine. Back to flashback.

"Did you use your powers?"

Long story short, I dominated the scrabble board that evening. In the flashback segment Jim will see a memory I made up of me throwing my fists high in the air with a look of pure happiness on my face as Esme looks dejected, but proud I learned such a valuable word. Let's freeze on that moment of triumph. No, not just freeze. That cool artistic thing where it's sort of like freezing but it's slowed down to a glacier pace, where my smile stays solid and sure as the background seems to move, and Esme has a frown, but her shaking head is slow, and you can see she's still sort of proud of me.

"Gunther, answer my question!"

That's exactly how it happened. It wasn't our first huge fight where she stormed off to bed after screaming how it was a foreign word and refused to check the dictionary. I definitely didn't wonder why my success elicited such a reaction from her. This wasn't where I realized it might've been a mistake asking her to move in with me.

Not how it happened. Not at all. Does that make me an unreliable narrator? I don't know. The real question is, would you trust me if I said no? I guess that's your answer, then.

See! You learn great things in an info dump.

"Gunther! Get out of this flashback right now!" The alarm was obvious in his voice.

Alright, alright. Let's see if you were paying attention. In medias res. In the middle of the action. It's usually meant for the beginning of a movie or book. But let's plop right back into what's happening.

The large pendulum swung in front of me, the ax on the bottom a breath away from my shoes, but I couldn't turn back yet, considering all I had gone through before.

Nope. I will not say what. Unreliable narrator right now. Do you believe me?

Jim groaned. **"Gunther, what percentage are you at?"**

No idea. That's Milla's job.

"I, and everyone with a second screen, watched you get almost eaten by that mythical shark with five eyes right before you cut to a flashback."

Yeah, I seriously regret creating that thing.

"Your percentage could be up a bit more if you used your power. I strongly advise you to get back to Milla so she can tell you where you stand."

No, I didn't use my power, and the shark creature didn't eat me. I swam as fast as I could. We shouldn't talk about it anymore, in case someone connects the dots and figures out where I am.

I ran past the swinging pendulum, aware it would track me the entire time I was in this hallway. It was supposed to be a moment of tension for Paldric and Alwin when they entered. They were supposed to walk down this hallway, expecting anything to pop out before they realize the pendulum had steadily got closer, making them run to the door. This will not have the tension, because I was already running down the hallway with the pendulum well behind me.

"Are you being honest with me? Have you used any of your powers?"

Come on, Jim. Didn't you listen to my info dump? Would you trust an unreliable narrator?

Jim sighed, and I could almost see him burying his head in his hands. **"Your life and the life of your characters are at stake."**

I swear I did not use any powers. If it makes you feel better, when I saw that creature for the first time, I would have peed my pants if I had the ability. How's that for consequences of one's actions?

"Fine," Jim mumbled. **"What exactly are your intentions once you finish these obstacles?"**

To make sure the shield is still here. That's all I need to know. And I'm being careful to *not* reveal anything as I do it.

"Alright. I'll just stay silent."

Thank you.

"Unless you use your powers. Then I will call Devin."

Thanks for keeping me accountable, Jim.

I opened the door and ran inside, panting. My clothes were soaking wet and clinging to my body as I went up the thin walkway to where the shield waited on a stone slab. I stared at it, knowing it was real and not a decoy. I turned, moving cautiously over the narrow walkway that would lead to my certain doom if I fell, but I tried not to think about that.

"That's all you're going to do?"

"Yes." I kept my arms out to balance. "My goal was to check if it was here, and it is. It means the necromancer is... well, I don't know what it means, but he doesn't have the shield."

"Get back to Milla for a percentage report."

"Yeah, I'll get back to info dumping and flash backing so the Rogue doesn't see where I am."

"No." It sounded like I caught him mid drink. **"No, Gunther. Don't do that again. It's too dangerous, and too tempting for you."**

"Well, what would you suggest? I can't describe everything I just went through. It makes what I did in the beginning pointless."

Jim paused long enough to take a drink of... something. I couldn't tell what it was, since the Guardians were literally talking heads all the time to me. But I heard him swallowing. **"As a mystery writer, I've always used the oh so common red herring trope. Let me explain it in detail."** His voice had taken on a dull lecture quality.

"Thanks, Jim. You're a lifesaver."

I ran as the second screen went up to the ceiling, masking what I was doing as Jim started narrating.

"As one might guess, it is a thing us narrators use to distract the reader from figuring out the real clues. It is most prominent in mysteries, but other genres are of course welcome to such a fun trope. It is a shiny, juicy clue that leads to nowhere. The

origin of the word comes from hunting dogs. While tracking, the dogs would follow a scent, but the more powerful scents, one of those being a red herring fish, would distract them. Apparently, they are quite aromatic. There are many subgenres of the—what just dropped from the ceiling?"

Don't worry about it.

"**Wait, is that—**"

"I'm fully aware of it, thank you," I said out loud to cut Jim off.

"**Subgenres of the red herring trope, like setting up someone in the group to be the secret villain or a mole, and for them to be perfectly inno—oh that sounds gross! Is that—**"

"Do! Not! Describe! It!" I couldn't help but shout.

"**Holy—is that what... oh, it's about to drop! Gunther! Run!**"

"Remind me to never drive you anywhere!" I shouted back. "Red herring, Jim! Get back to red herrings!"

"**Many mystery tropes rely on this, to give the reader something they think is the real deal, but it's a distraction, much like this info dump distracts you from what Gunther's doing.**" I could almost hear Jim's teeth grinding with anxiety, struggling to keep his voice dull. "**Had I been writing this, it would be incredibly boring, and we would fool no one. My dialogue was purely to distract—Gunther, GuntherGuntherGunther. That's not... no, no, no.**"

Shut up, Jim. Shutupshutupshutup.

"**Of course, readers love to pick apart red herrings,**" Jim said loudly to distract himself from what I was doing. "**So one must strike a balance of a believable red herring. My favorite sub trope of this is the weapon is not really the weapon after all. The gun being carried throughout the story before it's discovered to be fake. The knife in the body turning out to be just a prop knife.**

Kinda spoiled my own books there, but who cares? The problem is, I can only use these kinds of tropes twice before readers suspect it every time. I can use that to my advantage, though when—too many teeth. Why does that stupid shark have so many teeth?"

Sharks have a ton of teeth, alright!

"And five eyes? Why five? Why?"

Could you just get back to your monologue?!? I'm kind of busy here!

Jim sighed again. **"So, when I use these kinds of tropes, I play on the readers' expectations. I've only used the switched weapon twice, but then I got another book published where I placed heavy emphasis on the weapon to make everyone expect it would be a fake again, but I made it real to kill my fan favorite side character. A reverse red herring, which fooled a few readers. I was quite proud of myself for that."**

I broke the surface of the ocean, gasping and spitting. The sky was warm, but the ocean was not. The sun rose, and hopefully I could sneak back to the manor without dripping everywhere. I moved my wet hair out of my eyes with my hand.

"Need me anymore?" Jim asked.

"We'll see." I unfolded my glasses and placed them back on my nose. "I still don't want to describe where I am, but you did great. Thanks."

"Get back to Milla. I don't think you used any of your powers, but we've got to check. Oh, hey Grace. Come on in."

Out of breath, I nodded. My arms moved forward to swim closer to a certain place in Vaywell as the exhaustion hit. I didn't get any sleep last night, and though adrenaline was a great stimulant, I felt exhausted now that my secret quest was done.

There was something on the beach. It looked like fifty citizens out to meet me. Maybe it was for a good reason, but as I got closer, I knew it wasn't. I was too much of a cynic to believe this was a welcoming party. At dawn. With fifty inhabitants of the city. After trying way too hard to make sure no one knew I was coming out for a swim.

It was then that I saw Alwin, Paldric, Milla, and Tara kneeling on the beach, their hands tied behind their backs, knives to their throats.

"Grace, call Devin. I'll brew another pot of coffee," Jim said, sounding grim.

Chapter Thirty

THE NECROMANCER FINALLY SHOWS UP

The moment my swimming strokes slowed, four people ran into the ocean for me. I didn't struggle, mainly because my characters were kneeling in the sand with daggers to their throats. I could have saved them with my God powers, but I didn't know my percentage.

They dragged me onto the beach. Lord Adrijian appeared out of the crowd and headed straight for me. "Where's the shield?"

I stared at him, curious, saying nothing. I expected a new character, or the necromancer himself. Not one of my own.

"Search him! I need that shield," Lord Adrijian shouted to the men who dragged me out.

My soaking wet clothes clung to me, so it was clear I wasn't hiding the huge shield, but it didn't stop them from patting me down.

"It's not here," one of them said.

Lord Adrijian stepped closer. "What were you doing in the ocean?"

"Gunther? Jim's filling me in. Hold tight," Devin said.

"You're going to be alright, dear," Grace added for good measure.

I continued to stare at Lord Adrijian, sensed him as my creation, and yet he was doing something out of character. He was, admittedly, never super complex, but he was mine. The Rogue couldn't have turned him since the Dark Wizard was still on South Island, and yet a code blocked me from seeing what happened to him.

"Where is the shield?"

I held my palms out. "I obviously don't have it."

Lord Adrijian nodded to the guard, the one I had the pleasure of seeing at the front of his house. He pinned my hands behind my back, looking like he wasn't too sad about my situation as Lord Adrijian took another step closer. "But you know where it is, don't you?"

"The Dark Wizard hasn't touched him. His code is completely how you wrote it. He is still your character," Devin said.

Jim let out a groan. **"But the others have. All those characters on the beach are yours, and the Dark Wizard got them. The code was so expertly buried I didn't see it my first scan through. I'm sorry, Gunther. This time, it actually is my fault."**

He sounded so dejected, too. I would have comforted him, but his words chilled me. The Dark Wizard? Here in Vaywell? Impossible. Despite not seeing the code in the characters, there's no way the Rogue could have hidden the Dark Wizard from Jim. He couldn't travel that fast from South Island. Unless he has teleportation.

Does he have teleportation?

"Grace is checking now," Devin said.

My chest constricted. I ran through the Dark Wizard's powers in my mind. None of them included teleportation, but maybe I overlooked something. If I didn't notice fifty altered people on the beach loyal to the Rogue, I could have missed something else.

Lord Adrijian was so close now I could see tears forming in his eyes. "You will go back and get it for me."

"No teleportation. I'll dig more," Grace said.

"What happened to you?" I stared right at Lord Adrijian, trying to understand. I had little desire to get the shield, since I was running on almost twenty-four hours with no sleep. And I just made the journey he was ordering me to repeat. "I thought you were on my side."

Lord Adrijian narrowed his eyes. "On your side? What are you talking about?"

"Why are you working for the necromancer?"

"We have his wife." It was a voice I'd never heard before, stuck on a character I never created, in a story that should have been my own. The necromancer walked forward. He was deathly pale. And his black hair was a contrast to his skin. It looked like he had risen himself from the dead several times.

Which gave me an odd sense of pride. "I knew you were here. I knew it." The guard forced me to my knees in the sand. "How did you hide yourself?"

"My master, the Dark Wizard, knows many of your tricks, and is far cleverer than you." His voice was ugly and hallow, only an echo of what it once was.

"Ugh, are you one of those monologuing villains?"

The necromancer took out a jagged dagger and placed it against my throat. I closed my eyes because it was terrifying. Sometimes I forgot I'm an all-powerful God and couldn't technically die.

"Keep forgetting you're an all-powerful God," Devin said.

Yeah. I'll try.

Alwin attempted to stand. "Leave Gunther alone!" Paldric, too, struggled against his captors.

If he was a monologuing villain, I could use that to my advantage. I opened my eyes again. "How did you turn all these people against me?"

"The Dark Wizard is far cleverer than you," the necromancer repeated.

"The Rogue went for filler characters shuffling around on the streets. They were blank slates for him. He hid the code expertly well. I looked for the wrong things. Instead of finding new characters, I should have looked harder at the characters that already existed."

Don't, Jim. Don't feel bad. The Dark Wizard wasn't supposed to be here. We didn't expect this. "Where's the Dark Wizard now?" I asked the necromancer.

"You don't need to concern yourself with him. All you need to worry about is getting me that shield."

Fine. Grace, where's the Dark Wizard? Is he in Vaywell or on South Island?

"Give me a second."

"I haven't slept in a day, I'm soaking wet, and I just came back from that perilous journey. I'm not about to hop back into the ocean," I said to keep the conversation going.

"My master tells me you are impossible to kill, therefore this quest should be little trouble for the likes of you," the necromancer said.

"Not without serious consequences. If you value your safety, you wouldn't force me back there." I tried to stall to give Grace more time. I needed to know if the Dark Wizard was here.

"I am a necromancer. I am not afraid of death."

Grace gave a quiet hiss. **"Yes. Yes, he's in the dungeon. He's... he's got Lady Ana and is..."**

What, Grace? What is he doing to her?

"Trying to alter her code. Getting her to turn against you, too."

Torture. He's torturing them. How is the Dark Wizard *here*? I thought only the necromancer came here.

"He traveled here somehow, but the text is heavily encrypted. I'll start trying to crack it," Jim said.

You've been up all night just like I have, Jim. You must be exhausted.

"I'm brewing a fresh pot of coffee, remember?"

I'm trying hard not to be jealous of that coffee right now.

The necromancer got closer to me, and I did not like the chill that emanated from him. "You, of course, can go on this quest whenever you'd like. Take a nap first for all I care. Many people in this city are now servants to the Dark Wizard, and we asked them to remain in hiding. Try to cleanse the city while the Dark Wizard tortures the Lord and Lady of Vaywell. According to the family tree, with the monarchy gone, Lord Adrijian and Lady Ana are next in line for the throne. It would be so nice to have them under our control."

Lord Adrijian frowned, surprised, as other members of the city grabbed him and pulled him away. I winced. Lord Adrijian must not have realized he and his wife were next in line. The future king caught my gaze, deeply uncomfortable about ruling Veniloria even without the threat of being brainwashed by the Dark Wizard. "We shall also have Tara join them in the dungeon. My master is eager to meet her. To mold her to his will."

My eyes shot toward Tara, trying desperately to hide my concern, but it didn't work. Tara herself held still, like she could turn invisible if she stopped breathing.

"NO!" Paldric shouted. They whacked him on the back of the head with the hilt of the dagger. I winced in sympathy, already seeing the blood trickling from the wound.

"I'm told her molding will be quick, and she will comply to my master's will. Take your time on your quest, Gunther. See how long precious Tara will last."

"Don't do anything stupid, Gunther. Don't use your powers. You still don't know what percentage you're at," Jim said.

If I don't use my powers, I have to get the shield fast. The necromancer is right. It wouldn't take long to turn Tara against me.

"Take Alwin with you. My master is also keenly interested in him," the necromancer said.

They forced Tara and Alwin to their feet, dragging them away.

"No! Stop it!" Paldric said.

The sword. Does the Dark Wizard have the sword?

"He does," Grace said.

"Alwin! You don't have to activate the sword if you don't want to! Okay? Don't do it! I will go as fast as I can. Just hold on!"

Which is when a sharp pain exploded in the back of my head, and I was just glad I was already on my knees. I straightened my glasses before touching the back of my head, feeling the sticky blood there. I wanted to give in and heal my head. This stung, and the thought of entering the ocean with the Siludontia did not help.

"Paldric and the child will go with you. They have no real value to my master. Get the shield and get back here."

"It's too dangerous for Milla. She's just a kid. I can do it myself." The necromancer cut the ropes of Paldric and Milla before pushing them toward me. "Didn't you hear me? I'll go faster if I go alone."

"They either die while on your journey, or I kill them now." The necromancer held his dagger, ready to throw it at Milla. At a little girl. "They matter little to me." Milla whimpered, grabbing my arm. "My men will watch, and if she or Paldric remain above the ocean, they have orders to kill them."

Part of me wanted my looks to actually kill as I glared at the necromancer. It hurt enough knowing Alwin and Tara were with the Dark Wizard. I didn't want Paldric and Milla to get hurt, either.

My arm went around Milla, bringing her closer, still glaring at him. "Just twirl your stupid mustache and get out of here, villain."

The necromancer was confused. His fingers brushed his upper lip that could not grow facial hair, before giving me another curious look.

"You're at thirty-three percent," Milla whispered.

Thirty-three. Not bad for a mission that eventually proved useless. But now I had to return with Paldric and Milla.

"You have about eighteen thousand words left until we reach eighty thousand. Whatever these obstacles are, describe them as much as possible. See how much you can stretch it."

Sorry, Devin, but do you honestly think I'm going to leave my characters now? In the middle of all this? Finish book one only to watch the Dark Wizard torture them in the second book?

"Listen to me, Gunther." His voice had turned serious. **"This has always been about saving you. Once you are out, we can stop the device and make a proper plan to save your characters next. We don't have to react on the fly. As long as we narrate once a month, it will not break down. You need to leave your story. You are real."** They are not. That was the phrase Devin didn't say out loud, but the tone and the way he trailed off told me that's exactly what he thought. Yes, his ideas had merit, but there was still too large a chance that things could go wrong. My characters, my story, it was still in danger. I needed to save it.

"You will save it. As soon as you get out." It was Vince. He was here. Which made me realize something. They weren't supposed to talk about getting me out of my story. It was part of the contract. It was supposed to filter out all their lectures. I flipped through the data and sensed Devin had deleted it while I was sleeping. My heart pounded, feeling betrayed.

"We are doing this for your safety," was the only thing Devin said in explanation.

"If you value your characters' lives, you will get out of the story as soon as you can," Vince said.

No, thank you.

"Gunther! Don't—"

I turned Devin off. All of them. I shouldn't have, but I did. It was pure instinct. If Devin didn't realize I was going to do literally everything in my power to save them, then it was better if I didn't have his voice telling me they weren't worth saving. This story, with its two-dimensional characters and flimsy plot, was the last thing going for me. There was no way I could return to living in my parents' basement just to watch this story crash and burn. I can't handle another failure in my life right now.

"Thirty-four percent," Milla said.

I sighed as I stood up. "We'll get you the stupid shield. And once we do, we will storm the dungeons to get our friends back."

The necromancer smiled. "Do it, Gunther. Go insane. Destroy the world. I am looking forward to it."

There was no comeback to that. The city folk were already dragging Tara and Alwin away.

Milla slipped her hand in mine, and I squeezed it. "Come on, Paldric, Milla. We've got to go."

Devin, I'm sorry. I know you're still reading my thoughts. This is something I need to do to keep them safe. I will turn you back on soon. I promise.

The three of us walked into the ocean, and I tried not to focus on how everything in my life was falling apart. Again.

Chapter Thirty-One

PALDRIC AND I FINALLY TALK

"Stay close," I told Milla as she held my hand. "How long can you hold your breath?"

"I... I don't know."

"Don't be afraid, alright?" I moved closer to Paldric. "There will be a drop off once we swim farther. The cavern entrance is on the cliff side. Once we're inside, it's a quick swim to the top before we find air. It might feel like a long time to hold one's breath, but it doesn't take long. But we've also got to be fast. But... but there will be air."

Paldric looked back to see the men holding spears, their feet in the water, watching to make sure all of us disappeared under the surface. He glanced back at me. "We need to make sure we do this right."

"Yes. So, no heart-to-heart moments. No waiting until the last moment to confess something you think I don't know about you. No dragging this out. I know exactly what we'll face down there. When I tell you to run, run. When I tell you to stop, stop. Are we clear?"

"I understand," Paldric said.

"Good." The ocean was chest high on me, and Milla was already swimming. I braced myself to swim farther out when I froze. "Nope. I can't do this. Paldric, come here."

He did, confused, and I touched both our heads, sucking the blood back into our bodies and closing our wounds. Paldric frowned, touching the back of his head.

"Thirty-five percent," Milla said.

"Gunther—"

"There's also a school bus sized Siludontia down there deeper in the ocean that I already woke up, and it's pretty pissed."

Paldric's eyes widened. "A Siludontia? As in…"

"Shark. Fat shark with too many teeth and five eyes. Never has a blind spot unless you can see its gray tail. It stays on the deeper part of the ocean, and unfortunately the cave is near its hunting grounds, so be prepared once we get low enough. Stay close, and be glad you're not bleeding," I said.

The alarm grew in Paldric's face.

"Swim fast, alright? Because that shark certainly will." I held Milla so she could rest from swimming. She couldn't outswim a Siludontia if it was charging her, but Paldric and I could help. "Are you ready, Milla?" She shook her head, burrowing deeper into me and doing everything in her power not to cry. She couldn't go below the water if she was crying. "Deep breaths. Don't thrash around. I've got you. Nothing is going to happen to you."

"You're at thirty-five percent, Gunther." Her voice was an octave higher than usual.

Yes, I was. And I cut the Guardians off. The people who were my eyes on the Dark Wizard and the necromancer. I swam farther into the ocean, Milla following me.

"We can do this in less than ten minutes. It was supposed to be an arduous journey, but I know what to expect. It's like playing a video game after already going through it and knowing all the cheat codes."

"I... don't understand," Paldric said.

"It'll be fine." I took off my glasses and tightened my fingers around them. They almost fell into the ocean last time. It also kept me from seeing the frightened looks Paldric and Milla were giving me. "Just stick close. We'll go through them with as little drama as possible. This chapter is going to be so boring to read, it'll never sell."

"You're not making any sense. Again," Paldric said.

We waded in paradise blue water while a few feet from us we saw the dark navy water that held many unknown creatures. "I ramble when I'm nervous. My words are completely harmless, I promise."

"Harmless? When you've risen in percentage since I saw you last?" Paldric asked.

I prepped myself, taking deep breaths. "We'll be fine. Optimism, right? That's what you always tell me."

Paldric glared at me. "You are clearly panicking and trying to pass this off as optimism when it's obviously not."

"We've got to be fast to save Tara and Alwin. I don't know how long they'll last." I rubbed my eyebrow before taking a deep breath.

Paldric grabbed my arm to keep me from diving. I let out my breath, which made me suck in more air, and I had to admit my panic had taken over. My main character did not look amused. "Gunther, I am not an idiot. I don't skip to certain death with a smile on my face and assume the outcome will magically turn in our favor when every single one of us knows it won't. Doing so is what I'd like to call stupidity. You created me. Why don't you know me?" He didn't say this in an accusatory manner, nor did he say it with bitterness. He simply said it like he was commenting on the facts of a science project we were working on together.

My breathing paused, which was better. There was enough oxygen in my bloodstream right now. "I may have created you, but there comes a point where you come into your own and have your own life. I gave you ideas and principles that would make an interesting individual, but you're the one that lived them. It's how I've always wanted it."

"If you go down there in this state, you could get us killed. I don't want that to happen." Paldric pointed toward the navy blue part of the ocean.

My brows furrowed. "Fine. Let's have a heart-to-heart. Tell me what I don't know about you."

Paldric shook his head. "You know everything about me. What you don't understand is optimism." I couldn't argue with that. "It isn't just assuming everything will go my way. It's understanding that everything works out. That nature, the order of things, it's to our favor, even if we don't see it right now. Everything is ordered to produce what's best for us, whether or not we survive this."

I stared at Paldric. We clearly needed to have this chat ever since the argument in Paerra, but I couldn't comprehend his outlook on life. It was so alien. I pointed to myself. "I am the order who gave you that. And now I'm here. I've lost control of everything."

"You aren't listening, Gunther." Paldric took Milla, holding her close. "This is the very nature of creation. The rules that *you, as God,* live by, even if you aren't there. Things have a way of working out."

"If... if I wasn't... Paldric, do you not get it? I am here. I'm not in control. Things are spiraling, and I can't help but panic about it!" I put my glasses back on to see his way too calm face. "And even when I was in control..." I closed my eyes, not sure I wanted to talk to him in case he lost his optimism. If Paldric lost it, it would destroy him worse than what the Dark Wizard might do to him, but we couldn't ignore this conversation, either. "A dragon destroyed an entire village in a night. Your parents, they…" He watched me, curious. "You're just someone with a lot of plot armor."

"I don't know what that means," Paldric said.

I sighed, rubbing my hair. "You could die when I don't want you to. That's what it means. Because I don't have control over what the Dark Wizard does."

Paldric shook his head. "And what would happen if I died?"

I stared at him, once again finding myself back in my God role. I wanted to tell him there was nothing. He would cease to exist, because he was a character in a story, but it made me pause. There actually was a place after the story ended.

"When your journey is over, you will…" I struggled to find the right way to describe the extensive and protected database in the Guardian's headquarters. "You will find yourself in a grand afterlife. It's… it's called the database." He had no comprehension of what that was, so I might as well tell the truth. "There will be many other people of different time periods and creations. It will be a harmonious place of no strife, where you may do whatever you please for the rest of eternity. An enormous party, if you will."

Paldric smiled. "And my parents?"

I stared at him. "They'll be there too."

"See? There's nothing to fear."

I couldn't tear my gaze away. This knowledge of the database, where he would meet the characters of other stories, it filled him with a peace the Dark Wizard could never destroy. But the thing was, he already had that peace. What I said confirmed to him something he already knew, but that was impossible. There was no way he could know about the database.

And he almost had me, but I still couldn't believe in his optimism. If any of my characters died, they would remain in a coma until the story finished, sequels included. But if I cracked, I would never leave. The story would never end. He'd never see his parents again. He'd never see Milla or Tara or Alwin again.

"Paldric, it's…" I didn't know how I could explain it to him. It would simply be the difference between us. He would always be optimistic because he didn't have the full information. "It's alright. I'm glad we have someone optimistic in the party."

I almost took my glasses back off when Paldric stopped me. "You still don't understand it." He lifted one of his arms, pointing at the world. "Back in my town, we are experiencing autumn. Things are falling apart, and trees are letting go of their leaves. In a few months, it will be winter, and it will seem like death surrounds us. And then spring will come. You are not up there, and yet it will happen. This is how the world works. Fires ravish the land and cause damage, and yet seedlings grow from the ashes. Good things just… work out. Because evil things can't."

"I could go insane." I didn't want to fight, but he needed to understand. "No matter what I do, I could crack and destroy this entire planet. Every single one of you could die, and I wouldn't care."

"You might go insane, yes. And yet I firmly believe in a million years, you will get bored. And maybe, instead of destruction, you will try creation again."

It wouldn't work. Paldric simply wouldn't understand that while I was insane, he'd never see his parents again. I almost told him this, but what he said made me pause. "Actually…" my face softened in realization. "It wouldn't take a million years." I stared at him. "At most, I would be in my state for another forty, fifty years." Even in a cracked state, I would die eventually. And then the device, my story, would end, and my characters would enter the database and live on. Their coma state wouldn't be forever, because *I* couldn't last forever.

Paldric smiled. "See? It's looking better already." He hugged Milla before looking at me again. "Being optimistic isn't pretending things will all be fine and ignoring the bad. Optimism is, if I had to put it simply, not fearing the ending, however it happens, whatever it is. Everything in nature proves there is a renewal. Even the end has a new beginning, and there is always hope in beginnings. I don't know how it will be better for us, but I trust it will. Everything I see, everything around me, proves things end, and it's nothing to be afraid of."

I stared at Paldric, my mouth dropping open. The end. That's what I feared this whole time. Things not ending the way I wanted them to. I had a plan. An outline. The Rogue destroyed so many things when I entered my story. But I was still here. So were my characters. If I went insane and killed them, they would still live in the database once I died.

A huge load lifted off my shoulders. Going insane wasn't the worst thing that would happen to my characters. *I* would not be the worst thing. Paldric believed every ending would be okay. Ending of the seasons, ending of books. Ending of marriages. It was okay. Whatever happened now, whatever waited for us, even if it took a million years, something good would come out of it in the end.

"Thirty-three percent," Milla said, her teeth chattering.

My eyes fell on the little girl. I dropped a whole two percent. She smiled at me, and I glanced back up at Paldric. He patted my shoulder. "I don't ignore all the bad, though. If I see destruction, it is my duty to help new growth happen faster."

"You focus on the things you can change. Pour your energy into what you can, so..."

What *was* the worst thing, then? I stared at Paldric, hoping it would help. The worst thing to happen to him would be if he lost his optimism. If he wasn't interested in helping people anymore. As corny as it sounded, it was true. I doubted Paldric would ever lose his outlook, but I don't want to know how much torture he could withstand. I wanted to make sure he got to the database, happy to see his parents. It wasn't his physical death I feared now. It was the death of his character.

Which reminded me why we were in the ocean. Tara. She was receiving a death of character right now, and though I tried not to fear the end I couldn't control, this *was* something I could change.

"Alright, listen to me." I turned enough to see the men on the beach holding their spears. "There are four chambers in the cave below us. In the first one, arrows shoot through the entire room. It seems random, but I know the system, so follow me. In the second room, we must step on certain tiles to get through it, or poisonous spiders drop from the ceiling to chase us. The third one has a huge ax pendulum that eventually speeds up. Then we'll be in the room with the shield. Once one of us grabs the shield, the entire cave collapses, and the ocean spills into that room. Swimming up and out will get us back to the surface." I took off my glasses, holding them tight.

Paldric and Milla nodded. I swam out far enough to see the murky water with miles of sea below us. "Follow me. The cave opening isn't far."

I took a few deep breaths before diving into the water.

Chapter Thirty-Two

I Finally Describe the Obstacles. You're Welcome.

I kicked my legs as hard as I could. The temperature of the ocean turned colder the deeper we went. Due to book logic from my original outline, I could see the ocean perfectly without goggles. Extra plus because I didn't have to use my God powers.

The cave wasn't too far, but if someone didn't know where it was, they would have spent a long time searching for it. I sensed the shark swimming just below. I waved Paldric over and pointed at the small opening, ushering them in. He nodded before swimming over and entering the cave, guiding Milla inside. I followed, swimming fast toward air. My lungs weren't burning, but if I didn't know relief was coming soon, I would have panicked. At least we were in the cave, safe from the shark.

The cave had no light source, and book logic could only get me so far. Despite being able to see outside the cave, there was only darkness in here. But I knew there was air. There was going to be air. Even though the Rogue altered physical locations before the start of my story, he wouldn't think about altering this. I wasn't panicking. There would be air soon. There had to be.

I broke the surface, coughing. "Paldric! Milla!"

"Here, Gunther! We're here on these rock stairs," Paldric said.

There was an outline of a door somewhere above me, barely illuminating the cave. My two characters were there, panting. I swam toward the dim door. The rocks helped me find my footing, but my characters helped pull me onto the stairs. I coughed, my wet hair falling into my eyes. My fingers were surprisingly steady as I brushed my hair back. The exhaustion hit me as I placed my glasses on my nose. I'd already gone through this twice. Being perpetually wet was annoying. The only thing keeping me awake was a desire to keep my characters safe. And after seeing the dim outline of Paldric and Milla, I couldn't stop myself from hugging them. They hugged me back.

"We're alright," Milla said.

I again pushed my wet hair back. "Alright. Let's go. Follow me."

We made our way up the stairs and through the door. The room was lit with torches from my last time through here. I forgot to put them out. Getting out as fast as possible took my attention from extinguishing the torches, but no matter. It was nice to see.

I clapped my hands, rubbing them together. "Alright, there's a pattern to this. The elves created it to be simple, yet deadly. Once we move, we've got to keep moving. The only time we need to stop is right before the end, when arrows come from the bottom instead of the side." Milla took my hand, and Paldric came on the other side, giving her other hand a squeeze. "Follow me. Stay right by my side. You can close your eyes if it makes you feel better. Don't let go of each other."

Milla and Paldric nodded. I took a deep breath, then a step. A wall of arrows appeared inches from my nose, and as soon as they rushed by, I took another step, my characters following close. The arrows rained down from above, again right by my nose before I took three more steps as Paldric and Milla stayed by my side. Milla kept her eyes shut, and her grip on my hand tightened. She was doing an excellent job.

"Gunther." Paldric never used that tone before in my presence, but I understood the fluctuation. He forced his voice to stay calm because of Milla, but there was something causing him alarm.

"Yes?" I also tried not to tip Milla off with my tone.

"When convenient, check the door ahead."

I moved them forward, watching the arrows. Once we crossed the next batch of arrows, I checked the door. My heart plopped right into my stomach.

Shadows crossed under the door. Too many shadows. Thin, hairy legs poked through the crack. Thankfully, only the bottom. Once I noticed it, I heard the skittering of over five hundred spiders in the room next to us.

My eyes snapped back to the wall of arrows as my mind churned with panic. "Thank you for bringing that to my attention." I might have fooled Milla for the time being.

How did that happen? I closed my mouth and let myself scream, coming out as more of a whimper as I moved ahead.

"Gunther?" Great. Milla heard me.

"Thinking. I'm just thinking."

Step ahead, pause, step ahead, pause. Take three more steps, pause.

I must not have killed all the ones from when my foot brushed against a bad tile on my return journey. About five spiders dropped and headed straight for me. I thought I killed them all, but if two stumbled on a tile together, it would have broken another tile above them. Spiders can climb up the pit wall. And if at least two spiders stepped on another tile, causing five more spiders to fall...

Lovely.

We reached the end, and I pressed my hands against the wall. My lungs demanded air, even though we walked the whole way. I checked my characters. "I'm alright. Are you alright?" Paldric nodded, the look of worry still on his face. "Milla?"

She looked ahead, her eyes wide. "My arm hurts."

Both of us saw a lot of blood on her forearm. Paldric sprang into action quicker than I did.

"Let's see it, Milla." He got down on one knee and lifted her sleeve. "Yes, you did. But look, it's a nice, clean cut." He was already untucking his shirt and using his sword to cut a piece off the bottom. "It's going to sting, but this will help keep the blood in your body." Paldric wrapped her arm with the makeshift bandage as Milla nodded, tears in her eyes. "Don't worry. Once we get out, we'll have Tara look at it. She's good at this. You got sliced by an arrow, but it didn't hit bone."

"I'm sorry." She didn't hold back her sob.

Paldric tied the bandage together. "Sorry for what?"

"For being a silly little girl that always ruins things."

He focused on the bandage but shot his gaze to meet hers once she finished speaking. "What is this nonsense you're saying?"

"My brothers went on adventures all the time and they never let me play because I always mess it up by getting hurt."

"Milla, no." He placed his hands against her cheeks. "No, dear girl. It's not your fault for getting hurt. You have a body, just like Gunther and I, and we walked through about fifteen walls of arrows. It's a miracle you're the only one who got hurt. I'm not angry at you. You're not being silly. You got hurt. That's all there is." He went back to fixing the bandage, giving it a strong knot. "And if you got hurt every time you had adventures with your brothers, it was probably too dangerous for them, too."

She laughed, the first tears falling. "Yeah. They would always do things that might have..." *killed them.* More tears sprang to her eyes, frustration at wondering why the death of her family still hurt so much.

"Then it's a good thing you were there to stop them." Paldric patted her shoulder. "I'm glad you're alright."

Tears fell down her cheeks. "I miss them."

Paldric hugged her. "You'll see them again. Gunther gave a promise. It will still hurt, because you love them dearly, and there's always an ache when they can't be here with you, but you'll be going on adventures with them again. And they can be as crazy as you want them to be."

She hugged him back, burying her head in his shoulder. Paldric let her hug him as long as she needed.

Scenes tumbled into my head as I watched the entire exchange. Ones of safety. Of the oh so coveted happily ever after. Where Tara and Paldric were married, with children of their own, and Milla was there too. Adopted into their family like she was one of theirs. It made so much sense for Paldric to adopt Milla. Having her here brought out a fatherly characteristic in him I didn't expect, but he grew into that role as easily as he grew into his other positive ones. Being a father figure simply made sense to him. All of them would be fine. As long as we got that happily ever after. As long as Tara stayed herself.

Milla frowned when she heard skittering legs against the floor. It was undeniable now. She looked at me; the terror written across her face. "I don't like spiders."

Yeah, I know. Common phobia. Also, my ex-wife's fear. Between the spider room and the big hungry shark guarding the entrance, I was sick of Esme reading my story and wanted her to stop. I should have asked her, but I wanted to make her angry instead, because I have no maturity to make a relationship last. Aimee's words, not mine. I should have known this would come back to bite me. Literally.

The spiders got restless and fought each other in their aggressive need to kill. I braced myself against the wall, thinking. We could wait until the horde ate themselves, but it would take too long. My biggest concern right now was Tara and Alwin.

"These spiders are the size of my shoe, and that's not considering their legs." I talked to the air. It's what I did when I had writer's block. Talk it out. Not to Esme, because she never listened unless I mentioned something that wasn't fantasy. I learned to talk to the wall. "They have a deadly poison, slow and painful. I can heal it, but the less I need to use my powers, the better. When I open the door, they will come after us."

Paldric looked at the two torches above us. "Do they like fire?"

I didn't expect Paldric to answer, but his life was at stake too, so he'd be far more invested than Esme. "No, they don't. But there's only two torches, and about a thousand spiders."

"And we have a room that shoots arrows. If we can draw them out, this room should kill enough of them." It sounded great, so I picked up one torch. He looked at the door at the start of the room. "Do we open the door and run back to the beginning?"

I thought about it before shaking my head. "They are too aggressive, and we'd never make it back in time." I almost saw it with my mind's eye like a story scene. Us heading back in a slow, methodical way as hundreds of spiders descended, crawling over the dead bodies of their brothers to kill us. I shook my head again. "Not even sure their fear of fire will last long, but if we can kill enough, that will do."

Paldric lifted the other torch off its holder. Milla whimpered. He lifted her up with one hand. "You don't have to look, and I will make sure none of them bite you."

Milla nodded, wrapping her arms and legs around him as tightly as possible.

My hand rested against the doorknob. "Ready?"

Paldric had one arm around Milla, the other on the torch as he lowered it to spider level. "Ready."

The doorknob twisted open, and a black horde of legs shot through.

Chapter Thirty-Three

TO MY EX-WIFE, HATER OF SPIDERS

I gritted my teeth, working through the disgust of seeing so many legs and soulless eyes. No, I didn't have crippling arachnophobia, but when the horde tried to kill us, I understood how people could feel that way. My initial freezing was mostly because I knew exactly how poisonous those pincers were.

Arrows whizzed by, some from the walls, some from the floor. The spiders that got hit moved with the momentum, giving the impression they leapt into the air. It didn't take long for a small hill of dead arachnids to form.

The thing about spiders that I failed to remember in my state of panic was they weren't bound by the floor. In their desire to kill, they spread, heading up walls. Paldric kept his torch toward the ones on the ground as spiders crawled to the ceiling.

I backed away, keeping my torch high as a spider dropped toward Paldric and Milla. It instead landed on the torch, its legs curling in on itself as it caught on fire. I tossed the inflamed spider toward the horde. I hoped the flame would spread and tried not to think of the worst-case scenario if it did.

Milla screamed as a spider dropped on her hair. The burning corpse of their fellow arachnid clearly didn't deter the others from attempting the same tactic. It would start raining spiders soon. Paldric grabbed it with his bare hands and threw it far into the room of arrows.

"We've got to go!" I held my torch toward the spiders on the ground as they backed into the room of arrows. "Sprint to the next room. The path should be clear, since the spiders stepped on all the tiles. Run as fast as you can."

Paldric whispered to Milla, telling her to hold on tight because he was going to let her go. She nodded, squeezing him tighter. He pulled out his sword, still holding his torch. "I will follow you."

I nodded, then ran as I kept the torch low around my feet, giving myself a buffer from the arachnids wanting to bite my ankles.

Paldric and I sprinted into the next room, stepping on the spiders that didn't move out of the way. Despite the hundreds of dead ones in the arrow room, there were hundreds more in the tile room. I had never been so tempted to shoot flames out of my hands to purify the entire place, but I resisted. Pretty sure that would take at least ten percent of my sanity.

"Twenty," Milla whispered.

Yep. Not worth it.

We ran on the tiled floor, following the path the spiders gave us. Paldric used his torch to keep them from his feet, and the sword to kill the ones dropping from the ceiling. The pathway to the next door was slick with guts. We didn't cause too many to die. This must have been from their time killing each other out of boredom.

The path became less clear as the spiders were driven mad by the desire to bite us. We sprinted up the steps as I peeled a spider off my head before chucking it behind me. "Don't run ahead of me! There's a pendulum in the next room, and I don't want you to get hit!"

Paldric nodded, looking deathly pale. One spider bite was enough to kill slowly. Multiple spider bites would speed the process up. Something told me Paldric was a victim of the latter.

We entered the room with the ax pendulum and shut the door. I checked Paldric and Milla to make sure they didn't have any stray living spiders, since their guts still covered us. Then I waited a fraction of a second for the ax to swing before grabbing Paldric. He hugged Milla as we darted through the room. The ax followed us, slowly at first, but we wouldn't stay long enough for it to speed up. We sprinted through the next door before shutting it. All the doors swung out, which meant the spiders could follow us since there were no doorknobs on these last doors.

My main character was in a horrible state. I tore Milla from his arms and ordered her to brace the door. I hardly set her down when Paldric swayed dangerously, his face gray.

"You're okay." I grabbed his face and used my powers to cleanse the spider poison ravishing his system. I held him as he steadied himself, the color returning to his face. "Milla? Did you get bitten?"

She looked at me, those enormous eyes traumatized, but I didn't sense any poison in her. When this was all done, we needed to take her for ice cream or something. She didn't look at either of us. "Thirty-seven percent."

I patted Paldric on the back, a man true to his word. He protected Milla from the spiders. "You, sir, are incredible."

Paldric gripped his knees as he sucked in air. "Just to be clear," he said between gasps. "This... this was you? *You* created all this?"

Despite everything, a chuckle escaped me as I helped Milla lean against the door, running a hand through my hair as we got our breath back. The spiders tried to open the door, ramming their little bodies against it. "Technically, it was the elves, but yes. Blame it on me. It wasn't supposed to end up like *that*, but you can thank karma for the sweet revenge."

"I don't know what karma is." He still leaned over to steady his breathing. "But I'm glad you're here with me. Not for sentimental reasons, but because I hope you learned your lesson."

I snorted before taking Milla's hand and easing her away from the door. "The shield is over there. As soon as we touch it, the narrow walkway will be the first thing to crumble, so the spiders won't follow us. I'll carry you this time, Milla. Paldric, are you ready?"

He straightened, nodding as he lifted his torch. I dropped mine at the bottom of the door, and the shadows scurried away. For the moment.

Milla hugged me tight, almost cutting off my breathing. I gave her back a pat. "We're almost done."

We followed Paldric, easing onto a walkway as big as our shoes. I tried not to look down. Not that it would make a difference since I couldn't see the bottom, but the black emptiness would give me vertigo.

The spiders tried to open the door. The torch was enough to startle them, but they wanted to sacrifice some of their number to kill us. Many of them tasted Paldric and wanted more.

The door creaked, and the torchlight flickered. Milla whimpered, and I patted her again. "You are so incredibly brave, Milla. I hope you know that."

"I don't want to see them."

"You won't. They'll drown in this cave, and you'll never see them again. You are a brave little girl, and I don't want anyone to tell you otherwise."

"I'm not doing anything." She still buried her face in my chest. "I'm just being carried through all these trials."

The door creaked open, and a trail of spiders headed straight for us. Many of them, in their eagerness, fell off the edge of the walkway and tumbled to their deaths. The few that made it onto the walkway didn't get far before slipping into the void. I am glad, for once, I made them so big.

We approached the shield, and Paldric took a few seconds to eye the workmanship. I didn't blame him. It was a beautiful piece of art. The intricate design of the gold and silver almost made one believe the magical period was still here. The wood nymphs carved around the edge looked lifelike.

Paldric sheathed his sword, then glanced at me. I gave another hesitant look at the spiders inching ever closer. I nodded, holding Milla tighter and preparing to swim straight up. That was it. We just needed to swim to the surface, then we'd be done. We could focus on saving Tara and Alwin. I didn't know how much time passed, but the sooner we got back, the better.

My main character picked it up. He frowned, balancing the shield with one hand. "It's quite light."

"That's what you can expect from elvish made stuff."

The cavern cracked. Paldric strapped the shield on his back, making sure it was tight. I touched Milla, then placed a hand on Paldric. "We just swim straight up, alright? That's all there is to it."

The ceiling to the right of us collapsed, and a waterfall fell into the cavern. The dim light from the surface above was enough to illuminate the entire cavern. This recent development didn't bother the spiders one bit as they still tried to get us. The water below crumbled the walkway as the spiders dropped like their own waterfall of black legs.

I took deep breaths, preparing myself to swim in that ocean again when I saw it, and my entire body froze. The dim light from above, as well as Paldric's torch, illuminated him as he toppled over the edge of the cavern. How could anyone miss it? The school bus sized Siludontia tumbled into the cavern below, the torchlight catching the gleam of hundreds of teeth as three of the five black eyes glimpsed us.

Perfect.

Chapter Thirty-Four

To My Ex-Wife, Hater of Sharks

I will admit I was immature. I should have just talked to Esme and said, "Hey, you are so critical of my writing, and it takes a toll on my happiness. My writing group is better at critiquing my work without making me feel like a total failure, so maybe stop reading my stuff, or only talk about what you like."

Nope. Instead, I took her two biggest phobias and made them as bloodthirsty and manic as she always imagined the real animals to be. More karma for me, now that I lived in a reality where they wanted to kill us.

The funny thing was, she didn't even make it this far. She barely made it halfway when she informed me the fantasy genre was stupid. "If you and all your other fantasy writers put the same time and effort into doing something worthwhile instead of writing this disgusting escapism, all the world's problems would be solved! But now people would rather entertain themselves than fix problems!" she shouted in one of our last fights.

"You certainly enjoy how well I'm getting paid for it!"

"Really? This is being paid well? You know how embarrassed I was when my card declined at the restaurant my mother and I were eating at?"

"If the only financial problem you can think of is something that happened three years ago, I say my stories are doing pretty well!" Yes, I was shouting, no, I wasn't proud, but it wasn't like her tone was soft, either.

"It's because your best seller isn't fantasy! Stop pretending your book is so important when there are actual issues we face as a society! If you publish your book, you're giving people an opportunity to ignore those problems and it's nothing to be proud of! Fantasy is stupid, just like the authors that think they can write them!"

There were no words for that. Instead, I divorced her. Esme accused me of escapism, but you know what I didn't do? I didn't create a character that looked strikingly like her to get torn apart and swallowed by the Siludontia. *That* would have been escapism.

Anywho.

I passed Milla over to Paldric. She didn't notice the shark dropping into the cavern because she covered her face in my chest. "You take her, and you swim as fast as possible to the surface."

"Gunther." The worry was clear in his voice.

"I can distract him. Far better than you can."

The ocean water filled the cavern, and Paldric looked down. The torch was still lit, and we could see the dorsal fin breaking the surface.

"Get to the shallow end of the beach where he can't follow you." Milla whimpered as she put two and two together. It was better she realized it now instead of in the water. Panicking while in an ocean was bad. The water rose enough to wash the spider guts off our shoes as the sandpaper skin brushed against the ledge. "I will be right behind you."

My main character tossed his torch away. It extinguished in the ocean as he wrapped his arms around Milla, whispering words of comfort to her. I grabbed my glasses and leapt onto the Siludontia. I tried to grab him, but he was too big. "Go, Paldric! Swim as fast as you can to the opening!"

They dove into the water, and the shark headed straight toward them. I beat against his sandpaper skin, getting his attention. He tried to shake me off. When he couldn't, he swam closer to the opening of the cavern near my characters. I took a deep breath as he prepared to dive, even as water sprayed every which way, like in my mouth. The Siludontia dove low before he rose again, opening his jaws to eat Paldric and Milla. I beat against his gills to get his attention. My characters' legs dangled below the water, waiting for the ocean to rise enough so they could swim out of the cavern. We were all trapped with this stupid shark.

I rammed my fist into one of the shark's eyes. He finally moved his jaws to snap at me, trying to get anything. An arm, a leg, a head. He sensed me, but there was something more alluring about my other characters.

The waterfall leveled off with the cavern, and Paldric and Milla shot toward the surface. The shark followed, charging toward them. His body was built for water; Paldric and Milla's weren't. The more I beat against his face, the more I realized an important thing. Milla's arm was still bleeding. It drove the shark crazy.

The Siludontia's nose rammed against Paldric's feet, and all the air bubbles from Milla's body left. They still had a while before the surface, and now she had no air. Paldric grabbed her, trying to comfort her, but she panicked after gasping in shock under water. Paldric couldn't swim much faster, and his focus turned toward Milla, keeping her from slipping straight into the shark's mouth. The girl thrashed around, trying to breathe. Paldric struggled to keep his feet on the nose of the shark and not the mouth. He was slipping, and the shark waited to catch them.

I jammed my arm into the mouth of the shark, scraping it over the razor-sharp rows of teeth. Not only did my skin split open, but my arm became a battered, useless pulp that I forced myself not to feel. The shark turned enough for Paldric to kick off its nose. My main character continued to the surface with Milla in his arms. She stopped moving, her eyes closed.

The shark, however, clamped down on my arm, focusing his attention on me. Which is how I wanted it, but I would have wet myself if I had a functioning bladder. I freed my arm from his mouth, punching him in one of his eyes with my good hand. My air supply swiftly ran out, and Milla needed me, so I had to do this as fast as possible. I put on my glasses under the water, because I had no other place to keep them. I leapt on the Siludontia's face and gorged out all five of his stupid black eyes. After healing my arm, I leapt off his face, swimming as fast as I could. The shark focused on the blood, sensing it around him and knowing I should be there, but I was already breaking the surface, gasping and sputtering as I clutched my face, making sure my glasses made it. The beach wasn't close, so I swam like my life depended on it, though really it was Milla's. Paldric ran toward the beach, fighting against the water, Milla's unconscious body in his arms.

I kicked my legs, threw my arms into the water, urged my body forward. Sleep would come later. Milla's life was on the line.

The moment my feet hit the bottom of the shallows, I sprinted toward my characters. Paldric placed Milla flat on her back, listening to her heart. I dropped to my knees beside her, my hand on her chest, expunging all the sea water from her system and jumpstarting her heart.

Milla jolted awake, vomiting water. Paldric grabbed her, helping her sit up as buckets of ocean water came out of the poor girl's body. She gasped for air, clutching Paldric's arm, sobbing. "Forty... forty-three. Forty-three percent."

My body gave out, and I collapsed on the beach. Ten percent. An entire ten percent for that journey. The ocean lapped against the lower half of my body, but I didn't care. Milla was alive. Paldric was alive. I was alive. We had the shield, and I didn't hit fifty percent.

Paldric gasped for air. "Gunther? What did you do?"

I didn't answer, mainly because I wasn't entirely sure what he meant. I did a lot of things down there.

"Forty-three is awfully high," Milla said.

"I can't let you die." She didn't need to know that in my original outline, the dragon killed her and her entire family in chapter one. But now she was a different person. I cared about this little girl. She was a part of my family of characters now.

It didn't help that I was bone weary. I sprawled across the sand, tempted to sleep now, not caring to straighten my glasses. I had been awake for so long, my body demanded I do something about it. Whether God powers or actual sleep, it didn't care, just something. But Milla was right. Forty-three was high. We still needed to find the necromancer's secret lair here in Vaywell and stop them from torturing—

A cool metal blade touched my throat. Milla whimpered next to me as Paldric gasped. I cracked an eye open to see Tara at the other end of the blade, livid. As adrenaline returned to my system, I realized Tara never had this capacity of hatred. Someone else helped create it in her. And she aimed it all at me.

We were too late.

Chapter Thirty-Five

THE REAL CONSEQUENCES TO MY ACTIONS

I lifted my hands to show Tara I had no weapon. Lying flat on one's back after crawling out of the ocean, my glasses askew, should be a defenseless enough position. Her genuine anger scared me.

"Tara—"

"Don't." The sword dug deeper into my throat, driving away the desire to talk. "Don't you dare speak. Don't you dare pretend you didn't just create me for any other reason than to be Paldric's little whore."

The blade got way too close to my Adam's apple as I swallowed. Paldric got to his feet. "Tara, I would never—"

She pulled out a dagger and pointed it at him. The Dark Wizard armed her well. Paldric backed away, holding his hands up as she sneered at him. "I'm not interested in your excuses. That's all you've ever seen me as, isn't it? That's all both of you have seen me as!"

"Of course not. You cannot believe anything the Dark Wizard told you. He's lying," Paldric said.

Milla hid behind Paldric, whimpering. He dropped one hand to touch her shoulder, letting her know he was there. I remained flat on my back, the blade splitting into skin. I used the opportunity of having my hands near my face to straighten my glasses, even if I could barely see out of them.

"Tie them up." I had sensed more people coming, but not the necromancer. It shocked me when he started talking.

She barely removed the blade from my throat before multiple hands grabbed me and forced me to my feet. Ropes wrapped around my wrists as I glanced over the brim of my glasses. There weren't as many city folk, but it still made me uncomfortable. Paldric and Milla were also being held back, their wrists getting tied. Another filler character dragged an individual over to us, and as they came closer, I saw the blurry outline of Alwin, his face a mess of blood.

Alarm struck my heart. "Alwin. Are you alright?"

"Perfectly fine." A broken nose caused his voice to be more nasally. He had multiple cuts on his lips, and he struggled to stay conscious. "Don't do it, Gunther. I'll be fine." For a strange moment, I thought he could read thoughts. Or maybe I was that desperate to heal him with my powers.

Milla stared at the beach, surrounded by grown adults. "He's at forty-three percent."

The groan Alwin finally let out wasn't caused by pain. I winced, not sure I wanted the necromancer to know my percentage. Maybe he didn't understand what it meant.

Tara headed toward the necromancer, her back toward me. Not seeing her livid face gave me enough courage to start talking. "Tara, I'm sorry. If it makes any difference, this wasn't how I meant for this to go. I had an... an outline and everything, and I didn't mean for you to get hurt."

She froze, then turned around, a dark glare on her face. "You're sorry? You're sorry for assaulting me? For using your God-like powers to make me want you like that? You honestly think two silly words will make me forgive you for what you did?"

"I know it was wrong. And it hasn't happened since. I swear it will never happen a—"

She slapped me hard. I grunted at the sting of it, my glasses slipping down my nose. "You honestly think you're a good person?" I tried to meet her gaze, but she slapped me again. I grunted, tightening my fists, letting it happen. "You think I will bow at your feet and worship you because you haven't done that despicable deed again? That somehow you have earned my love and allegiance because you did the bare minimum?"

"Tara—"

This time she used her fist, and my lip split open. My glasses tumbled to the ground next to Alwin.

Paldric tried to stop her, but the city folk kept him back. "No, Tara!"

Once again, she pulled out her dagger and pointed it at Paldric. "Don't tell me what to do. If you really were a good person, you would've killed Gunther after it happened. Stabbed him through the heart."

"Killed someone to prove I'm a good guy? Are you even listening to yourself?"

"You've killed goblins without a second thought! Gunther is worse! He's unstable! He needs to be killed before the rest of us die. Do you honestly think when he cracks, he'll somehow save us while the rest of the world burns?"

She had a point. I hated to admit it, but she did. All my characters were in grave danger because I was here. And if I cracked, what would stop me from assaulting Tara again? Force her to do what I want before creating another woman with features I was in the mood for. Tara knew the frightening potential of my powers, and she had every right to be terrified. And livid. No wonder it didn't take the Dark Wizard long to break her.

"I need you to understand one thing, Gunther." She pressed the dagger against my throat again. I looked at her, not nearly as blurry because she was so close. I braced myself for whatever she had to say. "Even if you force me to like it, force me to enjoy what you're doing to me, deep down, I'm just faking it. Something tells me every woman you know always pretends to enjoy these sexual relations. She's doing what she has to in order for it to end quicker so she can actually accomplish something with her day instead of wasting her time with you." She chuckled, and I winced. "I've solved your problem. You cannot create women because none of them truly act like themselves around you."

After spending years with Esme, I was an expert at masking how much words hurt. A part of me wanted to deny everything, but honestly, how could I defend myself without saying something pathetic, like how my mother never lied to me? Which would open me up to a snide remark about my mother, and I just wasn't in the mood to be further emasculated. Better to cut my losses and let her have this victory.

Tara walked over to Paldric, busily undoing the straps of the shield around his chest. He couldn't do much else but let her as the city folk held him back. "Don't, Tara. Please."

"If you cannot see how Gunther is the enemy, there is nothing more to discuss." She finished undoing the straps and grabbed the shield, then returned to the necromancer.

"Thank you, Tara. I am pleased you see our side of things." The necromancer took out an equally beautiful sword before dropping them on the ground. City folk grabbed Alwin and dragged him over to the sword and shield before forcing him to his knees. The necromancer grabbed his hair, pulling back enough for Alwin to gasp in pain before cutting the ropes that kept his hands bound. "You will fill the sword and shield with your magic now."

Alwin placed his hands on his thighs and did nothing. He studied the sword and shield, his face steeling itself. I winced as I understood. My elf was practically immortal. Long life had helped acquaint him with death. Even though it pained him, threatening Paldric, Milla, and even Tara would not get him to hand over the energized sword and shield to the evil men. He met my gaze, as though realizing I understood this. No, wait. The longer I looked into his blurry eyes, the more I realized what he thought. He wasn't afraid to let them die, but he was terrified of how I would react if they did. I constantly put my sanity on the line to make sure everyone was safe. I might crack if he didn't do what the necromancer wanted. What he weighed in his mind wasn't preparing for everyone's death, but whether he wanted to risk my sanity.

My mind went through everything I knew about the necromancer. Villain. Evil. Created by the Rogue, but didn't have the connection like the Dark Wizard did. Typical monologuing villain.

"What do you honestly think you'll gain with all this?" I blurted out before I could stop myself. I needed time. Time to think. The villain needed to ramble as I got my thoughts together. "Are you seriously just a cookie cutter henchman? Don't you have a plan of your own?"

"The Dark Wizard will take control of Veniloria, and it would be wise to be on his side when he does," the necromancer said.

"Goblins, trolls, and shadow soldiers surround you on your little island. It's glaringly obvious you are the villains in all this."

The necromancer narrowed his eyes. "We, the bad guys? We, who welcomed the poor and destitute that his people exiled to our island?" The necromancer pointed to Alwin. "We, who refused to judge people because of some minor wrong choices they make."

I couldn't help but snort. "Is murder one of these minor wrong choices you ignore?"

"Don't consider yourself so high and mighty, Gunther, or I will have Tara remind you of the choices you've made." The necromancer picked up my sand covered glasses and placed them back on my nose. Honestly, it was pointless. I could barely see out of them. On the plus side, at least I couldn't see Tara. Instead, I focused on the necromancer through my smudged glasses.

"Then use this opportunity to tell me how wrong I am. Explain how you've baffled me by how the Dark Wizard is here, when he should be on South Island."

Humor trickled into the necromancer's eyes, and I stilled. He was about ready to gloat. Let him gloat. Let him think he had the upper hand because... well, he did. But at least I would have information.

"The Dark Wizard isn't here anymore. He's back on South Island."

I waited, hoping that with my silence, he would shove the information in my face, but he needed more goading. "And how did he get back there?" I asked through gritted teeth. The Dark Wizard had to be here to change Tara. The necromancer was lying.

He laughed. "I thought you were an all-powerful, all-knowing God." Good. He was rubbing it in my face. It would be any moment now. "No wonder you fell from the heavens. They must not need a useless God like you."

Paldric about said something, but I shot him a look. The necromancer was getting to it. We just had to be patient. My main character stilled, though he kept a dangerous glare pointed at the necromancer.

"Stop playing games. Just tell me where the Dark Wizard is," I said.

"I already told you. He's back on South Island."

"That's impossible. It took us a week to get here, and South Island is at least a hundred miles south. Unless he has teleportation, you are lying to me," I said.

Once again, the necromancer laughed. I let him have his villain laugh, because I needed him to give this information. "My dear sir. Do you not know what a necromancer does?"

It was then that I heard a roar. My face dropped, and my gaze turned to the sky. Far off in the distance, I saw the all too familiar silhouette of a dragon through the smudges of my glasses. I spent hours perfecting that silhouette to make sure it brought the perfect amount of fear when literally anyone saw it. I'm happy to report all my hard work paid off.

Chapter Thirty-Six

Jim Stumbled Into Genius Foreshadowing, Which Almost Makes Me Jealous of Him Again

The necromancer cackled at the terror on my face. Paldric was already forming a plan, and it was then my exhaustion hit. Here it was, almost mid-morning, and I'd been up for over twenty-four hours. I went through the trials more than once, battled a shark three times, and killed hundreds of spiders. Now, as the silhouette grew more detailed, all my battles paled compared to the dragon headed straight for us. And it was then my body no longer responded to adrenaline. Pavaldri was alive through whatever dark magic the necromancer possessed, which meant he had full control of her. We were going to battle. Again. Bound as we were. Surrounded by city folk. She was going to eat us and be done. That, or I save my characters and lose my mind. There was no way I could fight a dragon without going past fifty percent.

"That's right, Gunther. Understand you have failed. My master will use you to cleanse this world while he protects us from your deadly might. We will start this world anew."

I stared at the necromancer, knowing it was a lie even without touching the Rogue's code. The Dark Wizard couldn't be that powerful. He and the necromancer would be the first to drop if I cracked. The temptation to kill him was strong. But I would play right into the Rogue's hands. He was the real villain of the story. We'd have to fight off the necromancer as well as a dragon, and I needed to stay sane. I needed help. Desperate, desperate help.

"We will win." The necromancer took a step forward. "Once you cleanse this world of impurities, we will have our moment. We will destroy you and rebuild this world exactly how we want. Let our creatures run freely where they had never run before, and we—"

There was more to the necromancer's speech. That much was clear. He was on a roll, and no monologuing villain would leave that kind of speech hanging. To his credit, he didn't expect a dagger to plunge deep into his throat.

Milla screamed and looked the other way. My mouth dropped open as dark blood drained from his neck like water from a hole in a dam. Paldric, Alwin, and I watched the necromancer's eyes roll back to his head before he dropped to the ground, lifeless. We stared at his body for a few seconds before focusing on Tara. She was wiping the dagger on her dress. It hardly cleaned it as it, too, was splattered with blood.

"How... how..." Paldric tried to say.

"Well, I was trying to tell everyone in a code while talking with Gunther." She ran over to Paldric and cut his bonds as fast as possible. "I faked it."

"Ohhh," Paldric and Alwin both said. I stared ahead, trying not to react. Her words were simply that believable to them, which somehow hurt worse. Yes, I believed her too, but that was beside the point.

Once Paldric was free, he helped untie Milla as Tara ran toward Alwin, cutting his bonds before running to me, not meeting my gaze as the roar of the dragon got closer. We glanced at the sky, knowing we had a matter of minutes. She cut the ropes, and for a moment, she met my eyes. I sifted through what was a lie. She slapped me because I kept her gaze too long and she was afraid I would discover her deception. She knocked my glasses off because she assumed that held my power of reading minds. It was only after, when she understood the extent of her terror, that she attempted to tell everyone she was faking it.

Everything else, the anger, the hatred, the fear, she allowed herself to express with as much force as she could. It hadn't been a lie. The Dark Wizard gave her a way to feel that angry at me, and it didn't take long. It made me look away again in shame.

"I'm sorry about hitting you," she said.

I rubbed my wrists. "No, you're not."

She met my gaze again, then turned to be closer to Paldric. I took off my glasses to clean them as best I could on a soaked shirt. It was better than nothing. Paldric and Milla had the same sorry state of clothes, and Alwin and Tara had too much blood on theirs.

"You honestly think we won't tell the Dark Wizard what you've done? That you've betrayed him?" one of the city folk asked.

It was strange these filler characters let us untie each other. Their allegiance must be slim. Which meant...

"Paldric." I put my somewhat clean glasses back on. "Do your speech."

My main character looked over at me, frowning. "My what?"

"Your speech. You know, rallying the troops. Your heroic speech you did before. Uniting us against a common enemy and what not?" I gave him two thumbs up, waiting for him to get it. Instead, he stared at my thumbs, confused. I dropped my hands to my sides. "No, it's not about the thumbs. Come on! This is your moment to shine."

Paldric again gave me a questioning look. "I'm not—"

"A dragon is headed straight for us, and there's still lingering doubt in the city folk. Say the thing you always say. Fill them with hope. Let them know they can throw off the desires of the Dark Wizard. Also, their characters may be blank slates, but every single one of them possesses a deep pride about being citizens of Vaywell. And honestly, they have every right to be. This port city has lasted a thousand years, and it will last a thousand more. If we rally together, we can defeat the dragon. Awesome, hopeful stuff like that." I clapped him on the back. The city folk cheered, and I frowned, trying to figure out why they were excited when a literal dragon was heading straight for us.

Paldric gave me a humorous look. "I don't see why I need to repeat that. You did a pretty good job yourself."

The filler characters watched the sky, but also waited for my signal. I don't know why it made me uncomfortable. "Yeah, well, I'm also not the hero."

"You're just the one who created the hero."

Alwin took the sword and shield, both starting to glow with a blue-gray light. "Do you think we can defeat a reanimated dragon with two artifacts?"

I looked again at the dragon headed straight for us. "We'll have to."

And then I swallowed my pride and turned the Guardians back on.

Hi Devin.

"Gunther? Gunther! What were you thinking? Do you have any idea what you—"

Yes, hi Devin. Listen, I will gladly forget the fact that you deleted a part of the contract so you could keep convincing me to get out of my story. I will even listen politely to your entire lecture you prepared as soon as we're done. Right now, I need you to tell me anything you can about how to defeat a reanimated dragon.

"You will never turn us off again, do you understand? That was far too dangerous. Jim figured out the dragon twist while you were in the arrow room, and he could have warned you. We knew Tara was lying. You *cannot* turn us off again."

Do you know how to defeat this reanimated dragon headed straight for us?

"Stab it in the heart with the elf blade. Should kill it for good," Jim said.

Oh, hey Jim. I thought you'd be sleeping by now.

"My blood is infused with caffeine right now. Couldn't sleep even if I tried."

Lucky. I'll just have to work with adrenaline.

I turned to my characters. "Alright, listen. If we can stab that dragon in the heart with the sword, it will kill it."

"Where's the heart?" Alwin asked.

"Chest cavity area. Guarded by a ton of reinforced scales that will cut one to ribbons without the elf armor." I stared at the dragon, getting ever closer to Vaywell.

"The dragon is meant to spike your percentage, which means its focus is on you, and only you. The Dark Wizard and necromancer honestly believe they will survive your cracking. They

need you to burn the world. I strongly advise you to not do that. You are dangerously high. This is not a smart move," Devin said.

I told you before. I can't leave without making sure my characters are safe.

Devin sighed. **"Vince? Any suggestions?"**

"There's not much we can do. We already know he can't get out of his story by dying. And his word count isn't enough."

"There is no way he can fight a dragon at his percentage," Grace said.

It's better for me to fight her instead of my characters.

"Um, no. Your characters aren't going to snap and destroy everything," Devin mumbled.

The wind picked up, sand blowing every which way as I partially ignored Devin. "Alright, so I am the focus of the dragon's attention." I walked over to Alwin and motioned him to give me the sword and shield. "Which means if you return to Vaywell, Pavaldri won't attack the city until she's done with me, or I'm done with her. All of you, go back and wait."

The filler characters nodded and ran back to the city, leaving Paldric, Alwin, Tara, and Milla there, staring at me. "Are you insane?" Paldric asked.

"He's at forty-two percent," Milla said.

"He dropped a little?" Tara asked.

"Yeah. Whatever you told him made him think."

Alwin kept a tight hold on the sword and shield, narrowing his eyes. "It's still way too high to fight a resurrected dragon."

I kept my hand out to Alwin, gesturing toward the sword and shield. "I'm trying to save your lives."

"By putting your sanity at risk?" Alwin backed away. "Absolutely not."

"And you being here, in danger, also puts my sanity at risk." I shouted, not because I was angry, but because the wind made it harder to hear. "I can't let any of you die. You are all way too important to me."

"We're going to be fine. Whether we survive this or end up in the database, all of us would rather be here with you," Paldric said.

The database. The afterlife. They will be fine. I would never see them again. Not unless the Guardians published the book. Which they wouldn't, because it broke way too many rules. I blinked back tears that might have been caused by sand getting in my eyes. "I can't lose you."

"And we don't want to lose you, either," Milla said.

I rubbed my face. It was too late to argue. The dragon tucked her wings into herself and dove toward us, the wind almost toppling Milla over. "Alright. It's too late to have a discussion. Alwin, hand me the sword. You keep the shield. Everyone protects each other. And stay away from me. Please."

Alwin nodded before handing me the sword right as the dragon slammed into the ground and roared.

Chapter Thirty-Seven

I Am Just as Surprised as Anyone That This is Happening Again

Her roar deafened me. The ground still shook after she landed, and Milla almost collapsed to her knees before Tara grabbed her arm to steady her. I saw Pavaldri, my dragon, almost zombified. The brilliant scarlet scales were dimmer now, some of them falling off in places. The dark magic sealed the tear I made in her stomach with a pure black scar. It looked as though she bled black tears of blood where Alwin stabbed her eye. Purple flames filled the sockets of her eyes, and when she looked at me, I sensed how much she wanted to eat me.

"Stay away!" I shouted to my other characters.

Pavaldri roared. She dug her claws into the ground; the earth shook again as she headed straight for me. I ran in the opposite direction of my characters, knowing Pavaldri would follow me.

I would appreciate any advice, Guardians.

"Elf sword through the heart. That's all we've got so far, but we're working on alternatives."

Thanks, Devin. I would have said it dryly if I spoke it out loud, but I was too busy sprinting from a zombie dragon.

"Kill this dragon as quickly as you can. The more you dawdle, the more your percentage goes up," Vince said.

Dawdling. Right.

Pavaldri heated her fire, and I dove to the side as a blast hit the ocean, causing it to boil. The Siludontia hated this fresh development. Maybe those two could fight somehow. No, the shark was already retreating into the cool depths of the ocean. The smallest part of me felt disappointed. Not because he would be a great distraction, but the narrator in me drooled at the thought of a mega shark and a dragon fight. But I shook my head, focusing on my situation.

The sword was light in my hand as I scrambled to my feet. The dragon took three easy steps and grabbed me with her claws. Her squeeze would have killed me if I wasn't indestructible.

"Gunther!" Alwin shouted.

I stabbed the dragon with the sword, and she screeched, tossing me to one side. I kept my fist tightly over the hilt of the sword as I dropped to the ground, knowing my back would have snapped in half if I wasn't a God. Instead, the blow knocked the wind out of me, which was difficult enough.

Pavaldri limped, the sword cut burning her skin. She snorted, glaring at me with her purple flame eyes.

"Forty-four percent." All the air I struggled to get into my lungs left again. Milla was there, right by my side, in the line of danger.

"No, get back to the others." I grabbed her as the dragon hobbled closer.

"This is what I have to do. Keep you informed."

The dragon took a deep breath, ready to incinerate her bones. I grabbed her, covering her with my body as Pavaldri ignited a flame so hot it boiled the ocean.

And yet it didn't touch us. I cracked an eye open to see Alwin with the shield, bracing against the impact of the flames. I eased Milla away, so she wasn't as tightly against me and kept my hands on her shoulders. The little girl opened her eyes once she realized we were safe, despite the flames licking the shield. "Don't tell me my percentages until after the dragon is dead. You stay by the others."

She nodded as the flames stopped. Alwin grabbed her waist and ran off. I used the opportunity to check where the dragon's heart was, which was a good six feet above the ground. I could reach it with the sword as long as I dodged her snapping jaws.

I ran straight for Pavaldri, dodging her claws, swiping them with a sword lighter and deadlier than any regular weapon. Pavaldri once again tried to eat me, her teeth filling my view as I ran for her heart. I stabbed her mouth, black blood soaking me as the blade entered the top of her mouth as easily as stabbing butter. She roared, then jerked her head around like she was shaking a fly away. The elf weapon became dislodged, and me with it. I soared through the air, watching the ground come closer. My body still didn't think it was an all-powerful God, so it seized up, preparing to die.

I smacked the ground, getting a mouthful of sand. Every single Guardian sucked in a breath.

I'm fine.

"You shouldn't be, though. You've got to kill this thing, and we've got to end this story," Vince said.

I'm trying.

The dragon came for me again, and I struggled to my feet. My body convinced me I should be dead as my rubber legs refused to function. Pavaldri got ready to breathe fire when instead she roared in pain. She swerved, and I saw Paldric stabbing her with his regular old sword to get her attention. The zombified dragon scales weren't nearly as tough, and the sword buried inside her tail before snapping off. Paldric glared at the dragon, broken hilt in hand, ready to do whatever it took to give me time to recover like a heroic main character. The idiot!

I took another step. My legs wobbled before I fell flat on my face.

"Like with the troll, your body is having a difficult time feeling the consequences of your actions while also staying alive. It's going to take a minute," Grace said.

Pavaldri breathed fire at my characters, the shield in Alwin's fist the only thing protecting them.

"I don't have a minute."

My arms trembled as I forced myself up and grabbed the sword, wobbling over to the dragon. Every minute Pavaldri remained with a beating heart meant my percentage would continue to climb. I needed to kill her now, and unfortunately, I had a plan.

"Hey! Over here!" Pavaldri stopped breathing fire and turned her head impossibly fast toward me. "Yeah! That's right! Here I am!"

Pavaldri closed the distance between us. I held the sword in order to make myself look like a menace, almost a hero pose, but as soon as her shadow engulfed me, I dropped the sword tip, closing my eyes and bracing myself. I didn't want to see those teeth surrounding me again.

The narration device was a powerful tool. Though the story was ruined from chapter one, the device understood the theme of the story and would still play it out spectacularly. My theme? A nobody from a nothing town could defeat a dragon and save the world. I love fantasy for this very reason. The least likely person, the least interesting, the least qualified saved the world. Was it cliché? Absolutely. This was my escape, but not the escapism Esme tried to make me believe it was. All of us had dragons we battled in life. The monstrous creature that seemed impossible to defeat. I didn't write stories to help others escape their problems. I wrote them to remind people how to conquer them. Since this book was never getting published, I became the reader that needed the reminding.

Paldric's heroic journey became my own. He got the super cool armor and an elf that could backflip through a cavern to dodge dragon flames. The two of them had poses fit for a cover, and everything they did oozed coolness.

My fight would have none of that, but I didn't care. Just as long as the dragon died.

I tossed my glasses to one side before Pavaldri clamped her jaws around me and, remembering far too well from last time, tossed me to the back of her throat, swallowing me once again. I soared down her esophagus, clinging to my sword as it sliced through her. She shrieked as I dropped once again into her stomach. It was pitch black now, since I tried to use as little of my powers as possible. I sliced open her stomach and crawled out of the sack as she writhed around. The sword tore through the rib cage, slicing everything in my way. It felt like crawling through a cave full of hot pasta. The heart was somehow a glowing orb of darkness as I slid the sword right through it.

Pavaldri thrashed about, roaring and screeching as, using a phrase I never thought I'd say *twice,* I cut open my dragon and exited her body. My lungs sucked in the sweet, sweet air of the outside world before plopping into the shallow end of the ocean. The water was deep enough to immerse me, which helped to wash off the dragon innards. It was considerably warmer than before. As I broke the surface, I dreamed of the time when I would be dry.

I crawled out of the ocean, passing Pavaldri as she twitched and convulsed. My legs mutinously stopped working.

Vince groaned. **"It's not enough. He still has about four thousand more words before he hits eighty thousand. We can't end it here."**

My lungs filled with air as I tried to focus. Falling action. I needed to describe the falling action and then I would be fine. Maybe the after party. The celebration in Vaywell, when the people discovered the corpse of the dragon. Because we would have a celebration. Not because I was... not because I desperately...

"Gunther! You're at—"

"No!" I could hardly lift a finger at Milla. I was soaking wet and shivering. Not because of the cold. There was no cold. "Not yet, Milla. Not until I tell you." I could manage. Four thousand words without knowing my percentage. Trick myself into thinking I was normal. It would work.

Her eyes were wide, and her horrified look clued me in to how dangerous this was. She held my glasses in her hand but didn't approach me. Everyone here was in danger. There was no way I'd get out of Pavaldri and not be at fifty percent. Or worse. Milla's eyes told me it was worse. Tears and the salty ocean stung my eyes. "Psychology. Mind over matter." I wiped the water from my face. "I pushed the boundaries of every single narrator in existence. Did what no other has done. Lasted two weeks with my sanity in check. And I'll continue to last. Because death and destruction cannot be the end of this story."

They were blurry, my characters, but I could see well enough. Enough to watch Paldric touch Milla's shoulder, moving her farther away from me. Alwin placed himself in front of Tara, partially pulling out his sword to protect her.

"I'm fine! There's nothing to worry about." It was manic, how I said it. I tried to somehow force my percentage to go down. I coughed, rubbing my head. "This is fine. I'm going to make it. Stabilize at forty-nine percent. That's what'll happen. Not because I force it, but through sheer will."

"Gunther, you need to know your percentage," Devin said.

"This can work. I can stabilize. We have set the perimeters. If I believe I'll never last past fifty percent, then I won't last. But if I simply don't know... if I simply refuse..."

"This is for your safety," Devin said.

"I have four thousand more words. I will last. This is not how the story ends. I don't defeat the dragon just to go insane. It would be the worst book in the world."

Paldric and Alwin shot each other worried looks. I realized what this meant. I made no sense to them, and they always felt a spike of alarm when I babbled nonsense.

"Gunther is partially right. He lasted longer than any other narrator because he didn't enter for any selfish reasons. The Rogue forced him into it," Jim said.

"That has consistently been my theory why he's lasted so long. His mind is incredibly strong. He might last," Grace said.

"Not if he still denies the consequences. No matter what happened, Gunther, you need to face it. You need to understand how much damage you did to your psyche," Vince said.

I tried to breathe, but it came in quick gasps as I mulled this over, staring at my characters. They grounded me, helped me realize why I couldn't go insane. "I did this for you. For every single one of you." I met their eyes. "I love you. You are mine. I may be flawed, I may hurt you, and I might be too obsessed with your safety, but I love you. All of you are my reason to keep my sanity."

Milla nodded. "You're dropping. Fast."

"Ask Milla what your percentage is," Devin said.

"And even though I am fully aware I ignored the consequences for you, I can't help it. I care about you all, and I will never crack. I couldn't hurt you. Any of you." I had hurt them, though. Already. My eyes fell on Tara, who had her arms folded in such a way she was covering her breasts, looking terrified. The dragon stench lingered around me. I needed this to work. This story needed to be okay. It would be ironic for my marriage to end because of a lack of love, only for my story to end because I loved it too much.

Milla moved forward, and I watched her come. She held out my glasses that somehow survived a dragon's writhing. I took them but didn't put them on. Instead, I tried to not imagine what I could do with a world completely under my control. What would it be like to destroy the Dark Wizard with a thought and let my characters live like kings and queens? I wouldn't have to destroy them. Just their enemies. Let them have paradise now.

"Gunther..." There was a warning in Devin's tone.

My arms trembled. My breathing turned irregular. Four thousand more words. That's what I needed. Ramble. I needed to ramble.

The sand was warm; the afternoon already hot. I smelled the dragon everywhere. My eyes were dangerously heavy. Exhaustion hit me. I could just will it away. To keep going. I just needed to keep going.

Milla, despite me asking her not to, whispered my percentage to Paldric. His eyes widened.

Devin? Did you do that?

"Someone has to know."

"Don't tell me." Once again, I tried to point at Paldric. "I can do it."

If Devin could alter my story, that meant I was at least forty-five percent. It wasn't a surprising revelation. Honestly, I would have been more surprised if I *wasn't* at forty-five percent.

Paldric nodded toward Alwin. My elf helped me to my feet, yet kept a firm hold of me. It was for the best, since my legs still refused to work. At least, that's what I thought Alwin was doing until my main character hit me hard in the jaw.

"Ow! Paldric, what—"

"It's working. He's dropped some more," Milla said.

Paldric punched me again, jogging my memory. Last week I told him to punch me if I ever got too high. I winced, knowing if it was working, I should let it be. But Paldric certainly knew how to throw a punch.

The third punch darkened my vision considerably. I was on my knees. Alwin tried to keep me up, but I didn't fight the darkness. Maybe it would be good. Don't fight the consequences. Get knocked out. I didn't know if Paldric got in another punch, but I embraced the darkness, letting myself relax.

Maybe now I could sleep.

Chapter Thirty-Eight

THE AFTERMATH.
AGAIN.

A splitting headache caused me to groan as my eyes flitted open. Before I even touched my head I saw, on the ceiling, a number scratched into it. It was big enough to see without my glasses. Fifty-two. I stared at it, blinking, and assumed it could only mean one thing.

"Ah. Good morning, Gunther."

"Devin?" My headache sharpened, and I touched it, groaning.

"I expect that headache to hurt until you get out of your story. Are we clear?"

Right. Don't use my powers to heal it. Understood.

Despite everything being blurry, it was easy to identify my guest room in Lord Adrijian's manor house. I had little desire to get up, but I needed to check for other injuries. Sensing them pulse in pain was a good way to identify them. I sat up, groaning, but it was mostly from my head. I felt a bandage wrapped around my forehead.

"I'll guide you through these last few thousand words. We've already got another narration device prepped to receive the data

for the sequel. Once you arrive there, you're getting out. Are we clear?"

I nodded, then instantly regretted it. My elbows braced against my knees as I touched my head. It wouldn't take a large percentage to heal, right?

"It'll heal when you get out of the sequel."

"What's going to happen to my characters?" I asked instead.

"We'll hand it over to professional epic fantasy writers for them to take care of. They will write a sequel to keep your characters out of danger. A lot of walking, a lot of descriptions of feasts, very little danger. On top of all that, Jim programed the device to only need seventy thousand words instead of eighty. It's the lowest he could go."

I nodded, then hissed. How had I already forgotten my last lesson? I eased myself to a sitting position, touching my head. The professionals would let them amble around. With a Dark Wizard lurking in the background. Trying to get my characters to draw me back into my story.

This was going to be impossible. The device would know a plot needed to exist, so it would only narrate when something interesting would happen. Interesting like a Dark Wizard attacking.

"Your four characters are going to have meaningful conversations during these feasts. The authors we have lined up are the best. They are quick on their feet, and they won't let your characters get hurt. You must get out of your story. Within the hour. You pose a bigger threat to your characters than the Dark Wizard."

Deep down, I knew that. I really did, but the smallest doubt lingered that this could go wrong, and I wanted to be here when it did.

I saw my glasses on the side table and inspected them before placing them back on my nose. Someone had cleaned them.

"There is no scenario where you staying here doesn't end in complete disaster. Once we get the sequel started, you will write yourself out of the story. Are we clear?"

I looked up at the ceiling, giving no answer. Thinking about chinchillas, for some odd reason. Oh, and sugar gliders. Those were the cutest little creatures to ever exist.

"Gunther!"

It's okay, Devin. I get it. I'm a danger to everyone around me. But I need to make sure my characters are safe before I leave. And your lecture reminded me of how you deleted the part of our contract where you don't ask me to get out of my story.

The pause was long. I used the time to explore the expertly wrapped bandage around my head. Did Tara do this?

Devin finally broke the silence. **"Every second you stay in your story is dangerous. I know I lied, but there are too many people in this hospital hooked up to these devices for the rest of their lives. I can't just... not suggest you leave."**

I should be angry and turn him off again, but I didn't. My university had plenty of lectures dedicated to the dangers of the situation I was in right now. It was a miracle I lasted this long. It would be stupid to push my luck.

"The necromancer is dead, as is the dragon. It'll take the Dark Wizard and, therefore, the Rogue at least a week to reach your characters. We specifically have these authors lined up because they are skilled at taking pages to describe feasts. And with the story only needing seventy thousand words, this will be child's play for them. They will party, then your story will end, and the

characters will enter the database. It isn't a satisfying ending, but your characters will be safe, and that's all that matters."

Finally learning something, I didn't nod, but I did like what he was saying. The door opened, and Milla peeked inside. "Are you alright, Gunther?"

"I've had better days."

"You're at fifty-two percent."

"So I saw." I pointed toward the ceiling. Part of me hoped I got lower somehow during my chat with Devin, but it wasn't the case.

"You dropped fast. You were a lot higher." Milla walked farther into the room.

"Thanks for telling Paldric my percentage."

"Are you leaving us soon?"

"It seems like it."

"I hope you do." I couldn't help but smile. Children were blunt, and therefore it was part of her character. "I'll miss you, though."

The lump in my throat appeared. I knew, deep down, I had to give up my characters. Hand them over to professionals, but a part of me couldn't do it. The thought of them in someone else's hands made my skin crawl.

"Gunther..."

I didn't answer. I straightened my glasses. Despite wearing glasses for most of my life, I got used to how they felt. Every so often, though, I'd remember the sensation. Trying to ignore the true thoughts in my head, I noticed the rim, sensed them pressing against my nose and behind my ears.

"Gunther—"

The door opened again and Paldric and Alwin walked in. "How are you?" my main character asked.

"It doesn't matter what you've been told about your hunting skills. Your true calling is boxing." My main character was confused, so I rephrased it. "You, sir, are an excellent puncher." I rubbed my jaw as Paldric smiled. I still had a split lip and what felt like a healing black eye. "How long have I been out?"

Alwin helped me to my feet. "About a day. You needed it."

"Yeah, I did." I kept my arm around his shoulders to steady myself. Alwin didn't look much better than me, but at least we both would have time to heal.

"Still at fifty-two percent?" Paldric asked Milla, who nodded.

My steps faltered as my legs tried to remember they were fine. There was a knock on the door. Paldric opened it to reveal a servant, who bowed before handing a tray over. The smell was familiar. All too familiar.

"What's that?" I asked.

"It's coffee. A new import," Alwin said.

My eyebrows rose in surprise. "What? Coffee? How?"

"The strangest story of trade I've ever heard." Paldric accepted the tray and set it down on the small table by my bed. "Two days ago, this boat came to shore with these travelers who claimed a new crop from this island no one ever heard of. We don't know how our cartographers missed a vast island near Vaywell, but I guess they did. Honestly, it's quite delicious." Paldric handed me a cup.

Milla wrinkled her nose. "I think it's disgusting."

I drank, not caring that it didn't have my usual cream and sugar in it. I'd find some after I got caffeine in my system.

"What was the name of the island? I forgot what it was. I just remember it being unusual," Paldric said.

Alwin closed one eye, cocking his head to one side as he tried to remember. "Jimdon? I think that's what they said."

A smile crossed my face. Jim's thoughtfulness strangely touched me. His life was so perfect I couldn't help but hate him for a while there. And yet he did this for me. Thanks Jim. You really are a great supporting character.

"I'll pass on the gratitude. Don't let this give you any ideas, though."

No, I wouldn't do anything. Despite being at fifty-two percent, I loved my characters. I'd finish wrapping up with falling action, and then the sequel can get under way.

Paldric and Milla left to help with lunch. I could smell roasted meats as soon as they opened the door, and my stomach groaned in envy. Alwin helped me steady my steps. We left the room, and I placed my hand against the wall to brace myself as I continued walking. "I'll be fine, Alwin. Thank you."

He nodded and left to help. Devin? Am I at the word count yet?

"Less than fifteen hundred left. Make sure your conversations at lunch are meaningful with some character development, or the device will just summarize it into a brief paragraph."

My steps became surer, my headache not as bad. I looked out the windows of the manor house. Most of the city folk were down by the beaches, trying to clean up the dragon carcass there. I was glad we contained the battle to the beach. The clean-up would have been much worse if Pavaldri attacked the city.

I closed my eyes, trying not to think of the battle or how much power I used. Or how great it felt. A shuffling sound came from behind me, and I turned to see Tara. She stumbled upon me but didn't want to talk, so she tried to sneak away, and winced when my eyes landed on her.

"Oh. Hello, Gunther."

Chapter Thirty-Nine

WE WRAP UP BOOK ONE

I dropped my hand from the wall as Tara looked away. "Forgive me. I didn't see you there," she said.

"Oh, no worries."

She still backed away until there was a respectable distance between us before she pointed toward the magnificent dining hall. "Did you want to go this way?"

"Yeah." I rubbed my forehead before pointing at the cloth wrapped around it. "Did you do this?"

She shrugged. "You saved our lives. It was the least I could do."

"Well, I appreciate it."

We fell into an awkward silence again. I watched Tara, saw how uncomfortable she was, and knew I wouldn't need to wait until lunch to fill the rest of the word count. "Look, we need to chat."

She frowned. "Chat?"

"Talk. We need to talk."

Both suspicion and fear crossed her face. "Are you still at fifty-two percent?"

I understood her hesitancy. "Yes. I am. I don't want to lie to you."

She glanced behind me, her eyes searching for a familiar face before she met mine again, trying to smile. "What would you like to talk about?" There was a wavering to her voice neither one of us could ignore. She remembered the boundaries we'd set before, with either Paldric or Alwin present while we talked, but she didn't want to anger me by stating the request again. The eggshells she was walking on so I could remain happy made me uncomfortable.

I chewed on the tip of my tongue, trying to gather my thoughts together. I should go get Alwin or Paldric, but this conversation might make it so I leave. And it might be better if she sees me leave the story. "First of all, what you did, fooling everyone, stabbing the necromancer, that was... that was incredible. You saved our lives, too. Thank you." She said nothing, waiting patiently for me to finish so she could find Alwin or Paldric. "I also want you to understand that what I did to you was disgusting, and I will never do it again."

She hesitated, studying my face. "So, you'll be leaving soon?"

"My fellow Gods and I have a plan. We'll see if it works."

"Gunther, I..." She folded her arms, looking away. "I've been thinking a lot the past week. Don't misunderstand me, your actions were despicable, but I thought about the position you're in. I had to wonder myself if... if I had complete control over this world, I would have..." Her cheeks turned pink, and she still refused to meet my gaze. "I would have done something similar. With Paldric. And... and with Alwin. With both of them. Then forced you to apologize, made you grovel. Then..." she trailed off. I didn't bother finishing her thought, even though I knew exactly what she wanted to do to me. It surprised me how long Tara had been plotting her revenge fantasy, but it had softened recently. "Honestly, you *not* making that dragon explode the moment it touched ground was an impressive feat of mental power.

It's got to be difficult to *not* have things magically become what you want."

We both looked out the window at the beach, at the crew cleaning up the dead dragon. "If I could go back in time and stop myself from doing it..." I sighed. "I wouldn't. Because the truth is, I *can* go back in time. I can also make you forget it ever happened, but that would be its own kind of wrong. As terrifying as it is, we'll keep remembering, so I know how dangerous it is. And I acknowledge how terrifying it is for you, and... and I'm sorry. I'm sorry you'll remember how much I altered you for the rest of your life. How frightened you were afterwards. You and Paldric..." I stopped myself. The two of them hadn't even kissed yet. At least, not willingly on their own. So many things happened instead, and I placed their relationship to one side during this book.

"The narrators will develop their relationship in the sequel. You have my word," Devin said.

I smiled at her, relieved I wouldn't have to write a romantic sublot. "You'll be just fine. And I'll leave soon."

"Less than seven hundred words to go, Gunther. You're doing great."

Tara rubbed her upper arms. "Maybe you're right. I still wish it had never happened, but erasing it from memory would be worse. Just know if you ever control someone like you did me, I will help you understand how wrong you are. And remember, not even you predicted I would stab the necromancer."

I absently touched my throat before nodding. If anyone could figure out how to kill me, it'd be her.

She stood there, and I couldn't help but marvel at how she grew. I may have given her pushes and nudges, but she took the basic characteristics and made them her own. And I wouldn't have it any other way. "Thank you for not succumbing to the Dark Wizard."

She looked out the window. "I didn't want to. That's all I remember feeling as he was trying to convince me otherwise. I just didn't want to."

I felt myself relax. It seemed like such a straightforward thing, but that small desire saved her from being altered. It would help if she ever found herself in that position again.

"She won't," Devin said.

Tara waved at someone, and I glanced behind me to see Alwin leaning against the wall, his sword partially drawn, his eyes bouncing between us. Despite his healing injuries, my elf was still a force to be reckoned with. "It was good chatting with you, Tara." As I straightened my glasses, I backed away and tried to smile. "I'll never forget how monstrous I was. I will never go there again."

Tara nodded, the fear in her face slowly going away. Slowly.

I entered the dining hall, dozens of servants bustling about, getting food ready. Paldric laughed with another servant. He was always good at stuff like that. Good to the staff, good to strangers. Not afraid to trust them. It was his greatest strength.

"Alright. A few more descriptions of lunch, and we'll get the sequel under way."

It gave me an excuse to breathe in the tantalizing smell of roasted meat, trying to figure out the best words to describe them. My stomach groaned, even though I didn't feel hungry. It was tempting to stay long enough to eat lunch before I left.

"No, you're—"

I know, I know. My head turned, ready to describe the dining hall, when Paldric laughed again, then noticed me and waved me over. "Come meet Roger!"

Seemed like a good excuse to get more words. I walked over, trying to smile as I shook the man's hand. I stared at him, and everything inside me froze.

"Gunther?"

I said nothing. Thought nothing. Simply stared at the man in front of me.

"What? What happened?"

Why can't I sense him? Why can't I sense Roger?

Devin said nothing, but I already knew. I couldn't sense him because Roger wasn't one of my characters. Jim was right. This was the Rogue's MO.

"Don't get any ideas. We're starting the sequel now, and you're going to write yourself out of the story."

I ignored Devin. Not to the point of turning him off, because I wasn't that stupid. I stared into Roger's dark brown eyes until his smile dropped.

"Can I help you?" Roger asked.

Paldric was far too trusting. It was his greatest strength, and his greatest weakness.

"We've hit the word count. We need to end this now, and you need to get out of the book."

End it, Devin. Because I have a lot of questions for this man in the sequel, and I'm certain it will pad the word count nicely.

"You are going to leave the story. Do you hear me? You are leaving the story and we'll hand it over to professionals."

I looked at this man I didn't create, no smile on my face. My fingers tightened over his hand as he tried to pull it away. I refused to let him leave, especially now that I discovered him. Paldric's own smile dropped as he saw the change in me.

"Who are you?" My voice remained steady, but I made sure Roger understood I just murdered a dragon.

The Story Continues in Book Two...

ACKNOWLEDGEMENTS

To start out these acknowledgements I must first and foremost thank my incredible family who understand that sometimes I need to step away from life and write. If it wasn't for your loving support, this book would never exist. My characters thank you, too, for sharing me.

Also to my fans on Royal Road who read, commented, followed, favorited, and even threw a bit of money my way while I was writing this. You will never know how much it means to me that you believed in Gunther and the gang while they were in a rough draft.

Thanks also to Heather Frost who helped me through this entire publishing process and gave me plenty of advice and encouragement. Thanks for also being a fellow introvert and being totally fine with texting.

Thanks to the getpremades.com people for an awesome cover, emach55 for the map, and Kirra and Helen for your editing advice!

And, of course, thanks especially to all the people who I will remember were instrumental in the creation of this book at two in the morning after this book is published. Know that I shot out of bed in a cold sweat because I feel so bad not remembering what you did while creating this acknowledgements. You are the best!

About the Author

Ellen Taylor enjoys living with her husband and three boys, and also enjoys living in her head. She writes in her spare time, because sometimes she needs to be in control of chaos. Follow her on Facebook or Instagram for updates on future books at Ellen Taylor Books.

ALSO BY ELLEN TAYLOR

<u>Fiction</u>

The Altered Manuscript

<u>Non-Fiction</u>

Give Me Back My Children

www.ingramcontent.com/pod-product-compliance
Lightning Source LLC
Chambersburg PA
CBHW020127310726
48970CB00006B/1755